Some jobs come with unexpected benefits . . .

Alyssa runs her personal life just like her professional one: smoothly and efficiently. She learned in the worst way possible that investing her heart in a relationship only leads to disaster, and she won't take that risk again. Pleasure is still on the table though—as long as there are no feelings involved. Until a
one-night stand leaves a lasting impression.

When after-work drinks lead to an after-hours hookup, Grayson finds himself playing by Alyssa's rules—but she leaves him wanting more. Even when they discover they work for the same company, Alyssa is all business—on the outside, at least. As far as she's concerned, keeping Grayson at a safe distance is now part of her job description, even if it's her most challenging task. But when her living situation falls apart, Grayson makes her an offer she can't refuse . . .

The terms of their new merger are strict: roommates only; hands off. But every contract can be broken—and every heart can be melted—if the deal is sweet enough . . .

Also By Allison B. Hanson

Help Wanted
Never Let Go
Nick of Time
When Least Expected

Getting Down to Business

An On the Job Romance

Allison B. Hanson

LYRICAL SHINE
Kensington Publishing Corp.
www.kensingtonbooks.com

LYRICAL SHINE BOOKS are published by

Kensington Publishing Corp.
119 West 40th Street
New York, NY 10018

All Kensington titles, imprints, and distributed lines are available at special quantity discounts for bulk purchases for sales promotion, premiums, fund-raising, educational, or institutional use.

Special book excerpts or customized printings can also be created to fit specific needs. For details, write or phone the office of the Kensington Sales Manager: Kensington Publishing Corp., 119 West 40th Street, New York, NY 10018. Attn. Sales Department. Phone: 1-800-221-2647.

Lyrical Shine and Lyrical Shine logo Reg. U.S. Pat. & TM Off.

First Electronic Edition: December 2017
eISBN-13: 978-1-5161-0339-3

First Print Edition: December 2017
ISBN-13: 978-1-5161-0340-9

Printed in the United States of America

To all the people at DAS who spend their days on the job with me.
Thank you for your support in my writing job as well.

Chapter 1

Shutting the door as quietly as possible, Alyssa turned for the stairs to complete her escape. The phone in her bag buzzed as her feet hammered down the familiar steps. Once outside her building, she breathed in a lungful of freedom and frowned at the humid heaviness of the air.

It was going to be a hot day in Manhattan. Her lips pulled up, remembering how hot the night before had been.

"Morning, sunshine." She answered her friend's call knowing Mia would be anything but sunny this morning.

"Shut up. I hate you."

"Remember, it was *your* idea to go to ladies' night on a Wednesday when you had to be at work this morning. *I* said it was stupid."

"Are you outside already?" Mia brushed over her responsibility in their predicament.

"I'm going to the gym to shower. My apartment was…crowded this morning."

"The guy stayed?"

Yes, the guy stayed.

Grayson Hollinger III had sat down next to Alyssa the night before and offered to buy her a drink immediately. When she politely refused, he let out a breath of defeat and explained that his friend had promised him hordes of desperate women. She found his honesty intriguing. Paired up with the sexy smile and haunting blue eyes, she was more than interested. While she hadn't been desperate, she was willing to have a little fun on a Wednesday night.

Having nothing to lose but time, she proposed a simplified method to get them from point A to point B. She laughed now, remembering the shocked look on his face when she suggested they enjoy each other's company for the evening with no expectations or bullshit afterward.

The sex had been phenomenal. He'd even managed to get her to point B—something that had been nearly impossible for the last few years. When he asked to stay longer, she agreed, greedy for another chance with him. She hadn't been disappointed.

But now it was morning. Time to get back to reality.

Sure she wished she could have more with a man. Who truly wanted a life filled with strangers and uncertainty? Unfortunately, the option had been taken from her five years ago. These brief encounters for pleasure were all she was capable of now. She didn't deserve a happily-ever-after.

"Yes, he stayed," she answered Mia's question. "Which is why I'm going to the gym, so I can shower without waking him."

"So courteous," Mia chuckled, knowing it was more cowardice than courtesy.

"I'll see you at work."

"Yeah, about that."

"You'd better get your ass to work," Alyssa threatened.

"Travis stayed too. He suggested we spend the day in bed together. I have to say, his offer sounds better than yours, so…I'm calling in."

Mia was the opposite of Alyssa in most every way. From her short, black hair and chocolate eyes to her petite curvy stature. But the biggest difference was what they were looking for from men.

Mia was full of hope that one of the men she took home from a club would turn out to be Prince Charming.

Alyssa knew there was no such thing as Prince Charming. There were only short glimpses of happiness with strangers—and making sure her heart never got involved. That last part was fairly easy since her heart had frozen over.

"You remember what Millie said would happen if you called off again," Liss reminded her.

"Damn."

When their old boss, Ruth, had been fired, they thought they were home free. But Millicent wasn't much of an improvement.

"Do you want to end up like Kenley?" Kenley had worked with them for years before she was falsely accused of sleeping with her boss's husband and fired.

"Do I want to end up fired so I can get a new job with a dreamy guy who marries me?" Mia asked. "Yes. The answer is yes."

Maybe Alyssa had asked the wrong question.

"Get to work. I don't want to lose another work friend. I'll only have Freddie left and he can't sympathize on PMS issues."

"Fine. I'll see you soon."

Alyssa dropped her phone in her bag and headed off toward the gym, only to see the devil striding toward her. Liss might have looked for a place to hide, or an alley into which she could duck, but it was obvious by the glare in Sasha's eyes that she had already spotted her.

Better to get it over with.

"What the hell, Liss?" Sasha held up her phone. "You send me a text telling me I can't come home?"

"You've sent me texts like that so many times that I've started carrying a change of clothes in my bag." Alyssa held up her bag, grateful to have had it packed for her quick escape this morning.

"It's *my* apartment. You can't tell me not to come home to my own apartment."

"I pay rent too. So it's my apartment as much as yours."

"Well the landlord won't see it that way since my name is the only one on the lease."

It was always like this.

In the beginning, Sasha had been her friend. But friends don't always make the best roommates. Sasha had gotten the apartment in her name because Alyssa's past had adversely affected her credit score. They'd agreed to take turns, one of them getting the tiny bed and the other sleeping on the loveseat a week at a time. But eventually, Sasha claimed the bed because her name was on the lease and Alyssa's wasn't. It just spiraled from there.

"I knew you were working until two, so what were a couple more hours?" Alyssa pointed out. She'd texted her roommate at ten, telling her she had a guest. That should have been plenty of time for Sasha to work her magic and find an alternate plan.

She had a feeling the issue was more a matter of sticking it to Alyssa than of not having a place to sleep the night before.

"I have to go now or I'll be late for work. We'll discuss it later, okay? Maybe we can make up a schedule or something."

Without waiting for an answer, Alyssa hurried away knowing she was screwed and that pushing the discussion off until later probably wouldn't change the outcome.

* * * *

Gray was shaken awake by an angry woman. For a second, he thought the vixen he'd slept with three times the night before had morphed into this harpy by the light of day—but then it spoke.

"Liss left. You need to get out."

So this wasn't the woman he'd slept with. Alyssa had simply run off, not changed into a nightmare.

The woman tossed a crumpled piece of paper toward him.

"Get out of my bed, and no you can't shower here."

"You must be Sasha," he guessed.

"Yes. I'm Sasha. And this is *my* apartment."

"Okay, okay. I'm gone. Can you give me a second to get dressed?" He was still naked under the sheet.

"Sure." She flopped down on the sofa, six feet away, and crossed her arms as if waiting for a show.

Alyssa had warned him that her roommate might make a scene. She'd expected the other woman to show up at some point during the night and demand to be let in, which was why she had double-checked the chain on the lock to ensure their privacy.

Conflict wasn't Gray's thing, but he hadn't been willing to walk away from Alyssa the night before. He was more than intrigued by her suggestion that they enjoy each other's company and then go their separate ways in the morning without any pressure to continue the relationship.

The alarm on his phone went off, reminding him he had to be at work this morning. With a sigh of determination, he tossed the sheet aside and got up,

After getting dressed to a few impressed sounds from Alyssa's roommate, he checked for his phone, keys, and wallet before rushing out of the apartment. It had been a great night, but it was over.

He hesitated as he opened the wrinkled note from Alyssa, wondering if she was hoping for more—or worse, that she wasn't. He was new at this one-night thing. He knew he should want it to fade away in the light of day, but he couldn't help but feel a little saddened by that thought.

> *Grayson,*
> *I had a great time last night. Sorry there's no food. You can help yourself to coffee. Maybe I'll see you around sometime. Maybe not. No worries.*
> *Liss*

She hadn't even given him her phone number.

Sure Alyssa had talked a good game, but he didn't think it was really possible for people to have sex and walk away without any strings at all. He'd never encountered such a thing. *He* wanted some kind of string. On the sidewalk, he pulled out his phone and made a note of her address, just in case.

He took a cab to his apartment across town and showered quickly so he'd have time to stop for real coffee on the way into work.

When he moved to the city, he'd promised himself he wouldn't turn into a hipster coffee snob, but there he was in the immense line to order his double vanilla latte with foam.

The line shifted, and he looked up from his phone to notice a blonde woman in front of him. He tilted his head and studied her legs in the understated but sexy black pencil skirt. He knew those legs. They'd been wrapped around his waist for most of the night.

"Liss?" he said.

Her head instantly snapped up and she turned to face him. A look of confusion took over her subtly made-up face. With less makeup, she looked even prettier than she had the night before.

She allowed the patrons between them to go in front of her so she could stand next to him.

"What are you doing here? Are you following me?" she hissed, and tucked her damp hair behind her ear.

"No. This is where I get coffee." He looked up at the sign above the counter. "Every morning for the last year and a half to be exact."

"Really?" she said, her eyes narrowed in suspicion.

"Yep."

"I've never seen you here before."

"Maybe neither of us was looking before."

"Maybe."

"Let me buy you coffee," he offered. It seemed the least he could do since they'd been intimate.

"You don't need to do that." She pulled out her wallet as she ordered her double vanilla latte with foam.

His brows rose in surprise, and he quickly came up with a morning beverage alternative. She would surely think he was nuts if he ordered the same drink. Even if it was his normal drink. He wondered what the odds of that were as he ordered a mocha.

"Which way are you headed?" he asked.

"Up," she answered, pointing in the direction he was going.

"Me, too. Are we allowed to walk together?"

"Sure. I'm not far."

"I got your note and wanted to tell you I also had a really great time last night." *Great* wasn't the right word. From the ease of talking with her to the way they'd connected in bed, it had felt so different. Then she let him stay when he asked. Holding her while he slept felt right on so many levels.

"Great. We both had a great time." He smiled at her overuse of the word he found lacking. "But now it's the next day, and we agreed there would be no next day." Alyssa had made it very clear she didn't want anything from him but sex. Was there a reason? Had someone hurt her in the past? He swallowed down his urge to ask, knowing it would lead to him wanting to help.

If his past relationships had proven anything, it was that he couldn't help everyone.

"We're just two people walking up the sidewalk. Don't panic." He gave an easy shrug, at odds with how he felt. He wanted to see her again. Maybe they could have dinner and get to know each other better. Would that be so strange? People did it all the time.

"Suit yourself."

"I've had sex on the first date before, and it's generally kind of stressful because you don't know what to expect from the other person. Last night wasn't like that. I was completely relaxed. Maybe because I knew you weren't expecting anything," he shared.

"I was expecting *one* thing." She laughed and licked foam from her upper lip. He wanted to do it for her. "You delivered, which is impressive because, like you, I'm usually not able to relax enough to get to point B."

"Nice," he said as she stopped walking at the same time he did. They were standing in front of his building.

"This is me," she said.

"Seriously?" he choked.

"Yeah."

"This is me too. Hasher Borne, twenty-ninth floor."

"Hasher Borne, twenty-third," she said, eyes wide.

"Oh, shit. Do you believe in fate?"

"No way," she said firmly.

"Okay, good, because this could easily be misconstrued as fate interceding."

She laughed.

"What department do you work in?" he asked.

"I'm an account rep, but I've been trying to move up for years." She sounded irritated, but stopped herself from continuing what he was sure was going to be a rant. "What department do you work in?"

"Senior accountant."

"Oh." Her eyes flared and she looked away.

"What is it?"

"Nothing. Have a great day." She moved toward the front doors, but he stepped in front of her to keep her from getting away.

"There's obviously something. Even if you don't want to be friends, we are coworkers, and apparently, we both work for the number-crunching side of the business. What's wrong?"

"Have you ever had any family members work here?"

"No. None."

She seemed relieved, and explained.

"I've been passed over for a promotion to account manager three times because people up in your office have brought in their unqualified family members."

"Ouch."

"Yeah. I'm doing many of the account manager functions, but I'm not getting paid for it. And I don't have the fancy office up on twenty-nine."

"I think I might know who's responsible for that." Randy Taber had also filled their department with people from his large family. "It wasn't me. My family is in Connecticut."

"Why are you telling me about your family? You're sharing personal information." Yes, he was breaking the rules from the evening before. But in his defense, the rules should be null and void at this point.

"Are we really going back to the original plan now? We work together."

"No more so than we did before and never saw each other."

That might be true, but he'd be looking for her now. If for no other reason than to get a look at her in a pencil skirt. Wait. Should he be ogling someone who worked with him? She wasn't his boss or anything. Surely it should be okay. In fact, this might be the in he needed.

"Can I get your phone number?" he pushed.

"Why?"

"Because I had a good time. We might like to do it again sometime." Lots of times.

"I don't think so." She shook her head.

"Why not?"

"You don't seem to understand the concept of a one-night stand." This was true. The last time he attempted to have a casual fling, he ended up in a relationship. They'd been together for seven months when she told him it wasn't working. Despite his desire to figure out why, she simply moved on. He was hoping to move on as well, thus the reason he'd taken Doug up on his offer to go out on a Wednesday for ladies' night.

"I understand the concept, but if I meet someone I like sleeping with, why can't I have another one-night stand with the same person?"

"Because that would be a *two*-night stand." She laughed.

"Not if they're not consecutive," he reasoned.

This did make a little sense, but Liss shook her head. He followed her into the building and waited with her for the elevator.

"I think it's best if you stay on your floor and I stay on mine. We can nod if we see each other, and leave it at that."

He didn't want to leave it at that, but he agreed for now.

"If that's how you want to play it."

"Yes. I think it's for the best." They stepped in the crowded elevator and a few seconds later, they arrived on twenty-third floor. She stepped off, leaving him smashed between a woman with too much perfume and a guy with a coffee stain on his tie.

"Have a nice day, Grayson." She said his name in the same tone she'd used the night before. The tone that made his cock twitch. The door shut and she was gone.

"Damn it," he muttered, causing the people on the elevator to look at him.

It was fine. He knew where she worked, where she went for coffee, what club she frequented, and where she lived.

Fate was on his side. Not that he believed in such a thing.

* * * *

Alyssa couldn't help but smile as she walked to her cubicle.

"What's all this?" Frederick asked while making a wide circle in the air in front of Alyssa's body. "You look much too happy for a Thursday morning."

"Last night was ladies' night." Her smile grew wider.

"And did the lady get everything she desired on her night?"

"Oh yes." And more. Three orgasms were more than she expected from a one-night stand.

"I swear if I could give you my penis, we'd both be happier," he said, making her laugh. "You're such a guy when it comes to sex."

Freddie had no idea how right he was. She didn't want any of the emotions that women normally linked to sex. It was her experience that even if a man talked about marriage, family, and love, what it really came down to was sex. It had been a painful lesson indeed.

Now, her encounters were constant reminders that the only connection she was capable of having with a man was physical.

"I made it in before you?" Mia walked up, her brows crunched together.

"She got laid," Freddie said, while pointing to Alyssa with his thumb.

"I could *still* be getting laid if she hadn't forced me to come in this morning," Mia said with a fake snarl before flipping her straight black hair out of her eyes and walking off.

"Glad you could be here. Have a great day!" Alyssa called after her with a laugh. She could still hear Mia grumbling the whole way to her cubicle. She was in too good of a mood to care.

"This guy must have rocked your world." Freddie rolled his eyes and headed to his desk across the aisle from Alyssa.

Alyssa had to admit, the sex had been amazing. Gray had taken his time to make sure it was good for her. But how long could that last? She couldn't give in to his two-night stand theory. It was best to let things go when they were good. Like knowing when to end a beloved sitcom before you make a mess of it.

She nodded in agreement with her decision and got to work.

Unfortunately, her job was not as gratifying as her evening with Grayson Hollinger III.

With her business degree from Syracuse and her ambitious drive, she should have been working her own accounts by now, but she wasn't. For the most part, she was doing data entry.

But she would keep trying. Every time one of the family members got bored and left the company, it meant another chance for her to move up. Surely she would have her turn at some point. Until then, she would wait patiently.

Her bright outlook lasted only twenty minutes longer. Her phone lit up with a text from Sasha.

I don't think this roommate thing is working out anymore.

"Son of a bitch."

Chapter 2

As the meeting moved into its second hour, Grayson wondered how much force it would take to thrust his pen into his skull to end the misery. It wasn't as if he expected a room full of accountants to be exciting in any way, but there was only so much to talk about.

Yes, two plus two still equals four. Yes, having a positive number on the bottom line is still a good thing. The world is still rotating. Back to work.

He snickered at his imaginary meeting, and Doug raised a curious brow. Gray would explain later. If they ever got out of the meeting.

It wouldn't have been so bad, but he knew this meeting was the extent of his entertainment for the evening.

After spending the night before with Alyssa Sinclair, he knew his Thursday was going to be lacking.

While sitting at the conference table, zoning out, daydreaming about Liss in that skirt, and planning whether to order a pizza or Chinese for dinner, he realized his whole life was becoming pathetic. He could quite possibly be the only person from a suburb in Connecticut to be bored stiff with life in New York City.

He needed to do something. Something... real. His thoughts shifted to the woman he'd been with the night before.

He hadn't expected to strike gold when Doug talked him in to going to ladies' night. After all, Wednesday was probably the least sexy day of the week. Or maybe it was Tuesday.

After his initial crash and burn when he asked to buy her a drink, they eventually found common ground—getting both of them to point B, as she called it.

He laughed, causing Randy to look over at him before going back to the topic on hand. Grayson allowed himself to drift deeper into his memories. Maybe it was the way they'd connected, or the fact that he was in the world's most boring meeting, but he couldn't stop thinking about her. Every touch, every moan. He wanted to be with her again. Except Alyssa had been adamant about it being one night only. He'd have to find a way to change her mind.

"You left with that hot blonde pretty quick last night," Doug said as he sat across from Grayson's desk after the meeting finally let out.

"Wasn't that the point?" After Jade's announcement that things weren't working, he planned to give the relationship the normal six-month mourning period. But Doug convinced him to go out and "get back in the saddle" despite Doug's track record with romance.

"I didn't have any luck." Doug shrugged it off.

"What's the matter? Weren't they *desperate* enough for you?" Gray said with a chuckle.

Doug was a thirty-five year-old divorced father of a little girl he rarely got to see. Every time Grayson had to listen to Doug's stories about the cost of daycare and fighting his ex to get visitation, it made him want to pull out his wallet and double check his condom supply.

"At least the drinks were cheap."

"I only needed to buy one anyway."

"Seriously? You didn't even have to buy her a drink?"

"That's right." Gray couldn't hold back the smug smile.

"You suck." Doug flipped him off as he left Gray's office.

Doug would really be pissed off to find out it was the best sex he ever had. Grayson went about his day, catching himself smiling every once in a while. Alyssa's face in the line at the coffee shop was priceless.

At lunch, he glanced around the street at the crowds of people.

"Who are you looking for?" Doug asked.

"The woman I was with last night works here."

"Uh-oh. You want me to hide you?"

"No. Actually, I'd like to run into her again."

"Seriously? You just got out of a relationship. Give it a rest."

Technically it had been three months. "This coming from Mr. Family Man himself."

"We're not talking about me. I'm trying to spare you," Doug said. Grayson knew Doug would do anything to go back to his family, even though his wife had treated Doug horribly and used their daughter to manipulate him.

"I wouldn't mind seeing her again."

"It was a *Wednesday*," Doug protested. Gray laughed again and surveyed the crowd on the sidewalk looking for Alyssa's long, golden hair.

"I know. I'm as surprised that your idea worked as you are." With a sigh of disappointment he went back to work.

"You want to hit the gym after work?" Doug asked later that afternoon.

"Sure. We'll have to swing by my place so I can get some clothes."

While going to the gym with Doug wasn't what he'd been daydreaming about most of the day, at least he wouldn't be sitting home alone.

They took the elevator in his building up to the second floor—the metropolitan equivalent of trying to find the closest parking spot at the gym.

"You still haven't found a roommate?" Doug asked as they stepped inside his barren living room. The TV and the sofa had been Gray's, but the decorations had been Trent's.

"No. You want to move in?"

"Nah. I couldn't afford it."

"I'd be willing to lower the price for you."

"Thanks, but I'm saving up to get a place with two bedrooms. The caseworker says I can't keep Lucy overnight until she has her own room at my place. The apartment also has to meet all the other criteria of their inspection. Clean and safe. Do you know how much a clean, safe two-bedroom costs in the city?"

He did. He was living in one at the moment. And the empty bedroom was just sitting there.

"Until then, I'm going to stay in Queens so I'm close and can see her more. Besides, I don't want to move in here, and then have Trent break up with his girlfriend and want to move back."

"Fiancée," Gray corrected. "And no. He won't be moving back. They've sent out the save-the-date magnets."

Trent had paid his rent through the next four months, giving Gray enough time to find a new roommate, or for Trent's fiancée to change her mind and kick him to the curb.

Gray had to admit that he was kind of hoping for the second thing. Not that he had a problem with Tiffany or wanted his friend to be heartbroken. It would just be easier than finding a new roommate.

"Do you want me to put some feelers out to find someone?" Doug offered.

"You sure you don't want it?"

"I can't pay what Trent was paying, and I won't take charity."

"It's not charity. It's friendship."

"Friendship is me helping you find someone who can pay you what it's worth."

"Fine. But the offer's still open."

"I appreciate it."

"Are we doing this?" Gray asked holding the door while Doug inspected the kitchen.

"Yeah." Neither of them sounded very convincing.

* * * *

Gray didn't see Alyssa at the coffee shop on Friday morning, and wondered if she was avoiding him. He caught himself looking around, expecting to see her hiding behind a street sign or something.

By Friday afternoon, he found his *wanting* to see Alyssa again had turned into something a bit stronger. He headed out of the office a little early and sat on one of the benches outside their building. Waiting. He pulled a magazine out of his bag so he wouldn't look so obvious, but he couldn't fool himself. He knew exactly what it looked like. Stalking.

He would have missed her if she hadn't spotted him and stood in front of him.

"I'm pretty sure you're stalking me now," she said with her brows raised.

"Who said I was waiting here for you?"

She gave one nod and walked away. Shit.

"Okay. Hold up. I was waiting for you." She turned to look at him. "I wouldn't have to resort to this if you'd just given me your damn phone number." He smiled to let her know he was joking.

"What do you want?"

"It's Friday. I'm not really looking forward to going to a club tonight. I thought maybe you'd like to give us another go. I live nearby."

She rolled her eyes and walked away while mumbling something that sounded like, "One night means one night."

Gray laughed and chased after her as her heels clicked down the sidewalk.

"How about a drink? I never got to buy you a drink."

"No thanks. I have stuff I need to do tonight."

"We were pretty efficient together. You would still have plenty of time."

"Look. I'm sorry, but you have the wrong girl. I don't do any form of relationship. Whether it be marriage or going for a drink, I don't want any of that. I just wanted to have a good time and keep going."

"Okay. Got it. Sorry I bothered you. I feel the same way, except I didn't have a good time." This made her stop walking. She turned on him, scowling. "I had a *fantastic* time. The best time ever." He grinned and saw the corner of her mouth twitch slightly.

"I'll allow that. It was somewhat fantastic. I'm still not interested in a repeat. I have too much other shit going on right now."

"Sure. Fine. I get it. Take care, Liss."

"You, too." And with a small smile, she ducked down into the subway. Why did he feel so strange watching her walk away?

He shook it off and went home to get ready for the bar. He wasn't going out with Doug this time. He had plans to meet Trent and Tiffany. Nothing was more pathetic than being the third wheel. Hopefully, it wouldn't stay that way for long.

He sighed, remembering how easy it had been to talk to Alyssa. How direct she was. Her honesty was even more of a turn-on than her long legs and size Cs.

"So you said you went out Wednesday?" Trent asked with his head cocked to the side. "It's been a while since you've done that."

"Yeah. It turned out great though. I met this woman who was funny and hot."

"Wow. A funny, hot woman at a club," Trent said with a wink at Tiff who had once been just a funny, hot woman at a club, but was now the love of Trent's life.

"Her name was Alyssa, Liss. She actually works in my building."

"That must be awkward," Tiffany said as she pushed her fries toward Trent to share. Gray wished he had someone to share fries with.

"It's not awkward. Well, except that I'd like to see her again and she keeps blowing me off." Trent and Tiffany giggled at his comment, causing him to roll his eyes at their immaturity before laughing himself.

Two hours later, Gray bought another pitcher and sat down at the table.

"What's going on?" Trent asked.

"What do you mean?" He looked at the pitcher as Tiffany filled her glass. "Were you ready to go?"

"No. We just figured you would be."

As much as he hated feeling like a third wheel on their date, he wasn't ready to go home. He shrugged and poured himself another beer.

Eventually, he had no choice but to go back to his apartment alone. He wasn't even drunk enough not to mind it. He sprawled out on the sofa to watch television and fell asleep there, pretending it was an accident rather than the truth: he didn't want to sleep in his empty bed.

While Jade hadn't stayed at his place often—maybe that should have been a sign—he hadn't been alone. Spending the evening with Trent and Tiff forced him to see the truth.

He was a relationship guy. As many times as it hadn't worked out, he wasn't willing to give up. His parents made it look so easy.

Maybe Gray was making this more difficult than it was. His mother and father had met when they were both dating other people. Trent met Tiff in a club and wasn't expecting to fall in love. The right person might start out as a one-night stand. Again, his thoughts turned to Alyssa, but he quickly shook them off. She'd made it very clear she didn't want the same things he did.

The next night, he was determined to do better. It was Saturday. He put some effort into his clothes, and even put some crap in his hair so it would look like he didn't care about his hair.

He wasn't going to go out on the search for a girlfriend, he was simply going to meet someone and let it turn into whatever it was supposed to be. He sat down at the bar beside an attractive redhead. When she looked his way he smiled.

"I'm Kelly."

"Grayson."

"What do you do?" she asked next. He and Alyssa hadn't bothered to ask what the other person did for a living. Though looking back, that discussion might have prepared them for what happened the day after they'd been together.

Alyssa had said it didn't matter where they worked. The only thing that had mattered was if he could get her from point A to point B. He'd accepted the challenge.

"Accountant."

"You don't look like an accountant," she said with a laugh.

"What do you do?" He went along with normal protocol.

"I'm a life coach. Or I'm going to be."

"That sounds interesting. What kind of training do you go through to become a life coach?"

"I don't need any training. I'm a natural."

"Really?"

"Yes. I can meet someone and know what they should be doing."

Gray thought she might have life coach mixed up with palm reader, but he smiled and went along with it.

"And what should I be doing?"

"Definitely not accounting. In fact, you should walk into your office on Monday and quit that job. I can tell it doesn't make you happy." Grayson blinked. Accounting made him more than happy. It also made him a lot of money, which he enjoyed. Something else he enjoyed was having a roof over his head, which seemed in direct contrast to her plans.

"Actually, I like my job a lot."

"No, you don't."

"Yes, I really do."

"No, you don't," she repeated more adamantly.

It seemed Kelly was going to be more of a life dictator than a coach.

"I'll take that under advisement," he said before waving to an unknown person across the club and wandering off.

He'd tried two more times with the same disastrous results.

Finally at midnight, he thought he was onto something.

Desiree had just moved here from Miami.

"Thought I'd see what New York has to offer," she said.

"It has me." Gray said with a stupid grin. She smiled back. They chatted for a little while and she seemed like a fun woman who was struggling to find her way in the big city.

"Do you want to go back to my place? I have an early appointment, but that doesn't mean we can't party until it's time to go."

"Sounds good." Gray nodded. She hadn't said anything about it just being for one night. "Let's go."

He steadied her when she slid off her stool, noticing for the first time that she was a bit more drunk than he'd thought. Shit. He didn't sleep with wasted girls.

"Hey, maybe we can just stay here and talk for a while."

"No. No." She slurred. "Do you know where we can score some blow?"

The word *blow* had made him laugh when Trent and Tiffany giggled like fifth graders the night before. In this sentence, however, he didn't find the word amusing at all.

He held up his hands in surrender.

"And now I'm out. Sorry, that's not my thing. You should call a cab."

"Asshole," she spat as she stumbled away.

He ran his fingers though his hair, or tried to until they got stuck in all the hair product.

"This is ridiculous," he muttered as he headed for home, cursing Alyssa unjustly for ruining his life.

Chapter 3

"I don't know what to do," Alyssa said as she hung her head in her hands at her desk. On top of everything else, it was Monday morning.

The chat with Sasha had gone as expected. Keeping her out of their apartment that night she'd spent with Grayson had been the last straw. Now she needed to find a new place to live.

"It will be okay. We'll figure something out," Freddie said as he gave her the most non-sexual shoulder rub she ever had. "You can stay with Link and me for a little while."

"You can crash on my sofa but only until it gets hot," Mia offered. "In a few weeks, my bedroom will be sweltering so I'll need to sleep in my living room next to the air conditioner."

"Thanks guys," Alyssa said with a forced smile. "I'll figure something out." As desperate as she was, she didn't want to impose on her friends. That was what had gotten her into this mess. She couldn't imagine losing Mia or Freddie because they didn't work out as roommates. Besides, it was important she find a way to make it on her own.

"How long did she give you?"

"Two weeks, but I don't know if I want to take her up on it for fear she'll stab me in my sleep," Alyssa explained.

"You really pissed her off when you kept her out of the apartment." Freddie winced.

"I know, but if you had been with the guy I was with, you would have done the same thing. Besides, how many times have I needed to crash with one of you because she's done the same thing to me? It should go both ways."

"Everyone knows the roommate rules. It's the reason I don't usually have a roommate. I don't want to miss an opportunity if someone gets there first," Mia said with a chuckle.

"Unfortunately, the rules don't apply to her."

"Did you put a sock on the door?"

"I might have forgotten the sock." Alyssa laughed while they both hugged her.

"We'll take you out to lunch today," Mia offered as she and Freddie went off to their desks.

"Thanks." Alyssa appreciated her friends immensely, but lunch was not going to help in this situation.

The only apartments she found that she could afford on her own and wouldn't run a credit check weren't fit to live in or were in Jersey. Any money she saved on rent would go for transportation. Not to mention how early she would need to get up to get to work.

Thanks to her previous stupidity, she had bills that made it nearly impossible to support herself. She was haunted by her past every month when her credit card statement came.

With great reluctance, she sent her mother an email.

She would never ask her mother for money, mainly because she knew how tight things had always been for them when she was growing up. Her mom wasn't sitting on a huge savings that allowed her to just shell out a security deposit for an apartment.

What her mother could offer was Alyssa's old room. The thought of moving back to Albany made Alyssa's latte twist in her stomach.

If she didn't have to work late some nights at the office, she could get a second job, but even that might not get her on her feet.

"This sucks," she said to herself as she deleted the email and shook her head. She knew what she needed to do. Apologize to Sasha.

That night when Sasha got home from work at two, Alyssa was waiting.

"Hey, can we talk?" Alyssa asked.

"About when you're leaving?" Sasha said in a curt tone.

"Kind of. I was wondering if we might be able to work this out."

"You locked me out."

"You lock me out all the time." Alyssa worked hard not to raise her voice.

"Please." She put up her hand in a stop gesture. "I just think it would be better if I had the place to myself. There's really not room for both of us here."

That was true. There was hardly enough room for one person let alone two.

"Okay. I guess I'll work it out," Alyssa said with a sigh and fell back against her pillow on the love seat.

The next morning, she was determined to do something. She waited the hour after her supervisor came in to approach her about the possibility of a raise or overtime.

"As you know I have a degree in business. Would it be possible for me to take on a client instead of just doing clerical work?"

"You knew when we hired you that you would have to work your way up."

"Yes. I understand that. I have no problem with that. Except I've been here for almost two years and I haven't moved anywhere at all."

"It takes time. We don't have any openings at the moment. I'll keep you in mind when the next one comes available."

"Sure. Thanks."

Alyssa took a deep breath and went back to her desk, defeated.

On Wednesday, she finally sent the email to her mother about the possibility of moving back home.

There was no answer.

Thursday she sent another email and a text telling her mother to look at her emails.

No answer.

Friday afternoon she finally received an email:

> *Hi Sweetie,*
> *I'm sorry you are having trouble in New York. Of course you can come home if you need to. It just breaks my heart to see you giving up on what you wanted. How much money do you need? Maybe I can help a little.*
> *Love, Mom*

"Ah, shit," Alyssa said while rubbing her forehead. It might have been better if her mother had told Alyssa she couldn't move home instead of offering to help when she wasn't in a position to do so. The guilt was worse than being homeless.

"You know what you need?" Mia said when she stopped by Alyssa's desk. "You need another serving of that guy you had last week when you came in here all smiling on a Thursday."

"No." Alyssa shook her head.

"He took the stress away for a good day and a half," Mia added while Freddie nodded in agreement.

"Everything looks better with a hot guy lying next to you," he purred.

Alyssa shook her head again and the friendly advice dispersed, but it was too late. Alyssa was already thinking about Grayson Hollinger.

The next morning, Freddie was waiting when she came in.

"You are going to name your first born after me," he said holding up a sticky note.

"What have you done?"

"I've set up an appointment for you to see a room in an apartment close by."

"Oh, really?"

"Yes. The place sounds perfect. You'd have a roommate, but you'd also have your own room so even if he is a dick, you can stay away from him."

"A guy?" Alyssa's brows creased. "What is this guy's name?"

"Um. I didn't write it down. It started with a D. Dave or Drew or something. Doug, maybe. He seemed like a nice guy. He went on and on about the kitchen. So I'm thinking gay."

"How many times have I told you? Straight men like to cook too."

"I guess. I told him you'd stop by after work. Here are the directions."

"Thank-you." She took the note and nodded. At least it would keep her from hunting down Grayson. She'd been thinking about his offer for days. She needed a new place to live more than she needed a two-night stand.

After work, she walked to the building where the room was for rent. It would be nice to be able to walk to work. She put that on the pros side of her list. Being able to afford it was already on the plus side. Basically, pest free and a roommate who wears clothes at all times, were the last boxes to be checked. Everything else was workable.

She took the elevator, smiling at her wavy reflection in the stainless steel walls. It was a very nice elevator. No pestilence and it didn't even smell of urine.

Stepping off the elevator, she smoothed down her shirt and rang the bell, taking in the trendy carpet in the hall. She was halfway home.

"Please let the guy be wearing pants. Please, even sweatpants will do." She crossed her fingers for good measure until she heard the sound of locks and the door opened.

"What the hell?" she stared at the man who was wearing pants. Nice pants. Pants that didn't really matter because she'd seen him without his pants. "Grayson?"

"Hi." He looked down the hall and tilted his head. "How did you know where I live?"

"I didn't. I was given this address about a room for rent."

His eyes went wide.

"You're here about my spare room?"

"Your name doesn't start with a D," she pointed out.

"No. My friend Doug was helping me out."

"My friend Freddie was helping me find a new place."

"Hmm. Are you sure you don't believe in fate?" he asked with a smile. At this point maybe she did believe in fate, and Fate was a sadistic bastard.

* * * *

"Come in. Let me show you around," Grayson offered, opening the door wider. He made a valiant attempt to keep his smile at a normal level. He knew how skittish she was about things like fate and friendship.

"No need. I won't be moving in."

"Hold on. You didn't even see it."

"It doesn't matter. I'm not moving in with you."

"But you were willing to move in with a complete stranger?" So they had history—a very satisfying history. Not to mention short. "Wait. What happened to your roommate?"

"She's kicking me out."

"Because of what happened the night I came over?"

She turned to head back to the elevator, but he jumped in front of her, blocking her path. It seemed like it was the only way to hold a conversation with the woman.

"It wasn't working out anyway." She shrugged it off, but he could tell she was worried.

"But that means it's partly my fault."

"It isn't." She ducked around him, but he cut her off.

"Come inside. Let me show you my place. We can pretend I'm a stranger."

"Pretend?" She gave him a doubtful look, but she stopped her retreat.

"I know you have a thing against being friends with someone you've slept with, but a roommate is in another category altogether. There's nothing more than common courtesy and sharing some household chores."

"And if I were to bring other men home?" She squinted as if watching for him to hide an untruth.

"It's none of my business. Unless you were to yell out my name from memory. That might be awkward." That got a laugh. "We've already established that we are able to reach a common goal. It wouldn't be too much of a stretch to assume we'd be successful roommates."

Her shoulders sagged and she let out a breath.

"Fine. I'll take a look. Just a look."

He ran back and held the door, giving a little bow as she entered. She paused inside the door and looked up at the high ceilings, then down at the wood floors. He imagined she was comparing his place to her own. Her old apartment could probably fit inside his living room and kitchen. There were still two bedrooms and a bathroom to go.

"This is really nice."

"Thanks. I've been here for six years. My sister was dating one of those guys who flips properties and he got stuck with it. I was able to rent it for a bargain." But he still needed a roommate.

While he didn't know Alyssa that well, he knew the basics. She wasn't crazy. Or if she was, she was able to hide it well and was a functioning kind of crazy.

She walked through the kitchen, her fingertips trailing along the granite countertop. He shivered at the memory of having those fingertips trail down his chest and lower.

"Your room would be down the hall to the left."

"And this is your room?" She pointed to the door directly to the right.

"Yes."

He waited as she inspected the empty room. He heard the closet door open and close. It was a small closet, but it was still a closet.

"And the bathroom." He pointed to the last door. The bathroom had all the necessities— tub, shower, toilet, and sink.

"Did you clean before I got here?"

He stepped closer, wondering if something was amiss.

"No. Why?"

"Because it's clean."

"Oh. No. I like things clean. Would that be a problem?"

"No. I like things neat too." He would have guessed that from the way she'd put fresh sheets on the bed before they had sex.

"Good."

"Not good." She shook her head and looked up at him, hands on her hips. "It's not going to work out."

"Why not?"

"Because *you're* in it."

"Do you have a problem living with a guy, or is it me personally?"

"It's you."

The noise that came out of him sounded like a snort.

"You could have pretended it wasn't me."

"It's not that you're not great. It more that you *are* great."

"I'm great?" He couldn't help the smile that crossed his lips. No doubt it looked smug. He couldn't help it. He was apparently too great not to be smug.

"Not *that* great. A little great."

"I'll take it." His joke made her smile at least.

"We've had sex, and we work in the same building. For both those reasons, this won't work." She moved through the apartment toward the door and he knew she wasn't going to budge. "Thank-you for your time."

"If you change your mind, let me know."

"I don't have your number."

"I'm aware." He held out his hand for her phone and she laughed.

"Thanks, but I'm going to pass. Take care."

She opened the door and with a wave, she stepped out in the hall.

"You're kind of stubborn," he called as she hit the button to summon the elevator to his floor.

"I'm aware."

Chapter 4

When Alyssa arrived at the coffee shop the next morning, she spotted Grayson in line ahead of her. With a sigh she left, unwilling to face him. She'd tossed and turned all night—not an easy feat on a loveseat—worrying that she was passing up a great opportunity.

He didn't know the real reason she refused to take him up on his excellent offer. To him, she probably did seem stubborn. But there was more to it than that. Much more. And yes, she was also stubborn.

"You don't have coffee," Freddie pointed to her empty hands as she walked up to her desk. "Mayday! Liss doesn't have coffee."

"I'm staying over here where it's safe," Mia said from the other side of her cubicle wall.

"Guys, I'm not that bad."

"Remember the time Kenley said good morning and you freaked?"

"She was too chipper. Anyone would have gone off."

"Poor Kenley."

"Don't feel bad for her. She's happily married and they have a yacht." She was also pregnant. Liss was happy for her friend. It was nice to know at least one of them was capable of living a normal life.

"So? How was the apartment?"

"It was nice, but it won't work out."

"Why? Did the guy not wear pants?"

"He did." Though she did find herself imagining him without them. And maybe she'd sized up the height of the countertops to determine if they were adequate for kitchen sex.

She'd also imagined how frustrating it would be to lie in her bed listening to him in the shower. Naked.

She rolled her eyes at herself. Of course, he would be naked in the shower. *Get a grip!*

"I need to make a call."

"I'll bring you some coffee. Just in case." Freddie wrinkled up his nose and hurried off to save the villagers from the dragon's wrath.

Alyssa brought up her emails as the call went through. Kenley answered on the third ring.

"New Haven Custom Boats. This is Kenley."

"It's Liss." She dropped her voice lower so no one else could hear her conversation.

"What's wrong? Why are you calling so early?"

"I'm fine. I'm just wondering if I'm making a huge mistake and I wanted you to tell me I'm not." Freddie set the cup down and backed away. She gave him a smile and blew him a kiss, which he pretended to catch and tuck in his pocket.

"Am I just supposed to tell you you're not making a mistake, or were you going to tell me the scenario so I can make the call for myself?"

"I had sex with a guy."

"Many, as I recall."

"Not many. *Some.*"

"Several."

"Let's not argue over semantics. The point is you know how I feel about relationships."

"They're to be avoided like the plague," Kenley obediently filled in.

"Right. But Sasha's kicking me out and this guy has a spare room in a really great apartment and…and I passed on it, but now I'm wondering if I've made a mistake. I mean, I'm capable of having normal relationships with other people. Like you and Freddie and Mia. As long as I made sure he knew it wasn't romantic, I might be okay. So what do you think?"

"I don't have enough information to offer an opinion."

"It's two bedrooms with a huge kitchen, and—"

"Not about the apartment."

"Oh. The guy is nice, and we get along really well. He actually works here. The sex was fantastic. All three times. He seems—"

"Not about the guy," Kenley cut her off.

"Then what?" Alyssa didn't know what she was missing.

"I don't know why you refuse to have a relationship with a guy. You've never said." Right. She hadn't. She didn't talk about that. With anyone. Even her best friend.

"It's a long story."

"As you've told me many times. But you still haven't told me the actual story."

"It doesn't matter. The thing is I don't want more from this guy than a roof over my head and sex." There was a long silence. "Did you just roll your eyes?"

"Yes."

"Are you going to get to the part where you offer an opinion?"

"You want to have sex with the same guy?"

"It's possible. Other people do it. It doesn't have to mean anything."

"Casual sex with the guy you're considering moving in with?"

"Yes."

"The guy you said is nice and you get along with?" Why had Liss called Kenley? She should have known better than to try to have a conversation before she finished her coffee. She took another big swig, hoping to get it into her bloodstream fast enough to help get her out of this.

"I think you should sleep with him again and then see how you feel," Kenley said, shocking her.

"*You do?*" Kenley had been a virgin before she hooked up with the man who was now her husband. This was not the advice she expected.

"I think you should do it and see how you both feel before you decide anything about the apartment. What if one of you wants to be more than roommates?"

"I'm not going to want more." No way. It wasn't a possibility.

"He might want more with you. While you seem content to go through life without strings, normal people form attachments. I don't think it's fair for you to assume he's going to be content to live with you without wanting something more. And having sex with him might complicate that."

"So you're saying I should have sex with him again to make sure he's not going to fall madly in love with me?" She laughed at that.

"No. I'm saying you should have sex with him again to make sure it's something you can do without. If you do decide to move in with him, you'd have to give up the sex."

"Why can't we keep having sex?"

"Because having sex with someone you live with is halfway to being in a relationship."

"It is?" She let out a sigh. "Your logic seems sound. I think you might be on to something." And if it didn't work out, at least she'd have another evening of good sex.

"Glad I could help."

"I have to say, since you've been married, I haven't been able to offer you much assistance."

"I'm happy and secure in my relationship. It's an amazing thing. You should try it."

"Uh, oh. I've got to go. Seventy-nine emails waiting."

"Good luck. Let me know how it goes."

"Will do."

Alyssa spent her lunch break at her desk listing the pros and cons of hooking up with Grayson again.

No matter how she tried to force a different answer, it kept coming up the same.

* * * *

"I can't believe I'm doing this," Alyssa muttered to herself after work as she took a seat on the same bench where Grayson sat when he waited for her the week before.

Fortunately, she put on sexy panties and a matching bra this morning. She glanced down at her ho-hum black pants and tailored pink shirt. It wasn't particularly sexy, but he'd already seen the goods, maybe it would be enough to interest him.

Up until she'd gotten off the elevator, she'd been set on going back to her apartment with Sasha to try begging again. But she couldn't make herself leave.

She watched everyone rushing out of the building, eager to move on to the weekend.

Every tall, dark-haired man made her heart skip a beat, until *the* tall, dark-haired man she was looking for finally walked out of the building. Her heart pounded erratically.

She watched as he slowed down and glanced around the sidewalk as if he was meeting someone. Then he frowned and started walking again. She almost couldn't move, but seeing him made her want him all the more.

"Grayson!" she shouted to get his attention.

He turned toward his name and she almost melted at the big grin that broke across his handsome face.

Could he have been looking for her? That was a ridiculous thought.

* * * *

Alyssa was there, and she was walking closer to him.

He'd looked for her for the last three days since she turned down his offer to move in. He'd hoped if they ran into each other again, she might change her mind. He was getting desperate.

Every morning when he got his coffee, he would linger in front of the shop. Every time the elevator opened on the twenty-third floor, he prayed she would get on. Every night when he walked out of the building, he wished she'd be there waiting for him.

And here she was.

"Hey," he said, realizing too late he was smiling like a complete idiot. He was just so happy to see her, he couldn't keep it in. "How's it going?"

"Actually, I've had a pretty sucky day. I was wondering if you might want to hang out."

"Hang out? As in...?" He wanted to make sure he understood.

"You know what 'hang out' means, Grayson. Don't be coy. Coy only works with women you haven't already slept with."

"I wasn't trying to be coy. I wanted to make sure I wasn't getting my hopes up only to find out I misunderstood and you just wanted to get a pizza."

She twisted her full lips over to one side while she thought that over.

"Honestly, if we could work in a pizza, that would be awesome because I'm starving."

Grayson chuckled and nodded.

"I'm hungry too. It's early, and I assume we have all night?" he hinted.

"Yeah."

They walked together side by side. When he was forced to step behind her because of other people on the sidewalk, he used the opportunity to check out her ass.

"So is this just another one-time thing or have you reconsidered my offer to move in?" He was in uncharted waters. He wanted to have sex with Alyssa again. The first time he'd gone along with her invitation to have a one-night stand because he didn't really think it would be only one night. But now he didn't know what to expect. She seemed pretty serious about it not turning into more.

"It's a one-time thing. And if I were to reconsider your offer, it would mean we wouldn't sleep together anymore."

"I see. No wiggle room on that rule, huh?" Living together without sex seemed impossible. He really liked sex. And he really, *really* liked sex with Alyssa.

"None."

"You know, you wouldn't have needed to stalk me if you'd just agreed to exchange phone numbers," he said with a laugh.

"Fine. I'm ready to give it to you now."

"Seriously?" He glanced at her.

"What? Now you're spooked because I'm showing an interest in you? What is with guys? You all want what you can't have, but then when you get it, you don't want it anymore. Just forget it," she said, and turned to walk away.

"Hey, wait. I didn't say I didn't want it anymore. I definitely want it. Whether I have to chase you down or you throw yourself at me doesn't matter as long as I get to sleep with you again. I was only asking because I wondered what made you change your mind. That's all."

"I'm not throwing myself at you." Her brows moved up to her hairline.

"Fine. You were just resting on the bench when I happened to walk out of the building."

She seemed satisfied with his answer and nodded.

"I had a horrible week. I know you're extremely good at relieving stress. Why should I take the time to hunt down someone else who might not do as good of a job when I know where to find you?"

"I think that was my point *last* Friday," he noted.

"It was a good point. I just needed a little time to think it over."

"Stubborn." He gave her a crooked grin that made her smile.

"I like to think of it as strong-willed."

"It's all in how you spin it, I guess." He shrugged.

"So are you in, or do you just need to be right?" she asked.

"Oh, I'm definitely in."

They walked along the street among the hordes of excited people who were eagerly anticipating the weekend. Gray found he was eagerly anticipating his Friday night at least.

He looked up at the buildings and breathed in the smell of the city. There was nothing else like it.

Grayson reached over and took her hand in his, giving it a little squeeze. He didn't say anything, just a twitch of his lips to let her know he was happy. He liked that she didn't babble. It would have ruined the moment. She squeezed his hand back, making the moment even better. He was trying to keep his smile under control, but it was quite difficult.

It felt like he had rubbed a lamp and had two of his wishes granted: Alyssa. Sex with Alyssa.

His third wish would have been that she moved in, but he knew he was pushing it. He'd promised himself he would no longer enter into a relationship prematurely. He was going to let things play out and not try to force it to be more than it was. Alyssa Sinclair would put his new philosophy to the test, but it would be a lot of fun.

He squeezed her hand again, reveling in it being there. It was stupid to be this excited about a woman he hardly knew.

Sure, what he knew about her he liked.

Gray had gone through a long line of messed up relationships he thought he could save, but that was over. Now he was going to have some fun and let what happened happen. This thing—whatever it turned out to be—was a huge step.

As they got on the elevator in his building, his stomach growled. He was starving, but other hungers took precedence over his stomach.

Apparently, Alyssa was of the same mind because she had her shirt partly unbuttoned before he got the door locked. She let it fall on the floor and reached up to kiss him.

"I thought you were hungry," he teased against her lips as she started on the buttons on his shirt.

"Call it in. We'll be done with round one before it gets here."

"Holy hell," he said, pulling out his phone to do as she asked. "You're brilliant."

She was more than brilliant. She was sexy and skilled and…lots of other things he couldn't think of as she nipped the skin on his chest while unfastening his pants.

He stuttered out the order for the pizza and smiled when the nice gentleman said it would be there in thirty minutes.

Thirty minutes. He didn't have a second to spare.

He picked her up and threw her over his shoulder making her laugh as he took her to his cave—or room as it were. He tossed her lightly on the bed and jumped on top of her, kissing down her chest. He pulled her bra aside so he could latch onto one of her nipples and then worked over to the other one.

She was busy shrugging off her pants.

His memory had served him well. She was every bit as sexy as he remembered—and even more so now that she was in his bed.

He dug around in the drawer next to his bed for a condom as her hand grasped him, causing him to hiss with pleasure.

"Alyssa."

"You say my name a lot when we're together."

"Is that a problem?" Maybe it was too intimate.

"No. It's fine. Is that a thing for you?"

"I'm not sure. Maybe." He'd never given it much thought.

"Do you want me to say your name, or just use the usual God references?"

"My name might be nice. I know I'm not God." They laughed like old friends having coffee instead of two strangers getting ready to have their second hookup.

"I'm glad you finally let me talk you into a second time," she said with a playful grin.

He laughed and rolled on the condom, getting round one underway. Sliding into her felt like coming home after a long trip.

Somehow it was better than the times before. He felt even more comfortable with her, and he practically stumbled into point B without much effort at all. He would put more energy into it after he'd had sustenance.

Knowing she was satisfied threw him over the edge and he breathed her name as he climaxed. Her arms were still wrapped around him and he took pleasure in her touch.

They were catching their breaths when the doorbell rang.

"Shit," he said, not quite able to move yet.

"You stay here. I've got it." He managed to roll to the side and watched Alyssa get out of his bed and shrug on his work shirt to go answer the door.

A few minutes later, she was back with the pizza, paper towels, and two bottles of beer. She took off the shirt and crawled back in bed, handing him a beer.

"Naked dinner," she proclaimed as she picked up a slice and blew on it to cool the cheese.

"Damn it, you are too good to be true." If he knew she wouldn't run screaming from the room, he might have proposed marriage that second.

Chapter 5

Doug frowned at his phone as the bartender dropped off his beer. *I'm not going to make it. Something came up,* the text read. He had an idea what had come up. Or rather, *who.*

"Thanks a lot."

"You're welcome," the bartender said on her next pass.

"No. Not you." The woman paused, cocking her head to the side. He'd seen her in here many times. He knew her name was Chanda and she was amazing to watch in action. She could pour a drink with one hand and make change with the other while taking someone's order.

"I mean thank-you for the beer, but without the attitude."

"No problem." She nodded to the phone. "Did you get stood up?"

"No. I mean not by a woman. My friend isn't coming. He's with a woman." He winced as he played back his answer to make sure it sounded right.

"Friend abandonment is worse in my book."

He stared at the hoop in her lip as it pulled up into a smile. Then she was gone. Off to do six other things at once. Her brain must be so tired by the end of the night.

Rather than go home after his first beer, he stayed for a second and then a third. He had nothing waiting at his apartment but loneliness. He wasn't in a hurry to get back to that.

MacGregor's was full, but not over-crowded. There were a number of women there without a ring or a man at their tables. He made a few attempts, but didn't bother with a lot of effort. He was looking forward to having visitation with his daughter the next day, so he was okay to have a few drinks and go home.

Watching this bartender was making him exhausted anyway. He'd switched to soda after his third beer. He was thinking about heading home, when he caught the conversation a few stools away.

Two twenty-something men were hassling Chanda. They started by making comments about her boobs. She had very nice boobs, he noticed himself, but these guys were being crass. He frowned, but did nothing until one of the guys reached over and touched her while she was wiping off the bar.

She jumped back and scowled at the guy, who just chuckled and attempted to joke it off.

"Come on, I'll leave a big tip."

His unintentional pun made the jackass on the next stool bust up.

Maybe it was the liquid courage—though three beers over a four hour time frame didn't seem likely—but Doug was on his feet heading to her rescue whether she wanted it or not.

"Don't touch the lady."

"Lady? She's a hot bartender."

"Same rules apply to her that apply to your mother. Respect, dipshit, or leave."

It was at this point that Doug remembered he was alone, and there were two of them— both were bigger than he was. Together, they were a wall of angry muscle. Shit.

"Where's Mac?" Doug threw a look at his damsel who was not in distress, but safely on the other side of the bar. Mac, the owner of the bar, was large and Scottish. Despite the skirt—or kilt—he looked like he could kick some ass.

"He took a deposit to the bank. He should be back in ten minutes."

"Ten minutes?" Doug said and looked up at the ceiling. It would have been nice to know that before he spouted off about respect. "Baseball bat?" He held out his hand expectantly.

"Sorry. We're not allowed to keep weapons behind the bar."

"A baseball bat isn't a weapon," he argued.

"The lawyer said otherwise, unless we were heading to a baseball game."

"Great." Doug let out a breath, ready to face whatever these idiots were going to hand out.

"Not so mouthy now, huh?" one of them said.

"I already said what I wanted to say. Don't touch the lady unless she says it's okay. Were you going to say okay?" He checked with Chanda, just in case he could still get out of it.

"No. Definitely not." That's what he thought she would say. He squared his shoulders.

"The lady doesn't want you touching her."

"Then the lady might want to consider a different occupation."

"What does that have to do with anything? Are you implying that bartenders don't deserve the same social protections given to everyone else? I mean, maybe—just maybe—I could see your point if this was a strip bar, but even then, there's no touching the bartenders and dancers. So you see, you're making an incorrect assumption about the job requirements."

"God. Make him shut up already," the larger of the two said to the closer of the two—the one who pushed Doug. Hard.

Despite being ready for it, he stumbled back two steps. His fists automatically came up. Years ago, he'd taken boxing, so maybe there was some fragment of memory that would kick in to help him in this situation.

"Stop it," Chanda said.

"He started it." The big guy pointed to Doug who wanted to point out that he *hadn't* started it. That *they* had started it when the guy reached across the bar and touched her. But he was saving his strength.

The smaller guy grabbed Doug's shirt and pulled him closer. Doug moved to hit him in the stomach, but his swing was deflected and he was pushed up against the bar, the worn wood digging into his back.

It was bad enough he was about to get his ass kicked, but what really bothered him was how horribly he was going to fail this woman. He'd intended to protect her honor, but now it was likely she would have to call 911 to save his life.

Using his leg, he pulled the bar stool over. The heavy chair came slamming down on the bigger man's foot, but also caught Doug's shin, causing him to wince. At least he'd done something. The smaller guy had stepped away and Doug landed a shot to his jaw. The impact sent pain through his hand and up into his wrist. In his boxing days, he always wore gloves.

The big guy didn't wait his turn and stepped around his fallen friend to take a shot. But Doug backed out of the way, just as two police officers stepped into the bar.

The skirmish dispersed pretty quickly at that point. Chanda stepped in to explain, the two assholes were ejected from the premises, and the cops gave Doug a nod of acceptance. He nodded back and set the stool back up.

"You're my hero," Chanda said setting a drink down in front of him. "On me." She held out a bag of ice. "For your hand."

"Thanks."

"Thank you."

He was halfway through his victory beer when Mac came back from the bank. Doug fought the urge to go tell him how careless he was leaving his employee there without some kind of weapon to defend herself. It was common knowledge drunk people often became hostile or rude. Instead of getting in another throw down, he took a sip of his beer and let it go. His act of bravery hadn't gone unnoticed by the nearby women. They flirted and batted their eyes at him, but he didn't have the energy to chase after them.

He caught Chanda looking at him twice. She was probably considering a two-beer payment for his security skills, but he would take the attention as long as she provided it.

They made a few jokes about the incident. By the end of the night, she had promised to name her firstborn *Doug*, regardless of the sex of the child. And she had declared the date National Doug Day.

What she didn't know was how every time she said his name he felt his chest tighten up. Maybe it was the stress from the earlier altercation.

* * * *

Chanda put the last load of glasses into the sanitizer and turned it on as Mac collected his tips. With a nod to the last remaining patron he said, "Do you want me to kick him out on his arse before I go?"

"Nah. He's harmless." Chanda knew for a fact Doug wasn't drunk. She'd served him only five beers all night, and he was now stirring the remaining ice from his soda. Besides, he'd come to her rescue.

She hadn't told Mac about the incident. No one filed a report, and she didn't want him to think she couldn't handle things. She liked this job. It gave her something to do when she wasn't working her other job. It also gave her a steady paycheck—something sculpting and painting didn't always offer.

When Mac was gone, she wiped off the bar and went to stand in front of Doug.

"Time for me to go, huh?" he said as if it was the last thing he wanted to do.

"Soon. I have to wait until that's done cycling. Do you want another soda?"

"No, thank you." He pushed the glass away.

"I can't help but notice you struck out tonight." It had been almost painful to watch. His game wasn't bad, but he came off too desperate.

He grinned and she noticed how adorable he was when he smiled. "It's quite common."

"Maybe you try too hard."

He made a show of looking down at his dress shirt and khakis.

"I've got nothing else going on. Not many women are interested in a thirty-three-year-old man who's broke because he wants to take care of his kid." Maybe not, but money wasn't everything. She'd take a nice, broke guy over a rich asshole any day of the week.

"Why haven't you ever hit on me?" she asked.

"I only hit on pretty girls," he said, letting his shoulders sag. She frowned and let out an irritated noise. So she wasn't every man's cup of tea. She looked a little scary with all the piercings and tattoos. But she had nice boobs and she was put together okay. Who the hell did he think he was?

He looked up at her and his eyes went wide. Probably because she was now glaring at him.

"Oh, God. No. That didn't come out right," he backtracked.

She crossed her arms, pushing out her nice boobs that a certain someone must not have noticed.

"How was it supposed to come out?"

"I hit on pretty girls, because I might have a chance at a *pretty* girl. You're in the beautiful woman category. I don't hit on you because you are waaaay out of my league and it's a waste of time."

She stood up straighter, stunned by his compliment. She didn't think he'd be able to talk himself out his earlier comment, but she could tell he was sincere. To keep from grinning like an idiot she bit her bottom lip, catching her lip ring between her teeth.

Doug wasn't a bad looking guy. He had an adorable smile and nice eyes. He wasn't buff, but he was solid. She'd heard him refer to himself as chubby, but she didn't agree. She knew he had a nice sense of humor—and he was obviously brave. Plus he'd just called her beautiful.

"I thought maybe you weren't into the Asian thing." She shrugged.

"That's not it. I'm very into the Asian thing. I mean, not to the point of it being a fetish. Just the right amount of interest." He let out a breath and rolled his eyes. "You see now why I haven't hit on you?"

"Well, it doesn't seem like you have many options left. Maybe you should give it a try."

* * * *

Doug stared at the woman for a moment, unsure what her game was. Or maybe he'd thought about her so much he was having delusions.

"I don't even know what I would say. Even when I fantasize about you, we don't talk." He closed his eyes when he realized what he'd just said.

Her only response was a giggle. Great, she was amused. It could have been worse. She could have freaked out and called him a pervert. If she knew the kinds of things he'd fantasized about with her she might.

He ran his hand through his hair and laughed.

"Even if I had a chance in hell, it would be difficult to recover from telling you that."

"I'll give you a restart."

"Yes. Because a restart will make a world of difference."

"Come on. I'm giving you a chance here. You already have hero status. For someone who professes to think I'm beautiful, you seem to be letting the opportunity slip away."

"Fantasy you is not so bossy."

"Get used to it." She smiled and his heart sped up. He hated to break it to his heart that this was going nowhere. And his dick...Well, it never listened anyway, so he didn't have to bother.

"Okay. Here goes." He twisted his neck to the side and rolled his shoulders. "Chanda..."

She looked surprised.

"You know my name?"

"Of course, I know your name. I've been coming here for like two years. You bring me drinks. I like my fantasies to have names at least. It makes them more realistic."

She laughed and then waved her hand.

"Sorry. Continue."

"Chanda," he repeated and took a breath. "Watching you work captivates me." At this point, he didn't even care that he was embarrassing himself. He was a complete ass and this was more than likely going nowhere.

"Oh?"

"Are you completely creeped out yet?" He laughed it off, but knew it sounded bad.

"Oddly, no. Go ahead."

"Wow. All right." He folded his arms on the bar and leaned in closer even though no one else was there to hear him. "Even when I'm sitting at the table over there." He pointed to the corner table. "I can pick out the sound of your laughter over all the other voices and sounds in the bar. It's not that it's loud, it's just the best sound I've ever heard and I listen for it so I don't miss it."

It was the most truthful thing he'd ever said to a potential date. But why not? He had nothing to lose. Except maybe having to avoid his favorite bar because his drinks would now contain spit. He went in for the kill.

"And every time you smile, I find myself wondering what it would feel like to kiss you with that lip ring. Would it be cold? I mean, it's metal. But then it's in your skin and you'd be hot. At least 98.6 degrees, right? So the metal should conduct the heat from your lips—and now I sound like a science teacher."

While he was babbling, she'd stepped out from the bar and was on his side. Looking at her this closely, his throat worked to swallow.

She was small. Short, but well proportioned. Except for her breasts which were bigger than expected for her stature. She always wore tight T-shirts. Mostly V-necks. She was obviously aware she had a nice rack. He wondered if they were real.

She was smiling at him as she stepped closer.

"Come see for yourself." For a second, he worried he'd said something out loud regarding her boobs. It took a second for his brain to rewind back to what she could possibly be talking about.

When he thought he'd figured it out, he repeated the process. Surely he'd missed something in the conversation. She couldn't possibly be suggesting he kiss her to find out what the lip ring felt like.

"I'm sorry. What?"

"Kiss me, Doug. It was a nice line. Let's see if you can bring it home."

At another time, with another woman, he might have taken a second or two to plan out his approach and technique. But with Chanda, he just acted. Primal need took over in an effort to claim her mouth before she retracted her offer. Which she would do as soon as she remembered who he was.

His lips pressed against hers and his tongue reached out, needing hers. With a soft moan, she melted against him. Those firm but very real breasts pressed up against his chest. His arms wrapped around her tiny waist, and pulled her closer as he tilted his head to deepen the best kiss of his life.

Better than any fantasy he'd ever conjured up, he met her stroke for stroke, not relenting at all.

A horn blew outside, proving this was real. He would never add a horn to his fantasies. It was too distracting. Especially when it went off again.

Stupid cab.

Cab.

Hell. He'd called a cab. The beeping was for him.

Chanda pulled away, a surprised smile on her face.

"Is that for you?"

"No," he lied. He'd find another one. Or walk. To Queens.

"So what did you think?" She was waiting for his answer.

"Think?" He hadn't been thinking.

"About the lip ring."

He glanced down at it, noticing her lips were pink and glossy from kissing him. He shook his head and laughed.

"To be honest, I didn't even feel it. I was busy feeling so many other things."

She bit her lip and he wanted to lean over and do the same thing. But he'd already gotten more than he ever expected possible.

They stared at each other for a long moment. Just when he opened his mouth to say something—not that he knew what would come out—the chime on the machine behind the bar went off.

"I'm free to go," she announced.

"I'll walk you out," he offered. He didn't like the idea of her being alone. It was the reason he'd stayed so late. He waited while she grabbed her bag and locked up.

Out on the street, he hailed her a cab. When it pulled over to the curb, he opened the door and smiled as she slid inside and moved to the far side.

"You coming?" she asked, her head tilting to the side.

"With you?" She wanted to share a cab? He didn't think he'd be able to keep his hands off her in the small space.

"Yeah."

"I live in Queens."

"That's nice, but I was thinking you would come to my place."

"Oh." His brain only took a fraction of a second to put it together, despite it being the most improbable calculation he'd ever encountered. "Oh! Yes," he answered and got in the cab before she had the chance to change her mind.

* * * *

It was almost two in the morning and Grayson was exhausted, but happier than he knew possible. After the pizza, he and Liss had moved on to rounds two, three, and four.

"Will you stay tonight?" he asked.

"Do you mind?"

"I want you to stay," he said honestly.

"I want to stay too. Thanks." She snuggled up against him.

"What are you doing tomorrow?"

She let out a big sigh, and for a moment he wasn't sure if she was going to answer. Maybe she was going to bolt. He never knew with her.

"I guess I'll be working on my résumé so I can start sending it out."

"You're changing jobs? You don't like working at the same company as me?" he joked.

"Actually, I need to find a job in Albany. I'm moving back in with my mother." She let her head fall to the side in defeat.

"Why?" Grayson propped himself up on his elbow so he could look at her. He didn't want her moving away.

"Because I'm ready to go back home." This was a lie. She didn't even try to convince him. "It's just temporary," she added.

"Do you believe that?"

She shook her head and pressed her lips together.

"No. I'm going to get sucked back there and never be able to escape." Tears threatened, causing her eyes to glisten and her lip to tremble. "I'm sorry. I'm not going to cry. I promise."

"Are you sure? It looks like you need to." Gray winced and pulled her closer.

"What good will it do?"

"None, but it might make you feel better."

"Guys hate crying," she said.

"That we do, but sometimes it's inevitable." He stroked her hair and kissed her forehead. With her face against his chest, he wasn't sure if she let herself cry or not, but it was nice just to hold her. "I have to say, I'm rather insulted."

"Why?"

"I offered you a very nice room for a decent price and you're turning it down to move to Albany. You might as well tell me I'm worse than Albany."

She laughed and looked up at him.

"I like you, Gray. But I can't move in with you. It wouldn't be right. We want different things. Maybe we can meet up when I come to the city to visit."

"I don't see that happening. Besides, I don't know how I feel about hooking up with someone from *Albany*." He shivered this time, making it more theatrical. As if Albany was a slum. It made her laugh. Mission accomplished.

They lay there in silence for a long moment while he thought over the situation. In all reality he *should* be insulted. She was brushing off his perfectly reasonable offer and giving up everything she had here. For what? Just so she wouldn't have to spend more time with him?

"Liss?" He checked to see if she was sleeping.

"Yeah?"

"Why won't you move in here? Really? I mean, I'm not making you sign a lease. You would be free to try it out for a month or so, and if it didn't work out you could go with Plan Albany next month. I don't get it."

"I don't expect you to get it."

She didn't elaborate.

"This would be the part where you tell me the reason."

"I don't trust people." He got that. He had his own trust issues. Didn't everyone?

"I understand, but I'm offering you a room, not matrimony or even an exclusive affair. You wouldn't need to trust me any further than knowing I wouldn't steal your stuff or eat the last of your Oreos."

"Really?"

"Yeah. Really. It would be just like this, only you would have a home and not have to move to Albany."

"I'll think about it."

Thinking about it was a step in the right direction. He wasn't giving up.

Chapter 6

Alyssa found a T-shirt that smelled clean on top of his dresser. She slipped it on, taking a moment to notice how sexy Grayson looked stretched out in his bed with the sheet low across his hips. One small tug and she'd be able to see everything. She sighed and went out to the kitchen to start coffee and see if there was anything to make for breakfast.

The refrigerator shocked her. He had real food. Bacon, eggs. The milk wasn't even out of date. She opened a few cabinets to find a hodgepodge of cookware, including a skillet.

"Excellent." She put it on the stove and checked for plates. She found a toaster and bread. Things were getting better and better.

As the eggs cooked, she looked around his place. It was very neat for a guy's home. It wasn't huge, but the living room was bigger than her entire apartment.

Not her apartment for much longer, she reminded herself and flipped the eggs over. When they were done, she put the eggs, bacon, and toast on two plates. She poured coffee, adding tons of the vanilla creamer that she found in the refrigerator, and carried everything into his room.

He was just waking when she set the coffee on the nightstand.

"What is this?" he asked.

"Breakfast in bed."

"Seriously?" He looked adorable with his big smile and bed head. "I've never had breakfast in bed."

"It's awesome, unless you spill something," she warned while handing him his plate.

"This is the second meal I'm eating with you in bed with no clothes on."

"I have clothes on," she noted.

"Yeah. Mine." He tilted his head to look her over. "You make that shirt look good, Ms. Sinclair."

"Thanks." She laughed at the formality while he made "mmm" sounds about his breakfast. When they were done, he gathered their plates and took them out to the kitchen, refilling their coffees.

They sat in bed for a long time, talking about where they grew up, and where they went to school. She was surprised by how easy it was for her to share information about herself. He was safe.

Eventually, she realized she needed to get going. Staying for breakfast was one thing, but lunch would be overstaying her welcome.

"I should go," she said.

He nodded as they slipped out of bed. She followed him to the hall, still wearing his shirt. He'd put on a pair of boxers and she loved the way they hung on his lean hips.

In the hall, he opened the other bedroom door and leaned against the jamb.

"So did you think about it?"

She had, but she let out a sigh, unwilling to tell him he was breaking through her resolve. She didn't want to leave the city. She didn't want to move back with her mother. And worse, she actually wanted to live with him. But she had lived with a man before and it hadn't worked out. In a very bad way.

He reached for her, letting his hands rest on her hips. He picked her up and kissed her as he turned and then put her down inside the empty room.

"Please Liss." He whispered with his forehead pressed against hers.

"I can't live with you," she said, but without real conviction.

"Why not? What's the matter with me?"

"I'm not sure. I don't know you well enough to know what is wrong with you. Other than the fact you invite strangers to live with you."

"When I was in college, I moved into a dorm with a stranger. Guess what? He's still my best friend to this day."

"Do you hear what you're saying?" she said.

"I do. I think it would be fun."

"Fun? Fun because you would get sex and breakfast whenever you want it? Would I be like a slave for room and board?"

His head snapped back and he looked insulted.

"No. You would pay your rent with actual money, not services rendered. That's real nice, Liss." He frowned at her.

Why had she given him permission to call her Liss? She liked it too much.

"Sorry." She apologized for the low blow, but certainly if she'd thought it, other people would too.

"Just forget it. Move back to Albany." He made a wide sweep of his hand. "I was just trying to help."

"I'm really sorry. I appreciate your offer, I do. But I don't think you've thought it through. I don't do things like this. I'm all about fun and no bullshit, remember? And I think you're looking for something more."

He pressed her back against the wall and bent to look her right in the eyes.

"No bullshit, Alyssa. I want you to move in here because I think it would be fun. If you don't want to do the sex thing, we can simply be roommates. It's an empty room. I need to fill it; you need a place to live. Take it."

"And the price you gave me is what you would charge anyone else?" It seemed too reasonable.

"Yes. It also includes water." He winked at her.

"You're really serious about this?" she asked as excitement began flooding her system unwittingly.

"I'm an accountant. We think every minor detail to death."

"And I would *just* be your roommate? Nothing more?"

"Nothing more."

"And we won't let it turn into a romantic comedy? We are vowing not to have sex with each other if we become roommates?" Kenley had seemed sure if they continued to have sex he would expect more. While she knew she was invulnerable to such things, she didn't want to be put in a position where she had to hurt his feelings. And then lose her home. Again.

He looked up at the ceiling for a second.

"Just so I'm clear, why would we not be having the sex anymore?"

"Because people who live together and have sex are in a relationship. People who live together without sex or romantic ties are roommates."

"I see." He nodded. "My other roommate and I used to hang out, watch movies and things. Would that be acceptable?"

"I could probably do that." Kenley hadn't warned her about any of those things. She let the smile take over her face. "I can cook."

"We can share that job."

She thought of living there—a real apartment, with windows and an elevator. He had a washer and dryer, and real doors and bedrooms. Plus it was only four blocks from where she worked. All of it would be amazing on its own, but the best thing about the apartment was still standing in the doorway watching her reaction.

Grayson.

She had a lot of fun hanging out with him. Would that change? Would he still want more than friendship even if they didn't have sex? Would he get sick of her and kick her out?

Even if that happened, she would be no worse off than she was at the moment. At least this arrangement would buy her a little more time.

"Okay, but I have some questions," she said.

"Of course, I expected as much. Let's hear them." Gray smiled at ease.

"Since we won't be sleeping with each other, how do you want to handle guests?"

"We each have our own room. Guests shouldn't be an issue, so long as you don't bring home some loser who steals my TV."

"Okay, so we're responsible for anything our guests steal." Alyssa made it a rule.

"Fair enough."

"What about groceries?"

"Trent used to pay for the groceries because I cooked. How do you want to do it?"

"We could take turns. One week one of us buys and the other cooks and then we switch."

"That sounds like a good plan. I'm in." He was making this awfully easy. Too easy.

"What do you get out of this?" she asked, her eyes narrowed at him.

"Well, I know I like hanging out with you and you have a job. You're neat and I can trust you. I guess what I'm getting is a great roommate without having to do all the work of finding one."

"Okay. I'm in." She held out her hand to shake on the dumbest arrangement she'd ever made.

He looked down at her hand and stood straighter in the doorway. He reached for her offered palm, but then pulled back as if she had cooties.

"Before we shake hands and you officially turn into my roommate, I was just thinking maybe I'd get one more shot at Alyssa the hot girl who screams my name when she comes."

Alyssa smiled and leaned closer. Surely it wouldn't count if they had sex *before* they became roommates. He seemed to understand the rules. If they both knew it was just sex, there'd be no harm in extending the fun part a little longer.

"That is a great idea," she said, surprising him as much as herself. "One more time, and then we turn into roommates."

He picked her up and carried her across the hall. He set her on the bed and climbed over her. He was already pulling up the T-shirt she was wearing.

"This is mine," he said with a rough voice.

"Roommates borrow each other's clothes," she pointed out.

"You have to ask permission. Make that a rule."

"So noted." She giggled as he ran his tongue along the edge of her ear. His fingers gripped her hair and he sat up holding out a handful of her blonde hair in front of her face.

"I don't want the bathroom and the shower full of girly hair crap."

"One shampoo and conditioner per person," she agreed as his fingers moved down her stomach and slid into her, causing her to gasp. He had the best technique. He was a genius with his fingers.

"Also, one razor per person," he added with a slow smile as he watched himself stroking her. "And no sharing."

"Not a problem," she squeaked when he touched her in just the right spot. They were so great together. He had her gasping in mere seconds. As soon as her last tremor faded, he was moving inside her, toward his own release. She shifted and pushed up against him, causing him to finish with a groan.

"I usually shower at night," he told her between breaths.

"I shower in the morning."

"Would I be able to shave and brush my teeth while you were in the shower?"

"The shower curtain is solid, so that should be fine."

"I might want to get a new shower curtain. Clear."

"Are you changing the rules?" She propped herself up on her elbow to look down at him.

"No, ma'am."

"Are you ready to shake yet?"

He kissed her neck and moved to her ear.

"Just one more time," he whispered. "Then I'll be ready."

She rolled over on top of him, not sure if she would ever be ready to give this up. Why had she asked Kenley for advice?

Because Kenley was a normal person with normal feelings. She would know what other regular people expected.

Grayson seemed perfectly okay with it just being sex, but she couldn't risk hurting him. For both their sakes.

She wished she wasn't fucked up. Maybe she could have been happy with him instead of keeping him at a safe distance, for his own sake.

Chapter 7

By late Saturday night, Gray knew he hadn't had his fill of being with her. But since he was exhausted, he gave in and held out his hand to seal the deal.

Alyssa looked at it and kissed his palm, sending a jolt from her lips to his groin. Damn, how did she do that?

"How about we shake in the morning. I want to sleep here, if that's okay," she said settling in.

"It's very okay." He pulled her close, putting his face in her hair so he could smell her as he drifted off. He didn't care if they ever shook on it.

It seemed like a silly agreement. Why would either of them want to give this up? They were so damn good at it. No doubt she was worried he might get emotionally attached if they continued to have sex. He'd have to convince her he was up for this challenge. He could enjoy her company without taking it to the next level. Just because he never had a long-term, casual relationship with a woman didn't mean he couldn't handle it.

Sunday morning he woke up alone, but heard the shower running. A smile took over his face as he slid out from under the sheet to go join her.

The door was hanging open, an invitation that he jumped on. Her body was perfection in the misty shower with suds sliding over her curves down to her perfect toes. He nuzzled up behind her, noticing how hot her skin felt against his.

"Are you sure we need to keep the rule about not having sex?" he asked.

"If for no other reason than we need to leave the apartment at some point."

"I guess." He fake pouted. "But not until you move in."

"I was going to do that today. After we shook on our agreement."

"Today?"

"Yeah. I figure I can make it in three trips. The biggest thing I have to carry is an ottoman. The rest is just clothes and a few crates of hair products," she teased.

"I know a guy who has an SUV. I'll borrow it and we can move everything at once."

"That would be great. Thank-you. I really appreciate you letting me move in here. Really."

"Letting you move in here after we have sex in the shower, you mean?"

"Right. *After* sex in the shower."

Since she was already clean, she lathered him up, paying special attention to his favorite parts. She washed his hair. Never in a million years would he have expected shampooing to be so erotic.

Maybe it had something to do with her breasts in his face.

When all the soap was rinsed away, he dried his hands on the towel enough to wrestle the condom wrapper open. They should make special grips on them for water activities. Once properly covered, he pressed her back against the shower wall, hitching one of her knees up by his hip so he had access.

She moaned his name when he slid inside, and he wondered again how he was going to give this up. Surely they could come up with some way to make it work so they could have this too. He took contracts very seriously, even if they were only binding by a handshake.

After their shower escapades, they dressed and went out for breakfast. He tried once again to sway her on the sex thing, but she wouldn't budge. He had no choice but to agree to her terms and hope for the best. Once he paid the tab, he held his hand out.

"Roommates?" he said.

"Roommates from here out."

"Good. Now let's go move all your crap." He'd already contacted Trent to borrow his car.

When Alyssa let them in her old apartment, her roommate was still in her pajamas and looked like hell.

"Shh," she said with a glare, though they hadn't spoken.

"I'm here to get my stuff. I'm moving out today."

"You're moving in with him?"

"Yep."

"Did you tell him how he's going to have to deal with your screaming all night?"

"I don't scream all night."

"How would you know? You're sleeping."

"At least I'm not screaming out someone's name while I'm having sex in the same room as you. Who does that?"

"We didn't have anywhere else to go and I thought you were asleep!" Sasha defended.

"I'm going to wait downstairs. Let me know when you're…" Grayson motioned to the room and backed out of the awkward conversation.

As he went downstairs to avoid the drama, he found himself wondering if Alyssa *did* scream in her sleep and why. He also wondered what would happen when she was screaming someone else's name while having sex in the room across the hall from him. How would he feel about that?

He wanted to be an adult and say he would be fine, but part of him knew he wasn't that much of an adult. He pulled the Iron Man Pez dispenser from his pocket and took a hit.

It was too late now. They'd already shaken hands and she was moving out. He was committed to this relationship. Though he knew better than to use that word in front of his new roommate.

* * * *

"Are you kidding me?" Gray said as Alyssa carried down a bag of stuff. Since she hadn't had time to get boxes, she'd just tossed everything into garbage bags. It looked like they were moving body parts instead of her possessions.

"This can't be everything," Gray said doubtfully.

"This is it, I swear."

"You're perfect," he repeated his earlier sentiment with a wink. That wink made her stomach flutter, but she looked away.

They had a much better chance of making this work if they were just friends. Kenley was right, sex complicated things. Not that it had complicated anything between Gray and her yet, but sooner or later he might decide he wanted something more. Something she couldn't give.

After they moved her things into her new room, she went to the grocery store and stocked up on food since Grayson offered to take the first turn to cook.

"I'm impressed," she said as they ate dinner on the sofa.

"Really? It's a salad and chicken. Who can mess that up?"

"You'd be surprised," she said. "Sasha messed up EasyMac."

"You're living the good life now, princess." He winked at her and visions of him on top of her flashed before her eyes. *Calm down*, she told herself. She hadn't even made it one day and already she was lusting over him.

Allison B. Hanson

"Don't I know it," she allowed.

They did the dishes together and she couldn't help but smile at how nice it felt to have a companion. He stacked the clean dishes neatly in the appropriate cabinet and she nodded her approval.

"Are you a neat freak too?" she asked.

"A little. Except for clothes." He paused for a moment. There was something that he wasn't saying.

"What?" she pressed.

He shrugged before he continued.

"I hate that I have to dress up for work, so usually when I get home, I take my clothes off the second I walk in the door." He laughed and shook his head. "Don't worry. I'll make sure to get to my room."

"I don't want you to have to change the way you live just because I'm here."

"This is your home now too," he said considerately. She pouted at the idea of missing a naked Grayson when he got home from work.

Whose great plan was this?

Chapter 8

Grayson didn't know where to look when Alyssa came out of the bathroom later that night. She all but ran into him, wearing only a thin cotton tank top and shorts that were so short it looked like her ass got hungry and was trying to eat them. Her nipples were hard and poking through the fabric. It was a sexual fantasy overload, and he couldn't do anything about it thanks to the friends arrangement they'd agreed to.

He should have put in a clause stating that if a person looked this sexy when she left the bathroom, all rules were null and void. Why hadn't he thought of that?

"All yours," she said.

"Excuse me?" He coughed, hoping she meant she was all his.

"I'm done in the bathroom and I only left one shampoo and conditioner in there, per the agreement."

"Right. Thanks."

He hobbled into the bathroom and turned the water to lukewarm. He had a feeling he would be taking a lot of lukewarm showers in the future. When he picked up her shampoo and sniffed it, he was instantly flooded with memories of the two of them in his bed naked. His cock lurched, eager to make the fantasy a reality.

"Sorry. No can do. I shook on it." He frowned at his penis and picked up his own shampoo.

When he finished, he paused by her door for a second before heading to his room. He wasn't sure if he should wish her a good night or maybe ask for a kiss. He decided just to let it go. He rarely told Trent good night. He would use his past roommate relationship as a guide in this new relationship with Alyssa. From the handshake on, obviously.

He lay there awake for a long time, thinking of how stupid he was for agreeing to this. Eventually he fell asleep, but didn't stay that way for very long. He woke to the sound of a female screaming.

Some stupid instinct had him out of bed and running into her room to protect her before he even contemplated he might need a weapon. Fortunately he didn't. She was dreaming, just as Sasha had predicted.

He flipped on the light to find Alyssa thrashing around in bed as if being attacked by an invisible threat. The light woke her, and she looked around, her chest heaving. Yes, he noticed her chest heaving even in the middle of a crisis.

"What is it?" he asked as he sat on the edge of the bed. She was having a hard time catching her breath. She coughed a few times and he noticed her shaking hands. "Bad dream?" he guessed. She nodded confirmation as he took one of her hands and stroked it.

"You're fine. Do you want to talk about it?" She shook her head quickly. "Want some water?" He hadn't had a nightmare in a long time, but he remembered his mother bringing him water. Again she shook her head.

"I'm sorry," she said, her voice raspy. "I should have warned you about this. As Sasha mentioned, I scream in my sleep, but not all night. It happens sometimes. It should be better once I'm used to my surroundings. It's worse in new places."

"It's okay. I'm sure I'll learn to sleep through the blood-curdling screams." This was only a slight exaggeration.

"You're a good guy."

"So they say." He shook his head and stood up, trying to be the good guy and stop ogling her breasts.

"You can leave the light on," she said quietly. Was she still frightened? He opened his mouth to offer to stay with her, but closed it. He didn't need to find excuses to get into bed with her. He'd made an agreement, and he was keeping his word.

* * * *

Doug strolled into the office on Monday morning feeling like a new man. His first stop was Grayson's office. His friend had come to work after ladies' night with a smug grin. Doug wanted to give him a taste of his own medicine.

Except Gray still had the grin.

"Seriously?" Doug complained.

"What about you? You're smiling too. What's that all about?"

"I had a very good weekend."

"I thought you had Lucy on Saturday."

"I did. We had a great time at the park. But the smile is from the awesome sex I had on Friday night after you didn't show. And then had again last night." He nearly fell over when Chanda called Sunday afternoon to invite him over.

"Not that it's a competition, but the last time I had sex was Sunday morning, so I guess you win."

Doug had definitely won.

On Friday night, Chanda took him home to her warehouse loft. It was huge, but filled with half-finished sculptures. The two bedrooms were small in comparison to the rest of the space, but there was a bed, and that was all that had mattered once they got inside. Which wasn't easy.

It had taken longer than it should have to open the door, but he couldn't keep his lips off her, and she wasn't able to put the key in the lock when his face was stuck to hers.

Eventually, they got in and the clothes came off. He followed her up the stairs to her room and there he lost track of the sounds and the feelings. He never understood the hype about chemistry. He assumed it was something people made up to get out of a relationship. After all, his ex had told him that very thing. "We don't have any chemistry."

But it wasn't hype. It was real, and he had tons of it with Chanda. The reason he'd never understood it before was because he had never truly experienced it. Now he had.

He couldn't remember the last time he had sex with Julie, his ex, more than once in a row. Maybe their honeymoon? He thought he was too old for multiple sessions. He was wrong. He just needed the proper motivation.

Chanda provided plenty of motivation.

Unfortunately, his stellar mood was cut short when Randy called a meeting.

"I think we have more meetings about work, than we work," he whispered to Grayson as they took their seats in the conference room.

"I think you're right."

"First thing. The Knott account needs a new home." Everyone groaned, knowing it had been passed around like a plague. The owner was a crabby bastard who was never happy with anyone. "Lester is leaving and I'm not going to turn this mess over to someone new. So who wants it?"

Doug was careful not to make eye contact.

"Give it to Doug. He's used to getting his ass handed to him," Reynolds joked.

"Great, Doug. Thanks for volunteering," Randy said, and flipped the page on his tablet like it was a done deal. Doug might have stood up to them, but he had the fight beaten out of him years ago by his ex-wife. He'd learned it was just easier to go with the flow and not make a fuss.

The meeting went on like all the rest. Randy wanted to keep everyone in the loop. Apparently, they were moving one of the account managers up to a senior auditor position.

"So if you have any suggestions regarding the open position, let me know. We'll be conducting interviews next week."

They were dismissed shortly after, but as he waited to walk out with Gray, his friend had stopped to offer a name.

"Alyssa Sinclair."

Doug frowned as they went back to their offices.

"Are you sure that's a good idea? You're already sleeping with her—and living with her. Now you want to work with her too? You shouldn't put your meat where you get your bread."

"What?" Gray chuckled.

"It's a saying." Something his father had said.

"You get a sandwich when you put meat and bread together. Sandwiches are awesome."

Doug hoped for Grayson's sake, this turned out to be as great as a sandwich.

* * * *

By the third night of living with Alyssa, her screaming no longer had him running to her rescue. Though it was difficult to fall back to sleep when he knew she was probably lying in her bed with the light on trying to convince herself she was safe.

"You look like hell," Doug said Friday morning as Gray walked into his office. "Is it a good kind of hell or a bad kind?"

Before Gray had a chance to answer, he was interrupted by a tapping on the door. Alyssa was standing there with a paper bag.

"Hey," he greeted her with a tired smile.

"Hi. You were running late and I realized you left your wallet. So it's in here with the lunch I made you. Mainly because I noticed there was no cash in your wallet." She smiled and held out the bag.

"Were you looking in my wallet for a finder's fee?" he asked.

"Something like that." She laughed and Doug coughed, calling attention to himself.

"Oh. Alyssa, this is Doug. Doug, this is Alyssa."

"Alyssa. Very nice to meet you," Doug said. "I've heard a lot about you."

"Nice to meet you too. I have to get back downstairs. See you later. Have a nice day."

"You too. Do you want to meet at the bar after work?" he suggested.

"Sure."

"Text me when you're leaving."

"Will do." With that, she was gone.

"Uh-hum." Doug fake coughed with a grin on his face. "Are you guys dating?"

"No." He hadn't explained the situation to Doug, mainly because he was hoping the situation would change back to sleeping together.

"She brought you your wallet. She brought you lunch, and she is meeting you after work. I'm pretty sure that's dating."

"No. She's my roommate. We're not having sex." Grayson said, wishing it wasn't true.

"But you said you had sex on Sunday morning."

"Right."

"It wasn't with her?"

"It was. But we're not having sex now that she's moved in."

"I need to go. This is weird." Doug left the office while Grayson laughed.

He sent Alyssa a text while he ate his lunch, thanking her for the awesome sandwich. Made from meat and bread.

She texted back a smiley face, which made him chuckle. He had to admit, it did feel a lot like dating.

* * * *

At one-thirty, Alyssa received a call from Martin Hasher, the Hasher in Hasher and Borne. She assumed he'd dialed the wrong extension, but answered using her professional voice.

"Alyssa Sinclair, how may I help you?"

"Hi, Alyssa. Would you have a moment to come up to my office in about ten minutes?"

She still thought he had the wrong extension, but he had clearly said her name. He had to have meant her.

"Uh, yes. Of course. I'll be right up."

"Thank-you."

"Shit." She hung her head as soon as the receiver hit the cradle. Had he seen her dropping off lunch in Grayson's office? Did he know they were living together? Was he going to tell her company policy forbade coworkers from living together? She was going to end up like Kenley. Out on her ass without so much as a reference. "Shit," she repeated and picked up a notebook to head upstairs to her doom.

She waited in the guest chair outside his office for twenty minutes, making sure her irritation didn't show on her face. It was as bad as a doctor appointment when they say to show up fifteen minutes before your appointment, and then you end up waiting thirty minutes past the appointment before you're called inside.

"Ms. Sinclair?"

"Yes." She sprang up from the seat and smiled, her internal ranting forgotten.

"Please come in. Sorry for making you wait."

"No problem." *See? I'm accommodating. Please don't fire me.*

"Have a seat." He gestured to the chairs in front of his desk. "I've asked you to come up today for an impromptu interview. I have your employee file so I know the basics, but I wanted to discuss the possibility of moving you up to an account manager position."

She pressed her lips together to keep her mouth from falling open or shouting her excitement. She couldn't believe this was finally happening. She'd put her name in for job after job, and hadn't gotten a minute with the CEO. Now here she was interviewing for...

For a job she hadn't even known was open. She checked the job listing every day. Nothing had been posted for an account manager. She hadn't put in for the position. Why would he be considering her?

She hoped the answer was that they'd noticed how many times she'd applied in the past and decided to save time, but she doubted that was the case.

"The first issue would be to make sure you have a desire to make a change or an interest in the account manager position." Ah ha. They would have known she was interested in making a change if they had reviewed her previous inquires. "I see you're qualified, and I spoke to your supervisor to get her input."

"She suggested me for the job?" Alyssa was blown away. The woman wasn't nearly as awful as the manager before her, but Liss never got the feeling Millicent would want to help her get ahead. Especially since Alyssa was doing so much of her work.

"No." He flipped through the papers in front of him to find the answer. "It was Grayson Hollinger."

"Oh." She swallowed, letting that information soak in. "Yes, I do have a desire to move up in the company. I'm very interested in hearing more about the account manager position."

"Good. It's always nice to be able to hire from within when we have the opportunity." She wondered if they'd only taken on this strategy because they had run out of family members.

They went on with the interview. He asked questions and she knocked them out of the park despite not having had the chance to prepare. It was probably better this way. An ambush interview meant there was no time to worry or panic about the appointment. She still wasn't sure how she felt about Grayson's involvement.

Her mind was too busy acing the interview to spend brain power on her reaction to his interfering. She'd decide later.

"Well, I think that's all I need. We'll be making our decision and letting everyone know by next Wednesday. Thank you for your time."

"Thank you for speaking with me." They shook hands and once she was in the elevator heading back down to her floor, her knees began trembling. She was thankful for the delayed reaction.

She was useless the rest of the afternoon. She found herself staring off into space imagining what it would be like to have this new job. Not to mention the extra money.

When it was time to go, she sent Grayson a text:

Heading out. See you at MacGregor's.

Right behind you.

She waited for him outside the pub, still cycling through an endless array of emotions. When he walked up with the big smile she picked the first emotion and went with it.

"What have you done?" she snapped, knocking the smile right off his face.

* * * *

Grayson stared at her, stunned. "What do you mean?" he asked, feeling like he was being led into a trap.

"I had an interview today with Martin Hasher for a position I didn't even know was available."

"Really? That's great. I hope you get it."

"So I can work with you? It's not enough that we live together, now we must spend every second of the workday together as well?"

"We wouldn't be working together, Liss. I might occasionally have questions and need to see some of your reports, but for the most part, I don't interact with account managers." Was she angry that he'd tried to help? "They asked us if we knew anyone internally who would be good for the position. I gave them your name. If you're not interested, you can pass. I know you've been trying to move up so I thought I'd throw your name in the ring."

"Why didn't you tell me?"

"I didn't want you to get your hopes up. Randy Tabor is notorious for hiring his friends and family members. If he went that route, I didn't want you to be disappointed. I wasn't sure he'd even give Martin your name."

She twisted her lips to the side and nodded.

"Thank you."

He stood very still, unsure if this was a trap.

"I'm sorry. I thought you were trying to control where I lived and worked."

Was this her issue with relationships? Had someone tried to control her? He couldn't imagine Alyssa putting up with that.

"I'm not trying to control you. Was that a problem with someone in the past?" he asked, unable to help himself.

"No. But I've always been independent."

"I hadn't noticed." He let the sarcasm ooze as he opened the door to the pub. The air conditioning rushed out, hitting him in the face.

There were two seats together at the bar, so he helped her get settled and then sat next to her. It was a different bar, but it felt very similar to the night they'd met. The night they first had sex.

He let out a disappointed sigh.

"Startin' early?" Mac said as he put coasters down in front of them. He had a Scottish accent that made it difficult to understand what he said after a few drinks.

"On the way home. Mac, this is my roommate Alyssa. Liss, this is Mac, my favorite bartender in the city."

"She's a fine bit prettier than your old roommate."

"Yes," Grayson allowed.

"What's your pleasure?" Mac asked Alyssa.

"For some strange reason I feel like a Scotch," she said with a chuckle. "I'm celebrating, so give me the good stuff."

"Aye, this one's a heartbreaker, Gray. You're in for it," the bartender warned, giving Alyssa a wink. He brought their drinks and went to help the regulars at the other end of the bar.

"Starting with the hard stuff?" Gray asked looking down at her drink. "I was hoping it would help me sleep."

"You still don't want to tell me what your nightmares are about? It might help to talk about it. Take the power away from your subconscious." She raised a brow at him and he shrugged. "My older sister is a psychiatrist. Stuff rubs off."

She took a sip of her drink and let out a big sigh.

"I dream that a man is attacking me."

"I kind of gathered that by the way you kick and hit, and yell things like 'No!' and 'Get off me!' Who's the guy?"

She shook her head and looked away.

"I don't know. I can't see his face, he's wearing a—I can't see." It was obvious by her body language she didn't want to talk about it, so he changed the subject.

He didn't know what she needed from him, so he backed off.

Since she was a lightweight and her drink was kicking her ass, he bought them dinner. When they'd finished eating, he helped her up to their apartment.

She fell asleep on the sofa while he watched TV. She jumped when he woke her up to go to bed.

"You seem pretty sleepy, maybe tonight will be the night," Grayson encouraged as he left her by her door. "Sleep tight."

"Thanks. You too."

Despite their wishes, Grayson was awoken by the screaming at 12:06 a.m. He sat up and waited until it stopped, then lay back down wishing he could do something, but he was powerless to help.

His door opened and the light from the hall illuminated Alyssa's silhouette in the doorway. She just stood there.

"You okay?" he asked.

"Would you mind...would it be okay if I stayed with you?" she asked. Her voice sounded so sad he wouldn't have been able to turn her away even if he'd wanted to. He didn't want to.

"Sure." He slid over and she climbed in next to him. He draped his arm over her waist as she snuggled up against him, her back against his chest. His face was near her hair and he closed his eyes, breathing in her scent. He could do this. Casual.

They both fell asleep and slept peacefully the rest of the night.

* * * *

Doug frowned when he walked into MacGregor's on Friday evening and found two new people behind the bar. When he'd left Chanda's place last Sunday, they didn't have future plans. He'd been so absorbed in his post-sex high that he hadn't thought to ask her schedule.

"What can I get you?" the younger male bartender asked.

"Uh, is Chanda working tonight?" Maybe she would be coming in later.

"No. She's off tonight."

"Oh. I'll have a beer." He pointed to the brew list and tapped his fingers as the guy went to get it. Mac noticed him and came closer.

"You're Doug?" His accent was so thick it took a second to piece it together.

"Yes. I'm Doug."

"Chanda isn't working tonight."

"Yeah. He told me."

"Did she give you her number?" Mac tilted his head in confusion.

"She did. I just wasn't sure if I should bother her."

Mac's face broke out in a wide grin.

"Nah, you probably shouldn't bother her."

"So you're saying I *should* call her?" Doug asked as Mac walked away laughing. Weren't bartenders recognized for their ability to give their patrons good advice? Maybe not in Scotland.

Doug looked down at his phone and sighed.

Chapter 9

Chanda tossed a lump of clay aside and frowned at the line she'd just created. It wasn't the way she'd seen it in her head. She lifted her ribbon tool to take another try when her phone vibrated.

She wiped her hands and answered, seeing Doug's name on the display. "Hello?"

"Hi." She could hear the familiar sounds of the bar in the background. "You're not working tonight."

"No. I have the night off."

"That's nice." She smiled at his words. One of the things she enjoyed about Doug was the way he didn't know how to be a player. He was honest to a fault.

"Is it?" she teased.

"Of course. It's nice for you. I'm sure you're enjoying your time off. Are you sculpting?"

"Yes."

"Good for you."

"What are you up to?"

"I came to see you at the bar. Now I'm trying to figure out how I might get an invite to come watch you sculpt."

"Watch me sculpt?" She laughed, assuming that was not what he really wanted to do. Maybe he was a player after all.

"Yeah. I saw your art when I was at your place, but I don't know how it works. I'd like to see you making it."

"Are you for real?"

She heard him sigh.

"You probably don't like people watching you. I get that. Would you like to get breakfast on Sunday morning?"

He was serious. She could tell. He actually wanted to watch her work.

"Come over. I'll show you my stuff."

"You're sure? I don't want to mess up your mojo or anything."

"I don't think you will. Maybe you'll even inspire me." He laughed at that and with a "see you soon," he hung up. Chanda put her phone down and drew the perfect contour through the clay. He already inspired her.

It didn't take him long to get to her place. He smiled when she opened the door. He kissed her and she smiled back.

"So what are you working on?" he asked, genuinely interested.

She showed him her drawing and what she had so far.

"It doesn't always turn out like the drawing. I sketch it out as a guide, but then as I'm sculpting, I sometimes deviate if the clay wants to go in a different direction."

"Can I try?" he asked.

"You want to help?" She looked at her project with worry.

"No. I don't want to touch that. That's yours." He looked over to the pile of clay. "Maybe I could work on something of my own. Something way smaller." He shrugged.

"Why would you want to sculpt?"

"My ex-wife accused me of not taking an interest in her hobbies. To be honest, I'm not even sure what they were besides spending all my money on shoes and fighting with her mother. But I do understand what she meant, and while this is more than just a hobby to you, I find I'm very interested in it. Mostly because I can tell how much you love it when you talk about it and I want to see why. But I'd also like to have something we could do together. Besides...well...I'm not saying we're going to do that again, but... I mean...I hope we will...if not, that's okay."

"Doug, go cut off a lump of clay and put it on this board."

"Excellent."

Doug definitely wasn't a player. He was a refreshing change from the guys she normally dated. And he wanted to share in her love of art. No one had ever suggested such a thing. She found herself hoping he liked it.

* * * *

An hour later, Doug was filthy. He had clay in his hair as well as on his shoes and—thanks to her pulling him close to kiss him—he had clay down the back of his shirt. But he'd never had more fun than he had while making his little sculpture and laughing with Chanda.

"You're sure it doesn't have to look like anything recognizable."

"I'm sure. It just has to look like what you see it being."

"I think you hang out with Mac too much. I don't know what either of you are saying half the time."

She laughed at his joke and he smiled. He couldn't remember a time he'd smiled so much that didn't involve his daughter.

"What are you doing tomorrow?" he asked casually as he used one of the wooden tools to carve an indentation into his piece of art.

"Tomorrow is Saturday. Don't you have Lucy?" He'd explained how he only had his daughter one day a week, and how he couldn't keep her overnight because she didn't have her own room at his apartment. He didn't want to hide anything from Chanda. She already knew he was just a regular guy. And for some reason she seemed to like him the way he was. He didn't get it.

"Yes. I'm thinking it would be nice to take her to the Met. Would you like to go? Maybe you could give us the inside scoop on some of the art."

"You want me to meet your daughter?"

"Would that be a problem?"

"That's kind of serious isn't it? Would I be Aunt Chanda, her father's friend?"

"No. You would be just Chanda. And you *are* her father's friend. But if you want to call yourself my girlfriend, I'd be okay with that too." Very okay. Though he wouldn't push for that. He would only hope.

They had a wonderful time at the museum. Lucy was sleeping heavily in his arms as he carried her into Julie's house that night. Chanda waited with the cab, but that didn't keep Julie from noticing her.

"Who's that?"

"Chanda."

"Chanda?" Julie sniffed and Doug fought the urge to defend his girlfriend. Julie was a miserable person who wanted him to pay for his failure to make her happy. There was no reason to stoop to her level. "She looks like trash." Or maybe there was.

"She's a great person, and Lucy loves her." It was evident by Julie's reaction that he'd said the wrong thing. He hadn't said it to antagonize his ex-wife—he did that just by breathing—but because it was true. Chanda was fun and Lucy couldn't get enough of her.

He should have known Julie was too quiet about the situation. Her normal response was to yell until he apologized. She didn't do that this time, but he realized it was only because she was too angry to even yell. Instead, she was seething.

The call came the next afternoon around three.

"Doug Phillips. How can I help—" His greeting was cut off by the sound of his daughter's crying in the background. "Hello? Julie? What's wrong with Lucy?"

He heard a door close and the crying was now muffled.

"She's in a timeout because she decided to give herself tattoos today. She said she wanted to be like Chanda."

This was not good, but not the end of the world.

"Don't they come off with rubbing alcohol? She's had them before at your sister's house."

"She didn't use temporary tattoos, Doug. She used permanent markers."

"Oh crap."

"This morning when she got up the first thing she asked me was if she could get her nose pierced for her birthday."

Double crap.

"I don't want my daughter exposed to this…this sleazy woman who looks like a wannabe rock star. Either you keep her away from Lucy or I'll contact child services and tell them I don't think you're helping to raise your daughter in a nurturing environment."

"Julie, I only have one day with Lucy. Are you really going to try to take that too?"

"I'm doing what's best for my daughter." No, she was punishing Doug and Lucy for liking someone more than they liked her.

Rather than risk a battle with child services, Doug agreed to her ridiculous conditions.

* * * *

After a few more nights of needing to sleep with Gray, Alyssa was finally able to make it through the night in her own bed. She couldn't believe she'd asked to stay in his bed like a little kid, but she slept so much better. She hated the nightmares and had downplayed the frequency, not wanting him to think she was crazy.

"I made it all night without a nightmare," she said in the morning when she came out for breakfast.

"Good for you." To her surprise, Grayson seemed disappointed by this.

She had to admit, at least to herself, that she had missed sleeping in his arms. A few times she thought she felt his lips by her ear, and she felt safe.

"I'm sorry I bothered you," she said, embarrassed.

"Don't worry about it. If I had a nickel for each time Trent needed to come to my room to snuggle, I wouldn't need to go to work right now," he joked it off. "Today's the day?"

"Yes. Martin said they would make their decision on Wednesday."

"Good luck. I'm sure they'll pick you. You're the best choice."

"You don't even know what kind of job I'd do."

"Right, but I know you'd be the best at it."

"Thanks."

"I'm going to gym tonight, so I'll be late."

"Okay. I'm making pork chops for dinner."

"Sounds good. Have a great day," he said with a smile.

"You too." As he closed the door behind him, she couldn't help but think the only things missing were the kiss goodbye and the wedding bands.

They sounded like a married couple. She laughed it off.

Fortunately, she knew it wasn't real. Despite the few times she found herself wanting to kiss him, she had held her ground on the just-friends thing.

She'd had her doubts about their living arrangement, but so far it was working. And if it stopped working because he got too attached, she would be ready to bolt.

She picked her most professional outfit in case it came down to who looked the part.

Freddie and Mia greeted her when she got to the office.

"I'm not sure how to feel today. I mean, I want the best for you, which is for you to get the job. But I want the best for me, which is for you to stay here. You see my dilemma?" Mia frowned.

"I understand. You know I will only be moving up a few floors. I can still come down here for lunch sometimes."

"I'm changing my wish so you'll get the job and I'll stop being selfish." Freddie blew her a kiss and went to his desk.

"I don't care what floor you work on. We will still get together for drinks sometimes."

"Definitely." Alyssa only then realized how long it had been since she'd gone out with Mia. She'd been spending all her time with Gray.

She needed to fix that before he got the wrong idea.

Alyssa didn't get the call on Wednesday. She'd tried to gain some distance with Grayson, but he didn't seem to notice. Instead, he came into her room to talk to her, even sitting on her bed for an hour while they discussed the guy at his gym who made sex sounds when he lifted weights.

She didn't hear anything on Thursday either. And Grayson seemed off that night when he got home. He didn't sing in the shower, or make any jokes about her getting in the kitchen and making him a pie, like he normally did when it was her night to cook.

"Bad day?" she asked.

"Not really."

"Do you not like sesame chicken?" she pushed. He'd only eaten one piece with two beers. Not that she was counting.

"I guess I'm not that hungry."

Red flags were going up everywhere. A man who was not hungry was a man with a problem. Everyone knew that.

She decided to back off, since he didn't seem to want to talk about it, and because they were only roommates. This meant her responsibility ended with paying the rent, not making him happy. Although she would have tried if she'd known how.

Then she wondered if this wasn't about him at all.

"It's the job? You heard they hired someone and you don't want to tell me?" she accused after storming into his room without knocking.

"No. I haven't heard anything. I'd tell you. I swear. I told you not to worry about it. They never do anything on time. I doubt you'll hear anything until next week." She nodded. It did seem like Martin moved at his own pace. As if he owned the place or something.

As the night went on, Gray seemed a little better. He wished her a good night as they passed in the hallway.

She took a deep breath as she got into bed, hoping for another night free of nightmares. As she reached for the light by the bed, there was a knock at the door and her heart rate kicked up.

"Yeah?" she called.

Gray poked his head inside.

"You got a minute? As a friend?" he asked.

"Okay." She sat up, making sure the sheet was tucked around all the important parts. "What is it?"

"I need your advice."

"On?"

"I let this girl move into my apartment. Smokin' hot. Only we're supposed to just be friends, which is great and I don't want to mess it up. The problem is, I hadn't considered the fact she would be walking around the apartment in shorty shorts and baby tees all the time with no bra. And since I've already had amazing sex with her multiple times, I know how great it is. So basically I have a perpetual hard-on so bad I'm light-headed from the lack of blood going to my brain."

She snickered at his gush of information.

"So you want to find a way to ask her to stop wearing shorty shorts?" she assumed.

"Hell, no. I want you to tell me how I can renegotiate this friends-only thing so I can sleep with her again."

Her eyes widened in surprise. She thought he was on board with this arrangement. He hadn't so much as hinted at having sex with her since they moved in together. She needed him to be the stable one, because she was already faltering after seeing him without a shirt while he brushed his teeth this morning.

"Uh...well..." She tried to come up with an answer that would dissuade him from pursuing her, but the truth was, she wanted the same thing. "Give me a sec."

She picked up her phone, her thumbs flying as she texted Kenley:

I want to have sex with Gray. Give me permission.

Gray leaned against the doorframe silently during the minute it took Kenley to respond:

You're an adult. You don't need my permission.

You seemed to think it was a bad idea. I'm not sure it would be a problem, Liss shot back.

The important thing is that you're honest with each other. So no one has unrealistic expectations.

Good advice. Thanks. Alyssa could work with this.

"Maybe you should just be honest with her and see what she says. She might be feeling the same way about how you walk around without a shirt."

"Honesty, huh? Okay. I'll give that a try. Thanks." He backed out of her room and shut the door, leaving her sitting there with a confused look on her face. Should she have specified that he should be honest right that minute?

Before she had time to think about it too long, there was another knock at the door.

"Yeah?" she said, trying to hide her anticipation.

"Hey," he said as he walked into her room, now wearing jeans and no shirt. Good play.

"Hey." She couldn't help but smile at his change in demeanor. "What's up?"

"Funny you should ask. I'm up, and I have been up all night. I want you. Bad. What would you say to adding some fun to our friendship? No strings, just fun." He even wiggled his eyebrows for dramatic effect as he laid on the smarm.

She needed to make him work a little.

"Nah, I don't think so."

His expression was priceless. His mouth was actually hanging open. She couldn't hold it in; she burst out laughing and he pounced on her, playfully holding her down and rubbing all over her with his bare chest.

"As long as you understand this is just about physical pleasure. No emotions."

"I understand. Maybe we should have shook on that instead of trying to ignore our base instincts. I might be new to this whole not-getting-emotionally-attached thing, but I have to say, it seems like you're doing it wrong."

"This is what happens when you take sex advice from someone who was a virgin a year ago."

"Are we doing this or chatting? I'm dying here. I'm going to walk around in nothing but a towel tomorrow," he threatened, making her laugh.

"Okay, okay." She started taking her clothes off, but he stopped her.

"What are you doing? You know I like to do that part," he scolded.

"Sorry."

"That's one of the benefits of having sex with the same person. They know what you like," he explained.

"Yes, *Grayson*," she said, using his name because she knew he liked it.

"See? That's hot." He smiled down at her as he pulled her shorts off. "So tell me what you like."

And just like that, this new plan was suddenly uncomfortable. She didn't want him knowing things about her. Personal things. She'd already shared more with him than anyone else. Granted they couldn't get much more personal than having sex, living together, and working together, but this was different.

It was the real her. She didn't share the real her with anyone. Not anymore.

"I like getting to point B."

"Right, but maybe you could expand on something to aid in that venture."

"You do great. Just do what you normally do."

"Come on. Throw me a bone." He peeled off her tight shirt and latched onto one of her nipples.

"You've already got a bone. Are we doing this or are we chatting?" she repeated his early words.

"We're doing it, but if you don't get to point B because you're bored of my same old moves, it's not on me."

"Fine. Just shut up already."

"You're so mean, I don't know why I like you so much." He chuckled as he rolled on the condom. Then he turned over to lie on his back with his hands propped casually behind his head.

"Seriously?" she complained.

"It was your idea, you should do the work." He was beaming adorably.

"It was not my—you know what? Never mind." She shook her head as she straddled him and slid down his length slowly, making him hiss through his teeth.

"Damn, you have the best ideas," he praised her.

She didn't laugh this time. She was too busy rocking up and down on him. His hands rested on her hips, pulling her down, guiding her pace.

"You are so unbelievably gorgeous with your hair hanging down in my face like that," he said.

She let her hair tickle his chest and purred his name at the same time. She was learning all the things he liked. It made her feel powerful.

He reached down between them to rub her as she moved. He touched her the way she needed. Apparently, he was picking up a few things too.

"Come on, baby," he said as he watched her.

As if she worked on voice command, she responded, clenching around him and collapsing on his chest as the tremors took her over. Her hip was cramping slightly, but it wasn't enough of a distraction to keep her from enjoying every mind-blowing spasm.

When her muscles relaxed, Grayson flipped her over in one move and began thrusting.

She moaned his name as her fingers clenched the sheets.

"Alyssa," he said. "Look at me."

She opened her eyes drowsily and let her fingers trail down his chest and stomach. She pushed off the bed to meet his next thrust and that threw him over the edge. His head went back and his eyes shut as he pushed in as far as he could possibly go. There was no room left.

He fell onto the bed next to her, breathing heavily. After a short time, he traced small circles along her ribs with his fingertips.

A few minutes later his breathing slowed back to normal.

"I'm so glad to be your friend, Liss," he said, making her laugh.

"Are you going back to your own room now?" she asked as she made herself comfortable under the sheet.

"Do you want me to?"

"I don't know. If we didn't live together you would go home, right?"

"Not necessarily. I didn't the first time at your place. I didn't make you leave when you came here."

"Do you want to snuggle?" She laughed at him. She didn't want him to go. She liked sleeping next to him. He kept the bad dreams away.

"Would it be too much to ask for you to act like a girl sometimes?" he said, settling against her. Clearly he wasn't leaving, so she cuddled up against him.

"Because girls like to snuggle? That's a stereotype."

"Most girls like to snuggle. I'm sure there's been a study."

"If I were like most girls, you wouldn't have had to twist my arm to get me to move in here," she pointed out.

"That's true, but I want to stay and snuggle."

"Was it so hard to just say that?"

"I guess not." He kissed her hair.

"Gray?"

"Yeah?"

"We're not together, okay? Like in a relationship. I don't do relationships." She wanted to make that very clear. The sex had been fun. Living with him was great. But she couldn't take that next step. She didn't want him to think they were on that path.

"Why is that?"

"I don't do trust."

"Right. That's fine. I'm good with the snuggling and the sex and the sharing my home with you. I don't need a label."

"Thank you for understanding."

"Good night, baby," he whispered and she closed her eyes and let sleep claim her.

In the morning, Gray insisted they stop for coffee and walk to work together. She went along with it because she was just too relaxed to care. She'd been honest with him, and he seemed to get it. She was free to enjoy the sex and the roof over her head guilt-free.

It wasn't until ten when she saw Martin Hasher's name on her phone that she remembered the job that hadn't been offered to her on Wednesday or Thursday.

"This is Alyssa Sinclair."

"Hi Alyssa. Can you stop up?"

"Yes. I'm on my way."

The whole way up in the elevator, she told herself this was a good sign. Surely they wouldn't make her come all the way upstairs to tell her she didn't get the job. That would be a waste of everyone's time.

She saw Grayson as she walked to the office in the corner. His eyebrows went up, and then he smiled and gave her a thumbs-up. He must have thought it was a good sign as well.

Unlike the last time, she wasn't made to wait in the sitting area. She was sent right in.

Mr. Borne and two women were sitting at the small conference table talking.

"Alyssa, thank you for coming. This is Megan, Director of Human Resources and Lindsey, Executive Account Manager."

Liss smiled and nodded as she sat in the chair he'd gestured to.

"We'd like to offer you the position of account manager. These ladies will go over the details. Welcome to the executive floor."

"Thank you for this opportunity."

"Be at the meeting on Monday morning so I can introduce you to the rest of the staff."

"Yes. Thank you."

He left and she spent the next half hour filling out forms and having her mind boggled with instructions.

When she left, she looked around before sneaking into Grayson's office and shutting the door behind her.

She let out a little squeal.

"I got the job!"

"Awesome. I knew it would be you. You were the best choice. You should have seen the other clowns they led in and out of here." She laughed as he came closer and bent to kiss her.

"What are you doing?"

"I'm happy for you, so I'm kissing you in celebration."

"We're working."

"Not at the moment. I'm on break."

"We can't do this at work."

"We can't even kiss behind a closed door? Come on. I did get you that nice job. I kind of think you owe me." He smiled.

"I'm pretty sure those are the exact words they used on that sexual harassment video they made us all watch."

"You're accusing me of stealing my lines?"

She laughed.

"If you're not going to play nice, get out of my office."

She gave him a big kiss and opened the door.

"Thank you for believing in me," she said.

"Thank you for believing in me too."

She knew he wasn't talking about work. He was talking about trusting him not to get attached. So far, he was living up to his end of the bargain. Maybe she could have her cake and eat it too.

It was Friday and she had gotten a promotion.

Life was good.

Chapter 10

As soon as Lucy was buckled in and the cab started for the Bronx Zoo, she turned to him very seriously and asked, "Where's Chanda?"

"She's working today." This wasn't entirely a lie. She would be working later that day, but she wasn't working for the next four hours.

He hadn't told Chanda about Julie's conditions. In fact, he'd kept his distance. How was it going to work for him to be dating someone who wasn't allowed around his daughter?

"Awwww. I drawed a picture for her of a picture she liked at the Mets." He smiled as she pulled out her picture of a picture.

"And this one is us." She held out another with three somewhat square bodies on it.

"It's beautiful. What is this on my arm?" He pointed to a flower on the largest person's appendage.

"That's me. I have a tattoo."

Doug didn't know what to do. He hadn't gotten a Dad Manual with his child.

"Sweetie, if you want to get a tattoo when you're a grown-up, Daddy won't mind. As long as you've given it a lot of thought. And it's not a boy's name."

"Okay."

"And if at some point when you're an adult you want to dye your hair a bright color or have a giant needle shoved through your nose so you can put a hoop through it, I will support you, I promise."

Lucy's eyes were wide. Maybe he'd overdone it slightly.

"But until you're as old as Mommy and Daddy, you can't have real tattoos or piercings. You understand?"

Lucy nodded and frowned.

"I wanted to be pretty like Chanda," she said in a small, pitiful voice.

"You are beautiful, just the way you are. Why don't we call her and see if she can join us?"

"Yay!"

Doug put his phone on speaker and dialed her number. She picked up on the second ring.

"You're calling me?" It was no wonder she was surprised. He thought he'd been doing the right thing, but what he was doing was reinforcing Julie's feelings that people with tattoos and piercings were lesser beings.

"No. Lucy and I are calling you."

"Hi, Chanda! Please come to the zoo with us. I want you to see my favorite animal and I drawed you a picture."

He heard Chanda laugh on the other end.

"Don't you want to spend time with your daddy?" she tried.

"I want to be with both of you."

"I can't very well say no to that, now can I?"

"That worked?" Doug laughed. "I thought her special powers only worked on me."

"I guess not. I'll meet you there."

They spent the entire afternoon going from exhibit to exhibit. Each one was Lucy's favorite. He and Chanda held on to each of Lucy's hands and swung her in the air, making her giggle.

To the rest of the world, they might have looked like a normal family. He and Julie had never done things like this with Lucy.

"Thanks for changing your plans so you could come with us," he said. Lucy took it as a prompt.

"Thank you for coming with us, Chanda."

"Thank you for inviting me. I'm glad you have room in your special day with your dad."

"I'm supposed to share," his daughter reasoned.

"Even your favorite things like your dad?"

"Yes. I have to share everything. Especially when the new baby comes."

Doug stopped walking, causing the rest of them to stop too.

"New baby?"

Lucy covered her mouth. "Uh oh. I'm not s'posed to say anything about the new baby."

"Your mom is having another baby?"

Lucy nodded, looking upset.

"It's okay, sweetie."

"Are you mad? Mommy said it would make you mad."

"I'm not mad at all. I'm happy for your mom. I know she wanted to have another baby." Just not with him. Every time he suggested they have another baby, she told him he didn't make enough money to afford a second child. Everything came down to money with Julie.

Doug refused to grill his daughter with questions about whom his ex might be dating. It wasn't any of his business.

"Can you make us pancakes for breakfast tomorrow? The bunny kind?"

Doug bit his lip and looked up at the darkening sky. He'd love nothing more than be able to take her back to his place. He knew she'd be asleep as soon as they pulled away from the zoo. He used to love carrying her to bed. She always looked so peaceful. And in the morning—energy restored—she would clap at his sorry excuse for animal shaped pancakes.

"I can't. I have to take you back to your mommy's tonight."

"But I want to stay with you and Chan."

"We would like for you to stay with us too. But I'm not allowed."

"Because I don't have a bedroom at your place?" He hated when she picked up parts of their grown-up conversations.

"That's right."

"It is?" Chanda asked, her brows pulled together.

"I only have a one bedroom apartment. Child services requires Lucy to have her own bedroom or she can't stay overnight."

"But your bed is big enough for her."

"She's not allowed to sleep with me."

Chanda's eyes went wide. "Are you kidding me?"

"I wish." He shook his head. "She slept with me the first three years of her life, kicking and snoring the whole time, with two extra rooms down the hall. Now I have to provide a separate room."

"Even if she doesn't use it?"

"Right."

"That's ridiculous."

"Not my rules."

"Mommy says you can't afford it because you're broke, Daddy." She looked him up and down. "What is broke? Member when I broke my pinky?"

"I do, sweetie. It still makes me queasy." Seeing his baby girl with her finger hanging in the wrong direction, and the big tears.

"Why don't we get some cotton candy for the drive home?" he suggested. It worked on Lucy. Chanda, not so much. She was biting her lip ring and looking irritated. "It's okay."

"No, it's not." Chanda shook her head and squeezed his hand.

At Julie's place, Doug took a deep breath before opening the door and carrying his sleeping daughter up to the house. Julie met him halfway glaring at Chanda.

"I told you I didn't want Lucy exposed to trash."

"Shh. She's sleeping, and Chanda is not trash."

"Do you think child services is going to see her as someone who should be around a child?"

"You're not going to threaten me with this anymore. Chanda is in my life and she is great with Lucy. Lucy and I talked about tattoos and piercings, and I don't expect to have any more trouble with that."

"We'd better not."

Doug turned away as Julie rushed into the house. He'd hoped their conversation was quiet and far enough away that Chanda hadn't heard. It was obvious she had.

"Your ex is threatening to call child services because of me?"

"She felt threatened so she's acting out. She's not really going to call." At least she hadn't all the other times she manufactured reasons why he was unfit.

"Maybe I should stay away from Lucy."

"What would that teach my daughter? I want her to be able to look inside someone and not make judgments. Your tattoos and piercings tell me you're a hell of a lot tougher than I am. I nearly fainted in the ER from Lucy's broken pinky."

* * * *

"So I made us an appointment for Wednesday morning. Can you go in to work an hour late?" Gray announced while sitting in her new office on Monday. He liked their morning routine. Especially after their new nightly routine of sleeping together.

She was easy.

Not like that, but in the good way. In the way that made him happy to spend time with her.

They weren't dating. They were...well, he didn't know exactly, but it was great. Thus the reason he scheduled this appointment.

"What is this appointment for?" She scrunched up her nose.

"I don't want to say." He knew the seriousness of the issue would make her freak out for no reason. She didn't do relationships.

"Right, because you know I'm so big on trust I would just go to some appointment without knowing what it was for."

"Fine. Blood tests." He crossed his arms, braced for her rebuttal.

"Is that code for something else less painful and more fun?" she asked, affixing a label on a folder.

"No. I get a screening every few months. You said you've never had one. It's an unsafe world out there, Alyssa. You need to be checked."

"I've never had sex with anyone without a condom. Not once. Ever."

"Me either. Stuff still happens. Come on." He tilted his head to the side because he knew she thought it was cute. He was starting to know things about her, despite her efforts to keep him out.

"I hate needles." She winced as he smiled and walked over slowly to stand in front of her. He bent down and pulled up her shirt to reveal the large tattoo up her ribs.

"That's strange. Is this a sticker then?" He used his index finger to pick at it, making her laugh.

"Shut up. It's not the same thing."

"Because that needle kept jabbing you for hours and hours and this would be once and done?"

"I need all my blood. I can't spare any."

They joked around a lot. It was all part of the "keep things light" campaign, but this was serious.

"Liss." He looked her in the eye. "I know you don't trust easily, but I'm doing this as much for you. I want you to know your health and well-being are important to me. It might be uncomfortable, but it's important."

"Fine. Okay. I'll go."

"Wow. I won an argument. I didn't even have to bring up how I got you this new job." He joked to lighten the mood again.

"Don't push it."

"Do you want to stop for a drink after work tonight?"

"Don't you want to go *out* out?" she asked.

"What do you mean?" He took a sip of her coffee before he headed for the door.

"You know. Like a club or something?"

"No thanks. I like living with you. I have fun with you. I enjoy the sex. I'm not asking for anything else."

"Except my blood."

"A tiny little bit. I promise. You'll survive."

"Okay." She still looked nervous.

"Now." He kissed her forehead. "Get back to work. Stop thinking."

"I never think at work," she joked.

"That's my girl." He gave her a wink as he opened the door. "See you at the meeting later. Have a great day."

"Thanks. You too."

* * * *

Alyssa was the second person in the conference room for the meeting. She wanted to make a good impression. She should have realized Mr. Borne would show up to his own meeting seventeen minutes late.

Grayson had sat next to her despite the stay-away look she gave him. Now he was sitting so close, she was certain everyone else around the table must be able to tell they were having sex. Or maybe that was just guilt because his hand was on her thigh under the table and was moving under her skirt.

She kept her gaze on the screen at the front of the room where Craig Something-or-other was going over projections for the next quarter while she focused on breathing normally.

What was it about Gray? Yes, the sex was mind-blowing. Her response to his touch was a result of that knowledge. His no-nonsense approach to things was refreshing.

He seemed honest.

Donald had seemed honest too. She thought she knew everything about him. And maybe she did. She just didn't know the other person he became when she wasn't around.

Using the remnants of her willpower she reached under the table and removed his hand from her leg, placing it back in his own lap. While doing so she grazed something hard and swallowed.

They were in a business meeting for Christ's sake. Her first meeting in her new position. She needed to pay attention, but for the life of her all she could do was wonder if she would be able to sneak into his office for a quickie.

When the meeting was over, neither of them moved. She thought Grayson might have a physical reason for not getting out of his chair. Gray's friend Doug murmured something about playing with fire as he left the room.

"I shouldn't have touched you like that in a meeting. I'm sorry." His voice was low and serious. "You looked nervous and I only know the one way to make you relax. Though obviously that is not office-appropriate."

"Are you really apologizing to me, or are you sorry because you can't stand up right now."

"Yes." So both. She nodded. At least he was remorseful for his actions.

"I think it would be a good idea if we kept our distance at work," she suggested.

"I agree to your terms."

She nodded and stood.

"Liss?" When she paused he glanced up at her. "It's now time for lunch, and we can make it to our place and back in an hour. Even if we have to fix your hair afterward."

She swallowed and pressed her lips together to keep from smiling.

"Last one there has to do all the work." And with that she headed straight for her office to get her purse while he laughed behind her.

* * * *

Chanda was working the early shift on Monday. The lunch crowd usually consisted of the up-and-comers from the business district. They wore expensive suits and were hideous tippers. No rounding up with this bunch. Oh. No. They could do the exact math in their heads.

She was heading over to a table of eight when she recognized one of the members of the group. She'd seen Doug in his work clothes many times, but not in his work demeanor.

He looked up from a serious conversation and his eyes flared in surprise as she walked closer. He looked away and then back at her, not meeting her eyes.

What was this?

Her heart fell as she slowly realized why he hadn't greeted her with his usual smile. He was pretending not to notice her. Aside from the subtle headshake he gave her when she first approached, he wouldn't even look at her. She took the headshake to mean, "Don't."

Apparently, sleeping with the wild Asian bartender with the lip ring was hot on the weekends, but not acceptable with his starched shirt colleagues.

She bit back the pain in her heart and forced a smile to the group.

"My name is Chanda. I'll be helping you today. Can I start you off with some drinks?"

One by one, she went around the table taking everyone's order, not needing to write it down. She never forgot. Doug asked for water with no lemon. She'd see about that.

A few minutes later, she returned with everyone's drinks. Including Doug's, which was stuffed so full of lemons there was probably only a half cup of water in the glass.

"Uh, thanks," he said, looking at the glass in confusion.

Everyone ordered sandwiches or burgers except Doug who ordered a salad with no onions. She brought him a burger with extra onions.

It was obvious even to her she was being immature, but he'd hurt her feelings and giving him the wrong food made her feel slightly better.

"Thanks," he said as she put it down.

"I thought you ordered a salad," the guy next to him pointed out.

"This is good."

"So much for that diet, huh?" the other man chuckled while elbowing Doug in the ribs. She'd thought he was better than this. She glared at Doug and headed back to the kitchen.

She hadn't realized he was following her until she entered the narrow hall out of sight of the dining area.

"Hey," he called. "Chan, wait."

She turned on him, wishing she could shoot lasers from her eyes. The way he stopped, she thought maybe it had worked.

"What's wrong?" he asked.

She let out a humorless laugh. Was he kidding?

"What? No smile or hello for your girlfriend? Or am I not your girlfriend in front of your uppity coworkers?"

"Oh, shit," he whispered, his eyes wide. "You think I'm embarrassed of you?" Yes. Of course that's what she thought. What other reason was there for his behavior? She took a deep breath, wondering if she'd misinterpreted the situation.

"You're saying you're not?" She couldn't come up with another option.

"Of course not. I'd love to tell them you're my girlfriend. Maybe I'd get some respect."

"Then what is the problem? Why are you pretending not to know me?"

"The second I tell them you're my girlfriend, one of them will ask what you see in me. I don't know the answer to that question, and so far I've been able to keep you from trying to figure it out. I really don't want you to start thinking about it too much. So you see, it's better if they don't know. That way they don't start telling you all the reasons why you're too good for me."

"You're serious?" She knew he was. She could see it in his eyes. He believed these losers had the power to turn her off this sweet man.

"Every minute we're together is another minute I don't quite understand. I feel like I'm on borrowed time as it is. I don't want to do anything to turn up the clock."

She kissed him. Hard.

"You're so stupid." She laughed and shook her head. "Go sit down. I'll bring you your salad and a new water."

"I'm okay with the burger."

"No. I spit in it."

"Wow. That might be more of a deterrent if we didn't have our tongues in each other's mouths every time we're together." He gave her his wicked smile and her heart beat strong and true, healed by those dimples and the sparkle in his eyes.

"Go sit."

She quickly put together the salad he'd asked for originally and got him lemon-free water. She walked it out with a big smile.

"Sorry, baby. I brought you the wrong thing. I just hate that you think you need to be on a diet when I can't keep my hands off of you just the way you are." She let her hand run over his shoulders for added effect before she leaned down and kissed his lips. "I'll see you later tonight?"

"Y–yes," he stammered and then smiled. "Later." He swallowed and then addressed everyone. "This is my girlfriend. Chanda."

They all blinked in confusion. One man's mouth fell open much like she'd seen on a cartoon. Maybe she was missing something.

She looked back at Doug who was smiling at her. The usual warm tingly feeling enveloped her. If he was tricking her, he was doing a pretty thorough job of it. All she saw when she looked at him was the man who stood up for her honor. The guy who was able to both make her cry out in pleasure and laugh when they were in bed. The man who played dolls with his six-year-old and enjoyed every second of it.

"What the hell do you see in this guy?" one of the men asked with a booming laugh.

Chanda narrowed in on the pig-faced man as Doug muttered under his breath. "Told you."

"He's a great tipper," she smiled widely and trotted back to the kitchen.

Chapter 11

Alyssa sat next to Gray in the shabby waiting room. She didn't want to be here, but Gray was right. It was the responsible thing to do.

Every few seconds, he put his hand on her knee in an effort to keep it still. As soon as he removed his hand, she went back to jiggling it again. It was something she did when she was nervous. She remembered how sore the muscles in her legs were in the evenings during Donald's trial. That had been a lot of jiggling.

"Relax. It's one prick. You love pricks," he joked with a big grin. She smiled at his silly humor. It was one of the things she liked about him.

"Alyssa and Grayson?" the nurse called. Hearing their names said together threw her for a second. It sounded almost normal. She shook it off and followed Gray into the room.

The efficient lab tech gestured toward the chair and Gray made the same gesture to Alyssa.

"Ladies first," he said as he came to stand next to her. The tech affixed the rubber cord on her bicep. Gray took her other hand and gave it a reassuring squeeze. "You won't feel a thing," he promised.

"I can feel the alcohol swab is very cold," she challenged, knowing she was also going to feel the tiny pinch of the needle, followed by her body's life fluid being sucked out of her for a futile examination. Or at least she hoped it was futile.

Gray leaned down and kissed her hard on the mouth at the exact same time the needle pierced her skin. She didn't feel the needle, but she could tell it had happened. To her surprise, he kept kissing her until she felt the tech adhere a bandage and cotton ball to the inside of her elbow.

"All done," he said, giving her a wink as they traded seats. "It wasn't so bad was it?"

She shrugged. The kissing had been quite good.

"I don't think I'll be able to cook tonight," she played it up with a wince, letting her arm fall limp at her side.

"I'll take care of you," he promised. She flinched at the promise. Years ago, someone else had made that promise.

"You two are so cute. How long have you been married?" the tech asked as she put a bandage on Gray's arm.

"We're not married. We aren't even dating," Alyssa told her. "I have better taste than this," she joked, though only Gray laughed. The tech looked him up and down, probably not finding anything out of place.

Not that there was. He was perfect. At least for someone who was looking.

"You'll hear back with the results by Friday. It says here we can call Mr. Hollinger with the results of both tests?"

"Sure, that's fine," Alyssa agreed. She was doing it for his benefit, though it was a good practice to have screening done periodically. And it hadn't been that bad.

They held hands as they left the office.

It was no wonder the tech was confused. To anyone on the outside they looked like a happy couple.

"Thanks for forcing me to do that," she said as they walked to work.

"I take offense to the word *forcing*. I didn't *force* you. I asked and you reluctantly agreed."

"Whichever. Thanks."

"You're welcome." He leaned down and gave her a kiss when they were only a block away from work. Then they both let go of each other's hands simultaneously.

So far he was respecting her wishes. He hadn't asked her for anything she wasn't willing to give. Except maybe the blood.

He was perfect.

He knew her well enough to know she wouldn't want anyone to know about them. He knew what she liked in bed. He knew her favorite foods.

But there were plenty of things she didn't know about him. How he was raised, what he did when he was alone, or the search history on his computer. She didn't know this man. No one ever really knew another person. Not really.

Nothing ever stayed perfect for long.

Alyssa knew that.

* * * *

Gray missed the call from the doctor on Friday, but he got the message that everything was clear. With a little fist pump he tucked his phone back in his pocket.

"Good news?" Doug asked as he walked in Gray's office and flopped in a chair.

"Yep."

"You're not the father?" he guessed.

"Something like that," Gray said with a laugh.

"Going out tonight?"

"I don't know. Maybe. I haven't checked with Liss yet."

"I thought she wasn't your girlfriend."

"She isn't."

"Then you can go out without her."

"I could, but I don't want to. I like to go out with her."

Doug shook his head.

"I'm not one to define a relationship. Lord knows I have no idea what to call the thing I have going on right now. But I'm pretty sure when you live with someone, have sex with them and enjoy going out with them, *that* is a girlfriend."

"She's a roommate, coworker, and friend." That was what Alyssa was comfortable with and he was fine with that. It was obvious to him by this point that someone had hurt her. He didn't know who or what that someone did, but she admitted she had trust issues.

The last thing she needed was for him to agree to a friends-only arrangement and then change the rules on her. She wouldn't appreciate that.

Besides, he was learning a lot about himself. He'd jumped from one relationship to the next without ever taking the time to build a friendship first. Now that he was friends with Alyssa, he realized how important that step was.

Not that they were going to be in the relationship.

"Then can we go out tonight? There's someone I'd like you to meet," Doug asked.

"Can Liss come too?"

"See? That right there is a girlfriend," Doug protested.

"No. It's not."

"Say it with me...girrrrl friennnnd."

"It's not like that."

"Fine. You can bring your girlfriend who isn't a girlfriend."

Doug rolled his eyes and left Gray's office mumbling about how much he hated Gray.

Liss stopped in before lunch.

"You hungry?" she asked. He raised his brows and tilted his head. "For food." Damn.

"Yeah. I have time to grab something quick." Though he wished it was her he was grabbing. And not quick.

"Doug wants us to go out with him tonight," he said when they were out of the building, where it was safe to speak like regular people.

"I was going to make chicken nachos and watch Jason Statham blow shit up."

"Ooh, that sounds fun too. We can do that before we go out."

"Fine. I'm in. Maybe we can have sex before we leave. Can you do a British accent?"

"Top of the morning to ya."

"Irish."

"Right. G'day, mate."

"Aussie."

"Uh. By jove, I think I've got it."

She stopped walking to look up at him with her brows pulled together.

"Let's just stop this now before I'm so repulsed I can't ever sleep with you again." She yanked open the door to her favorite café and he preceded her inside, while fighting the urge to hold the door for her. She might not be his girlfriend, but she was still a woman and his father had ingrained certain manners in him.

He subtly pulled her chair out as the waitress brought water to the table. They ordered immediately and Liss frowned.

"That Wallace guy from mergers is over there with Martin's executive assistant, Wendy." Alyssa nodded in their direction.

"Ooh. Do you think they're having an affair?"

"Not everyone who eats together is having sex, Gray."

"We are."

"Shh." She glanced in their direction again as if they could hear the conversation from the other side of the room.

"They can't hear us."

"We can't look like we're talking about sex."

"How does that look?" he wondered.

"I'm not sure, but it's different. So, how is your day going? Are you ready for the meeting this afternoon?"

"You mean am I ready for a nap?"

She laughed and nodded.

"It would be more exciting if you let me sit next to you and spread your legs—"

"Knock it off. When we're at work, I am just a coworker. When we're at home, I'm your roommate. When I'm in your bed, I'm your lover. You have to keep this straight or everything is going to get messed up."

"When we go out for drinks are you my girlfriend?" He didn't know where the question had come from. He blamed Doug and his earlier dissertation.

She looked him dead in the face.

"I am never your girlfriend. Ever."

Got it.

* * * *

Alyssa knew she probably went overboard with her declaration at lunch. But it was important he knew there could never be anything real between them.

He'd been quiet as they ate and on the way back to the office. In the lobby, she went to check on something with the front desk clerk so she wouldn't have to ride up with him on the elevator.

This was work. It was important to keep it separate. She didn't want people to think something was going on. She'd just gotten this promotion. If everyone knew she was with Gray, they'd think she'd slept her way to the top. Even though there were technically six other floors to the top. Still.

Her phone rang.

"Speak of sleeping their way to the top," she said before answering. "Hey, Ken."

Kenley Carmichael—now Kenley Jackson—used to work with her until she was fired and wrongly accused of sleeping with their boss's husband. She moved to Connecticut where she did in fact end up sleeping with her boss who was now her husband.

"How are things?" she asked.

"Good. I got a promotion."

"What? And you didn't tell me? We need to celebrate."

"Sure thing. Why don't you roll yourself over here and we'll throw back some shots." Kenley was very pregnant.

"Maybe we'll have to postpone until after my confinement."

Alyssa laughed at the historical reference. Though it was an apt description, considering Zane didn't want her to do anything that could possibly hurt her or the baby. Like standing for more than ten minutes or walking.

"Zane is still being a worry wart?"

"He moved the yogurt from the bottom drawer to the top shelf so I won't have to bend to get it." She let out a sigh. "But the nightly foot rubs are nice."

"Hmm. Foot rubs, huh? Maybe I would get knocked up if it meant foot rubs."

"Really?"

"No. Not happening." They laughed together. They might have started out doing the same thing for Hasher Borne, but their lives had taken way different paths.

Kenley was married with a baby on the way, living in suburbia with her flannel-wearing husband. And Alyssa was still in the city, trying her best not to get attached to anyone.

"How's the new place?" Kenley asked.

"The new place is good."

"And the roommate? What did you decide?" There was a tone on that last word that hinted at her suspicions.

"We're sleeping together."

"I knew that was going to happen!"

"Yes. Yes. It was such a mystery. So I caved and we're having sex. That is the extent of it. I'm so glad I didn't listen to you. Gray is perfectly fine with how things are between us. He's not expecting anything."

"I see."

"What do you see?"

"I see you're happy."

Damn people who knew her so well. Why did she talk to people?

"Gray is a lot of fun. We enjoy doing things together. It's like being with you, but with a penis. So yeah, I'm happy."

"I've been replaced by a penis?" Kenley gasped.

"You did it first, Mrs. Glass Houses."

"Penises *are* handy to have around."

"Truth. But this penis knows there's no chance of us ending up together in some kind of happily-ever-after."

"You know, you still never told me why you don't want a happily-ever-after." She'd never told anyone. The only person in her life who knew was her mother and they had silently agreed to never speak of it.

For a moment, Alyssa considered telling Kenley her story, but she wasn't ready.

She couldn't go there. She couldn't dredge it all up.

"I can tell by the delay you are not going to tell me now."

"No. I can't."

"That's okay. You will when you're ready, and I'll be here to listen."

She didn't think she'd ever be ready.

* * * *

Due to a demonic formula haunting his client's spreadsheet, Gray got home after Alyssa.

"Honey, I'm home!" he called.

She came out of the bathroom wearing the shorty shorts and tight T-shirt that drove him mad. She said they were comfortable, but he found them to be the opposite. Every time she wore them, his pants grew uncomfortably tight.

"*Honey*? Really?"

"It was a joke. Would you relax?" It wasn't as if he could force her into a relationship.

"The last time you told me to relax was when you forced me to go to the doctor's office." Right. He'd forgotten about that.

"Since you insisted on keeping it all business at lunch, I didn't get a chance to tell you earlier. I heard back from the doctor's office today with the results from the screening."

"And you couldn't find a way to fit it in the conversation?" Alyssa put her hand on her hip.

"Apparently, you have bitchy blood. The symptoms include using sarcasm to keep people at bay."

"Wow. That was some test," she said as she popped the cap off a beer and handed it to him. "To bitchy blood and the fact that it's Friday," she toasted as she tapped her bottle to his.

"Other than being bitchy, your blood was perfectly fine. So was mine." He leaned down to kiss her neck, right under her ear. It was one of his favorite places to put his lips. He could smell her vanilla-scented hair and feel her heart beating.

The beer wasn't the thing he wanted.

In one quick movement, he pulled her shirt over her head and began walking her backward down the hall to her room.

He unhooked her bra and let her shorts slide down over her hips. No panties. He moaned at this development. Normally he was quite fond of panties, but for some reason finding none was wicked hot.

She climbed back on the bed and he followed as soon as he got his own clothes off.

Kissing his way down between her breasts, he stopped to suck each of her nipples before continuing on his journey. After circling her navel with his tongue he moved lower, and lower until—

"You don't have to do that," Alyssa said as she shifted to get away.

"I know I don't have to. I want to. It's a perk of passing your test." He smiled up at her and ducked down again, only to have her squirm away.

"You really don't need to."

"What's the problem here? I said I want to."

"I just don't...do that."

"Why not?" he asked, not moving from his position between her legs. She was always rather adventurous when it came to sex. He didn't understand the hang up.

She let out a sigh and looked up at the ceiling, no doubt realizing they weren't going any further until this was discussed.

"Wait. Are you one of those girls who sees it as a chore?"

"Probably because guys always seem to act like it is. Then they take a two-second pass and expect to have a parade thrown in their honor."

"I'm sure some guys are like that. I'm not one of them. I assure you, you will want to throw a parade when I'm done."

"It doesn't really do anything for me," she admitted.

"How is that possible?"

She shrugged instead of answering while she continued to wiggle away.

"Have you ever explored this with a guy? Like, tried different stuff. Mapped out what you like and don't like?" he pushed, wanting to get to the bottom of this mystery.

She shook her head quickly and looked up at the ceiling.

"Okay, then let's figure this out," he suggested with a big grin.

"How about if I do you instead?" She started to sit up and move away. Gray thought maybe there was something else going on, although he had to admit her offer did make him throb.

"You can't accept pleasure from someone without reciprocating?" He raised a brow at her.

Her lack of an answer told him everything he needed to know. He was right. She didn't want it to be about her, and most guys were okay to let her bow out of the spotlight. Gray wasn't.

"We can either do what I want to do, or I'm taking my toy and going back to my room," he teased, hoping a joke would make her less tense.

"Why do you care so much?" she balked. "I'm giving you a free pass."

"You might have been with guys who just wanted to get off as quickly as possible, but we're not all like that. Some of us think it's hot when the woman gets off too."

She let out a sigh of annoyance.

"I don't think I can relax enough," she confessed.

"Do you trust me, Liss?"

"Trust? Really?" she complained. "No. You know I don't trust anyone."

"I don't mean with big emotional stuff, I mean with this." He nodded down in the general area.

"I don't know." Her answer was more of a whine.

"Haven't you liked everything I've done so far?"

"I guess so."

"Will you trust me with this? It will be fun. Give me ten minutes and if you're not into it, we'll move on."

"Do you have a timer?"

"There's one on my phone." He pointed at the nightstand, knowing she wouldn't actually use it.

"Proceed," she said stiffly while squeezing her eyes closed.

Gray laughed and shook his head. It would appear he had his work cut out for him.

He was up for the challenge.

Chapter 12

"I've never been so disappointed in my life," Alyssa said, stifling a laugh after they'd caught their breath.

"Excuse me?" Gray propped himself up on his elbow, looking indignant. She let him suffer for another second before she explained.

"I wish I could purr." She smiled and stretched out against him like a cat. "It's the only noise that could possibly express the way I feel right now, and I can't do it."

"I don't want to be one of those people who says, 'I told you so,' but..."

"Go ahead. You've earned it."

"So you enjoyed yourself?" he asked with a grin.

"You couldn't tell?"

"I think I could tell you enjoyed yourself like three times."

"I guess you've earned the right to be smug too."

"Thank you," he said with a big smile as he lay back on his pillow. He obviously didn't need her permission to be smug. Smugness was seeping out of every pore. She found it adorable.

She didn't want to tell him he was right about something else too. His little exercise had led to an exchange of trust between them. He'd been patient with her as she worked out her insecurities enough to tell him what she liked and didn't like.

She'd had sex many times, but she never let go and enjoyed herself as much as she did tonight with Gray. The first waves of regret seeped in threatening her happiness.

Couldn't she just have this one time to enjoy being close to a man without the guilt? He'd made it all about her because he wanted her to feel good.

He didn't understand. He'd done something nice for her. He deserved a parade that wasn't clouded over with her issues.

"At the risk of making your head so big it won't fit out the door, I just want to say thank you for taking the time."

He turned his head to look at her. He was still smiling, but it was more natural now.

"It was hot," he told her, then looked away. It was obvious he wanted to say something else. She would have pressed, but she wasn't sure she wanted to hear it.

"We're still going out with Doug later?" she checked.

"I kind of wish I would have said no so we can just stay in and do this all night."

"Stay in? It's Friday."

"People do it." He shrugged as she went to get ready.

An hour later they were walking into MacGregor's. The place was full. Gray offered to go get their drinks while Doug scoured the place for a table.

She was impressed when a few seconds later, he was waving her over to a booth. Gray carried the three pints over to their table as she scooted across the bench.

They all made the same sound of appreciation when they swallowed that first gulp.

"So you're a woman," Doug said.

"Kind of." She smiled over her glass.

"I can vouch for her. I've seen all the parts." Gray's smug smile was back.

"What do you think of me? Am I okay looking?" Doug asked.

"What's this? Don't I tell you you're sexy enough, Dougie?" Gray joked, but she could see the sincere doubt in Doug's eyes.

She made a show of looking him over and then nodded.

"Yeah. You're good. In the right circumstances, I'd be attracted to you."

"Really?" It wasn't a hint for more praise; he seemed truly shocked.

"I've told you a million times, you're good." Gray waved at him. "Your ex-wife really did a number on your self-esteem."

"I didn't get hot girls before my wife either."

"Your wife *was* hot. I saw a picture of her with Lucy."

"She was the only hot woman who ever wanted to be with me. That's why I married her."

Alyssa laughed at his expression, but she could tell there was a slight truth to his statement.

"You're cute. You have nice eyes and the dimples are sexy."

"I have dimples too," Grayson pointed out.

"We'll deal with your insecurities later. I have my hands full with Doug's right now."

Doug turned and pointed toward the bar.

"See the hot girl behind the bar?"

"Yeah."

"Do you think we're well matched? Do you think I'd have a shot with her?" He was only looking at Alyssa as Grayson choked on his beer.

"You want to shoot for Chanda?"

"I'm asking Liss if she thinks I have a shot."

The petite bartender had the words *Wild Thing* stamped on her forehead. Doug looked very corporate boardroom in his button-down and khakis.

"Yes," she answered confidently.

"*Yes?*" Gray and Doug said at the same time with equal looks of disbelief.

"If you smile and talk to her like you talk to us, without all the schmoozy pick-up lines and crap, you would have a good chance."

"Wow." Doug looked completely perplexed for a moment, and then he laughed. "So that's how I did it."

"Did what?" Gray asked.

"I'm dating her. Like for real. We're together. The first time, I figured she didn't have anything better to do, but it's been a few weeks now. She's met Lucy. I'm really into her, and she seems to be into me. I just couldn't figure out why."

Alyssa laughed at the look on his face.

He pulled out his phone to text something. A few seconds later, Chanda pulled the phone from her back pocket. Alyssa could tell by the smile on the woman's face that she was totally into the sender.

She looked up, ducking to the side to see them, and then waved and blew a kiss.

"Holy shit." Grayson sat back against the booth.

"See? I told you." Doug ran a hand over his hair. "I'm worried I'm going to mess it up."

"So don't mess it up," Alyssa offered.

"I think I'm in love with her. I have to keep biting my tongue so I don't blurt it out."

"*Most* women like to hear it when a guy falls for them." Gray shot a look at her. She couldn't miss the inflection on the word *most*.

"You have to know if she's serious before you go throwing that word around. If she's not, it will have her running for the hills." Alyssa stuck out her tongue at Grayson.

"How do I know if she's serious?" Both men looked at her for an answer.

"Hell if I know, but good luck to you. Here she comes."

Chanda didn't hesitate when she got to the booth. She slid in on Doug's side and gave him a quick kiss and a smile. Then she turned to them and gave them a smile as well.

"Chan, this is Grayson and Alyssa. Guys, this is my girl."

"We've met," Gray said. "When you bring me drinks on Fridays."

"Which I'm happy to do." She looked at their glasses. "You're set for now I see."

"Is it time for your break? Can you sit for a second?" Doug asked, hope in his voice.

"Sure. I have a few minutes. My name isn't on the outside of the bar. Let that Scottish bastard earn his keep," she joked, causing Alyssa to laugh. She liked the woman, and it was obvious Doug more than liked her.

"Chanda is also an artist. Sculpting and painting, but she can also draw a mean caricature on a napkin when given the opportunity." Doug beamed with pride and wrapped an arm around her. It wasn't a possessive gesture, more that he just couldn't keep his hands off her. "Gray and Liss work with me."

"It's very nice to meet you. I'm sorry you're all so bored for the major part of your existence."

"I see Doug has told you what we do."

"He even tried to make it sound exciting," Chanda laughed and leaned in for another kiss.

"Speak for yourselves. I happen to like my job," Alyssa said.

"That's because you've only been doing it for two weeks. You haven't noticed how much it sucks yet."

"It pays the bills," Alyssa noted. Now that she was paying less in rent, she was getting closer to paying those bills off. They were the last part of her past weighing her down. A few more months and she would be free of the financial debt at least.

* * * *

Watching his friend with Chanda made Grayson want all the things he didn't have with Alyssa. Things he might never have because of the walls she refused to let him through.

It was obvious something had happened to her. Something bigger than a run-of-the-mill betrayal like he'd experienced.

At the time, it had hit him hard. He thought the dual betrayal of a girlfriend and best friend would keep him from ever trusting again. But he found himself ready to commit to someone. Not everyone was his whore of an ex-girlfriend or his backstabbing ex-best friend. Grayson was over it. He wanted what Doug had. He wanted the girl to actually be his girl. He looked over at Liss and smiled. She smiled back, but he could still see the storm clouds in her eyes.

Blurting out his feelings wouldn't work for them. He needed to convince her that he was safe. There had to be a way to convince her that being in a relationship wasn't terrifying. Except that would ruin the small bit of trust he'd managed to earn. He was in a no-win situation.

* * * *

Gray wasn't in bed when Alyssa woke on Saturday morning. She could hear the shower running so she knew there was no sense to get up yet. She rested her arm across her forehead and thought about the night before.

When they came home from the bar, they ended up in his bed. She assumed he would be tired and just want to get to it so they could sleep, but there was something different.

He continued his campaign to take his time making her feel good. In many different ways.

Normally she wasn't comfortable accepting pleasure, but Gray had convinced her he was getting pleasure out of it as well. This knowledge allowed her to relax enough to make it amazing. The guilt was still there, hiding in the darkness, waiting for the moment she was alone to pounce. But she wasn't alone when she was with Grayson.

She didn't realize she was smiling until Gray walked in the room, grinning around a toothbrush. Not *a* toothbrush. *Her* toothbrush.

"What are you doing with my toothbrush?" She pulled the sheet up to cover her naked body since he was wearing boxers.

He shrugged with his mouth covered in foam.

"I just grabbed one out of the cup," he mumbled before he returned to the bathroom to spit.

"There are only two toothbrushes in the cup. How could you possibly get confused as to which one was yours?" she yelled at him across the hall until he walked back into her room.

"What's the big deal?" He shrugged it off as he came to sit on the edge of the bed to kiss her with his minty fresh breath.

"It's gross."

"I had my face between your legs last night, why can't I borrow your toothbrush?"

"It's not the same."

"I beg to disagree." His blue eyes were practically sparkling.

"Do you want to beg to disagree or find yourself begging for something else?" she threatened.

"What about French kissing. Our tongues are in each other's mouths." He had a point, but she wasn't ready to give him credit for having a point.

"Just don't use my toothbrush." She pointed at him as she got up and made her way to the bathroom.

"Fine, but our toothbrushes were touching in the cup anyway."

"Still not the same thing." She shut the door, but not before she heard him mutter, "Is too."

They spent the weekend doing mundane household things like laundry, dusting, and mopping the kitchen floor. His neatness gave hers a run for its money. When they were done, they watched television, ordered take-out, and ended up in bed together.

It was the most perfect lazy weekend ever.

Since they were both running late for work the next morning, they got ready in the bathroom together.

They were brushing their teeth, and Gray was trying to talk around his own toothbrush, making her laugh because she couldn't understand what he was saying.

He reached out to turn the water on at the same second she went to spit and she ended up spitting toothpaste all over his arm.

That caused another bout of laughter.

As he washed off his arm, Alyssa caught a glimpse of them in the mirror and nearly froze at the image of them.

They were still laughing, but it was something more.

She was happy.

Not just fun orgasm happy, but deep down happy. It wasn't acceptable. Giving up these little things with a man was her penance for destroying someone else's happiness.

"Hey, it's okay." Gray frowned, no doubt confused by the change in her expression. She smiled as best she could and brushed it off. It wasn't his fault. She wouldn't make him pay for her stupidity.

"I have to say, I like your toothbrush better than mine. This one sucks," he said, clearly trying to lighten the mood. She swallowed and went along with it.

"I'll pick you up a new one when I stop for groceries tonight," she offered.

"Thanks. Hey, can you get those cookies with the stripes and the hole in the center? I love those."

"Sure. If you think of anything else we need, text me."

They both stopped for a second, letting the situation soak in around them. It was very domestic. She didn't want him to read too much into it.

"This is a perfectly normal roommate conversation," he stated calmly.

"Really? Did Trent ever buy you a toothbrush?"

"Well, no. We did split a box of condoms once. Condoms and dental hygiene are just a few aisles apart." He shrugged and seemed perfectly fine. She thought back to her living arrangement with Sasha—before she turned into a demon—and nodded. She'd stopped for tampons on more than one occasion. Tampons were only a few aisles from dental hygiene too. His logic seemed sound.

Chapter 13

"I swear if you don't wipe that fucking smile off your face I'm going to hack my doughnut all over your desk."

"Good morning to you too, Doug," Gray said as he sat at his desk unloading his messenger bag. "What's your problem?"

"I'm sorry. I asked Julie if I could keep Lucy overnight on Saturday. We were having so much fun with Chanda, and Luce begged me to make her rabbit pancakes for breakfast."

"And Julie said no."

"She said no with that hoity-toity attitude that drives me nuts. I actually think she enjoys torturing me. How did I not know she was evil when I married her?"

"Women are cunning beings. Maybe we would notice if we could look away from their boobs for a few seconds."

Doug laughed at that and shook his head.

"I don't just enjoy Chan for her boobs—as wonderful as they are. It's her. She has this way of looking at things that blows my mind. It must be the artist thing. I see something and then she mentions things like lines and color and depth, and bam! I'm seeing it completely differently and it's beautiful."

"Maybe she's a witch. Have you eaten any apples she's offered you?"

"No apples. And trust me, if she was a witch I think she would have used her powers to turn Julie into a toad. She was as angry as I was. She loves Lucy. And Luce loves her too. I'm telling you this woman is everything I didn't know I could ever have."

Grayson's thoughts turned to Alyssa and how she was everything he wanted in a woman. With the big exception of how she refused to be in a committed relationship. That was a bit of an obstacle. But maybe one day he could win her trust. He wasn't giving up.

"Liss seems to be more than just boobs to you," Doug noted.

"Yeah." Gray could only shrug.

"From what you've said, she's a great roommate. You're still sleeping with her, which must mean it's good. What more could you want?" It was a valid question. Was it worth it to push her until she left just to be able to say they were in a relationship? Then he'd have nothing. At least for now he had what she was willing to give.

"I don't know. On that first night, we decided there wouldn't be any bullshit between us. No expectations. Just honesty. The thing is, I would be okay with more if it was with Alyssa."

Doug wiggled his finger at him. "You like her."

"Yeah. I told you I like her."

"No. No. Not like that. Like her like *love* her."

"I don't," Gray said a little too quickly. "I don't," he repeated for emphasis. He couldn't, she'd made it clear that kind of thing was against the rules.

"We'll see."

"I hate to make your day even worse, but it's time for our meeting." Grayson wanted to end the conversation.

"I heard we're doing team-building stuff today. You want to be my partner?"

"No."

Doug fake-coughed the word *love* as they left Grayson's office.

* * * *

Teambuilding? Alyssa held in her groan and looked across the table at an expectant Grayson. His nod in her direction communicated his intent clearly. Did she want to be his partner for this stupid exercise?

A quick glance around the room provided little alternatives. At least Gray wouldn't cause her to cringe if there was any kind of physical contact involved.

She nodded back.

"Okay everyone pair up. Take out your phones and hand them over to the other person." There was a shuffling of people. Most people finding the person they worked with the most. She noticed one person take the opportunity to leave, and wished she'd thought of it first.

She stood next to Grayson away from everyone else and gave him her phone as he handed her, his.

"Pull up the contacts list. Ask your team member about a few random people in their contacts list. Listen to how they describe those people. Can you tell by the other person's body language and expressions how they truly feel about their contacts? We're going to take ten minutes, and then we'll move on to the next thing."

Grayson was already frowning at her screen.

"What is this? You hardly have anyone in your phone," he complained.

"You're in there. Ask me what I think about you." She wiggled her eyebrows and he moved on.

"Kenley? Didn't she used to work here?"

"Yes. She's my best friend."

"Tell me something personal about her."

"We complement each other well because she gets too attached to people, and I don't. When we have an issue, the other person can easily step into the role of devil's advocate."

"Did you talk to her about me?"

Alyssa shrugged, and then nodded.

"Is she the reason you're still living with me?" Another shrug and nod. "I like her. What about Mia?"

"She knows what I'll say before I say it. It's creepy."

"And your mom?"

"I think it's my turn."

She scrolled through tons of names. Four passes and she was still only at the letter D.

"What about your dad?" She gave up and took the easy route.

"My dad is great. Very encouraging. He has a wonderful sense of humor and I hope you'll get to meet him next month at my family's annual get together."

She choked on air.

"You're kidding. You're inviting me to a family event where I would meet your parents? What part of 'roommates only' are you not getting?"

"Trent has met my parents." He brushed it off. "My dad has taken up cooking since he retired and he thinks he's good at it. He isn't, but my mother praises him as if he's a gourmet chef." He shook his head and she could see how much he loved his parents.

"My mom is a great cook. Though when I come to visit, she thinks she needs to make all my favorite foods in one meal," Alyssa shared without knowing why.

"How often do you visit?"

"Not often. I usually send her a ticket to come here."

"I'm using my skills to see that you do not like to go home. Why not?"

"Bad feelings." That was all she was willing to say. "But not about my mom. She's a hard worker and so strong. I know she would be there for me no matter what. She's already proven that." Grayson tilted his head and opened his mouth to ask something else when Randy saved her.

"Okay everyone. Give the phones back. Next thing. Scroll through your photos and pick one to show your partner. Tell them about it. Partners, listen and watch that body language. See if you can see what the other person is feeling."

"For the love of God, please make it stop." Alyssa hung her head as Grayson scrolled through his pictures.

"This one." He held out a selfie of the two of them in bed together. She was sleeping on his chest.

"Is that drool?" She gasped, and reached for his phone, but he snatched it away.

"You mean this puddle on my shirt by your mouth? Yes. I believe that is drool."

"And that is your favorite picture?" Her voice couldn't be any flatter as she looked over her shoulder to make sure no one was paying attention.

"Show me yours."

She focused on the task and sighed, not liking her choices.

"There's this one." She held it up and he squinted.

"That's the back of your television."

"I needed to remember how the cables hooked up."

"Try again."

"Fine." She gave up and showed him her favorite picture. It always made her laugh.

"That's my—" He didn't say the word *ass*, but it was—in a pair of boxers that had a duck on the back and the words *Butt Quack*.

"I can't help it. I laugh every time." She tried to stop, but laughed again as his face went serious.

"I wish we weren't in the conference room so I could kiss you right now," he said so quietly she barely heard him. Laughter abandoned, they stared at each other for a long moment. She may have even leaned in slightly.

Fortunately, Randy called everyone's attention and they both snapped out of whatever spell had bound them.

"So did you learn anything about the other person? How much of it was non-verbal? Reading body language is an important skill and you can improve on it. It's a vital way to communicate with our clients. Learn how to spot unease. We don't ever want our clients to feel uneasy with us. If your client isn't confident, then you need to stop and explain things differently. Even if it's bad news, we have to make sure our client understands and feels confident in us." He paused to let that sink in and then clapped once. "Go out and make us money."

Those were always his closing words. Alyssa breathed a sigh of relief and went back to her office as quickly as possible.

* * * *

Grayson wasn't sure what had happened at the meeting, but it wasn't entirely bad. Although from the way Alyssa had run off, she was clearly spooked. He didn't need a lesson in body language to see that. She had shared personal information with him. She'd told him about her mother. That was a huge step for her. And it meant she trusted him enough to let him in. A little bit at least.

He called her a little before noon.

"Alyssa Sinclair," she said.

"Is it wrong that I'm aroused by your professional voice?" He used humor to make her feel comfortable when things got too serious between them.

"Thanks. What can I do for you?"

"Go to lunch with me."

"Do you mean food or a quickie at our place?"

"Whichever. I'll leave the details up to you."

"I can't do either. I'm skipping lunch so I can impress my new boss by finishing this project early."

"Come on. You gotta eat."

"I will eat. I'll eat at my desk while I work."

"That's sad."

"It will pay off in the end."

"So what are we doing tonight?" He moved on.

"I'm going for groceries, remember? It's my turn."

"Right. Do you care if I go out? Doug needs to vent before he combusts, and Chanda is working."

"Are you asking me if you can go out, after you asked me to buy you the striped cookies this morning? God, Gray. What the hell?"

"Relax. I'm sorry. It was more of a courtesy than asking for permission."

"Are you sure?" He wasn't sure. He was comfortable with her, and that comfort leeched out into other areas. Areas that could be interpreted as intimacy.

"I'm going out tonight. I'll see you when I see you. And don't stay up." He tried the tough guy routine, which just made them laugh.

"Do you mean I'll see you when you crawl in my bed to *snuggle*?"

"Women are supposed to like snuggling. There is something very wrong with you," Gray said.

"Yep," she agreed easily. "I've got to go. This report isn't going to analyze itself."

Gray chuckled and hung up, his heart happy.

He didn't love Alyssa. He was pretty sure of it. He hoped for his sake he didn't love her. If grocery requests and brushing their teeth together freaked her out, falling in love with her was a very bad idea.

That night after work, Doug wanted to go to a different bar than where Chanda worked so she wouldn't think he was a stalker.

"I don't think she would think that," Gray said.

"I don't want to overdo it. There is such a thing as too much of a good thing." He pointed to himself and laughed.

Gray caught himself checking his phone a few times, wishing the night would speed by so he could go home. He knew it was important to go out with his friends. It was healthy, and with the way he'd been feeling that morning, he felt it was necessary to get out and prove to himself he wasn't in love.

"Hi there." A brunette with bright red lips stood next to him.

"Hello."

"I'm Hailey," she said, though he hadn't asked, nor would he have asked given the opportunity. That was probably a bad sign.

"Nice to meet you," he said.

"It's kind of chilly in here," she noted, making small talk.

"Well, the air conditioning is cranked up and you're hardly wearing any clothes," Gray pointed out, remembering too late that strangers didn't converse with this much honesty. This comment threw her for a moment, but she rebounded quickly.

"Where do you work?"

"Sanitation," he lied.

"Really?" she looked him over in his dress shirt and slacks. "I hear they make great money."

"Oh, sure," he agreed. "And we get plenty of free stuff too. This morning I scored half a bag of chips and a bottle of shampoo." Alyssa would have laughed, Hailey didn't. In the short time they'd lived together, Alyssa had ruined his ability to communicate with other humans.

Hailey twitched and then pretended she saw someone she knew on the other side of the room.

"What was that about?" Doug asked.

"I'm just not interested." Which was a good thing since he'd totally blown it.

"She's not doing it for you?" Doug raised his brows.

"I think I'm going to head out." Grayson didn't want to get into all the reasons why Hailey didn't measure up to Liss.

"I'm going to go down and see Chanda. I think we've set some good boundaries here, but, you know." Yeah. He knew. He wanted to get back to his girl too. Except Grayson didn't have a girl.

Alyssa was lying on the sofa watching reality TV when he came in.

"Wow, it's early," she mentioned.

"Is it?" It felt like it had been hours.

"It's not even ten."

"Right. Well, it was kind of lame."

"Kind of lame at a bar so you came home to watch television and eat leftover Chinese with me?" She laughed. Obviously unaware it was the "with me" part that had him home so early.

"Sure. It was a long day. I just want to unwind."

"I bought beer." She held one up for him.

"Thank you, Genie. You only have two more wishes to fulfill."

"I bought the cookies you wanted, and your new toothbrush is on the counter. Consider me retired."

They snuggled on the sofa, drinking beer and making fun of the people on TV the rest of the night. He let her use the bathroom first when it was time to go to bed. It was only when he walked in the bathroom that he realized he was smiling.

He'd been in relationships before, but none of them had felt like this. This *un*relationship was the best thing that had ever happened to him.

Chapter 14

"Did you buy me a *Barbie Doll* toothbrush?" Grayson asked, holding it up as he walked into her bedroom. She tried to hold back the laughter and failed miserably.

"I thought it would be easier for you to tell which one was yours."

"Very funny."

"It sings," she added.

"I hate you," he said, making her laugh again. She could tell he didn't mean it.

"So what are you doing this weekend?" he asked, coming back into her room with the singing toothbrush.

She was laughing so hard she could barely answer.

"My team has a meeting next week and I'm presenting. I really want to impress them. I'm going to be preparing for that."

"It doesn't hurt to be prepared." He left to go back to the bathroom.

She listened as he went from the bathroom to his bedroom and then walked back in her room carrying a pillow. He traded it out for the one on the other side of the bed and got in next to her. He adjusted the pillow, and then let out a happy sigh as he snuggled under her covers.

She sighed and turned off the light, lying there next to him, looking up into the darkness of the room. She'd missed having someone to sleep with. Not just for sex, but just…there.

"FYI, the Barbie toothbrush sucks. It's so tiny I have to brush one tooth at a time," he complained.

She laughed again and let him pull her against him.

* * * *

The next morning, she awoke alone. Gray was in the kitchen.

Her heart squeezed happily at the sight of him in boxers and a T-shirt at the coffeepot. She decided the reaction was more about the coffee than the man. Though he was pretty damn sexy, even when he wasn't trying.

As she passed, he turned, pinning her to the counter and kissing her deeply.

"How's that to start your day?" he asked, while wiggling his brows at her.

"It would have been better if you didn't have morning breath," she joked.

With a laugh, he poured coffee into her favorite travel mug and added a huge helping of vanilla creamer.

"I know that's not true, because I used your toothbrush this morning when I got up."

"Seriously?"

"Well, I didn't have all day to spend brushing my teeth. I have to get to work."

"Whatever."

"So I was thinking about your upcoming meeting and I want to help."

"Help?"

"Yeah. Maybe you could bounce your presentation off me and I'll give you feedback."

"You are not going to want to listen to my budget findings for Pinecrest Parking Systems."

"Oh, but I am. I'm riveted by the thought of parking systems and how they spend their money." He grinned at her.

"You don't have a car."

"I used to. And I might want one again, if I had a safe place to park it."

"They have a sizable budget for safety upgrades."

"Good plan," he agreed with a nod while leaning over the eggs on the stove, the slope of his back inviting her to lean up against him.

"It's also convenient." She hopped up on the counter next to him before laying out her plan. "They need to spend more money in advertising. I'm going to suggest they get the extra income by not going to trade shows. According to the data, they're not getting enough of a return in that area."

"But they will from advertising?" He sounded doubtful.

"I spoke with marketing and got a plan. If they spend it in key locations, it can pay off." He nodded at this and they both went off to get dressed.

"So what locations?" he picked up the earlier conversation as they walked to work.

"I actually came up an idea that Diana in marketing loved. I'm thinking the subway. When you're crammed in on the train, everybody wishes they had a car. I'm going to suggest some less expensive spots on the platform. Seeing that option day in and day out might make more of an impression than throwing their advertising dollars all over the place."

"That's a really good idea." He held the door open and smiled.

There was something in that smile. Something comfortable. She nudged his arm with her elbow.

"Thanks for the coffee."

"Thanks for the crappy toothbrush." He winked as they got on the elevator and rode up together.

Grayson was good to his word. After their morning meeting, he came in her office to hear her presentation. He made comments and suggestions that were actually helpful.

"Maybe ease them into the new statement format in stages rather than dumping that on them right out of the gate. People like to feel as though they can trust someone before they're open to change," he suggested, taking it very seriously. "Well, most people like to trust someone. Maybe not you." He gave her a wink.

"It's not that I don't want to trust someone. It's more that I...can't."

"You trust me, right? I mean you moved in with me, trusting in the fact I wasn't going to steal your stuff or hurt you."

"You did steal my toothbrush." She raised a brow.

"Still. There had to be trust there on some level."

"Maybe," she allowed reluctantly. "A very small level."

"Whatever. I'm going to count it as an accomplishment."

By lunchtime, Gray's attention began to wane. He was no longer offering suggestions of the accounting nature, but was still offering suggestions in the naked department.

"Would you like to go home for lunch?" he whispered by her ear while she tried to type.

For a second, she let the joy of the moment envelop her. This was what she would have wanted. A man to support her ambitions as well as make her smile.

She took a breath and let that dream flow out of her as she exhaled and took the thing she could have. Sex.

"Sure. Let's go."

* * * *

"Let's go out," she said as they left work for the night.

"Out?"

"A club. Do you remember the place where you go to hang out with people and socialize?" Of course he remembered. He just didn't see why he needed to go to a club when Alyssa lived with him. They could have a drink and socialize in the comfort of their own home.

But he knew what she meant, and it was nice to see her take a break from worrying over the presentation, which she had already perfected earlier.

"Fine. We'll go out to a club."

"I'll buy you a drink, since you were such a big help today."

He knew he wouldn't let her buy him a drink as payment for doing something he wanted to do. Not to mention something he was already being compensated for by his salary.

Besides, he had fun helping her with her proposal. She was brilliant and should have been promoted years ago.

He showered after Alyssa came out of the bathroom. When he was dressed, he sat on the sofa, waiting. Alyssa was pretty quick about getting ready. She was gorgeous so there was only so much that she needed to do.

She emerged from the hall wearing a short red dress. Her blonde hair fell in waves past her shoulders and her face had a subtle amount of makeup. Just enough for a guy to see she would still be amazing without it.

He felt lucky to be able to walk into any place with her on his arm.

Ten minutes at the club, and Gray was ready to get out. He finished his drink and danced with Alyssa. Grinding up against her body had the effect he predicted. He frowned when they sat down again.

"You don't seem to be having fun," she noticed despite his attempt to hide it.

"Honestly?"

"Of course. That's the rule, right? No bullshit."

He nodded. "I would have rather just stayed home and snuggled on the sofa with you while watching a movie where things blew up."

"Hmm."

"Don't give me shit about it. You asked." He frowned at his hands on the bar.

"I'm not going to give you shit. I was just thinking it sounds nice. I wouldn't have to wear heels."

"Oh, no. You still need to wear the heels, but with your bra and panties."

"How about no heels, a T-shirt, and a pair of your boxers?"

"Deal." He held out his hand and she shook it before tugging him off his stool.

"Let's go."

Seeing her in his clothes did something primal to him. It was as if she were marked by him. She was his.

He smiled as she settled on the sofa in his boxers. She rested her head on his thigh and her long legs stretched out, taking up the rest of the space. He played with the long strands of her golden hair until the movie began.

This was so much better than a loud crowd or going off with a stranger. While he'd done this many times with past girlfriends, this was a contentment Grayson had never known before Alyssa moved in.

The movie was horrible, so he wasn't surprised when she started to fidget only ten minutes into it. What did surprise him was what she began fidgeting with.

She slipped her hand under the waistband of his shorts and was now stroking him with a phenomenal rhythm. She twisted around in his lap as he let his head fall back against the cushion. He closed his eyes, letting the feeling of her touch sink into his bones. Then he felt something else.

Warm, wetness surrounded him and he looked down to see her mouth gliding up and down his length.

"Liss?" he said shocked.

She paused and smiled up at him.

"What? You said this was one of the perks of having a screening."

He had said that, but then she hadn't wanted him to take advantage of that perk for her pleasure.

"Should I continue?"

"Yes," he answered, his voice coming out breathy and desperate. He watched as she ran her tongue up his cock while giving him a naughty look.

When she wrapped her lips around him again, he jerked. He tugged down his shorts a little so she had more room as she serviced him with incredible enthusiasm. She even moaned a few times as if she were enjoying it. The sound reverberated through his flesh, making him want to explode.

He made the mistake of opening his eyes and looking down to watch. Her lips were flushed red from the friction. She continued to slide down over him and pull back up with just the right amount of pressure.

He could feel himself building. Watching was too much, but he couldn't look away, and it was too late anyway.

"Liss," he groaned, giving her fair warning, but she didn't move. Instead, she kept going, taking in everything he gave her as he cried out so loud it echoed in the room.

When his breathing came back down to normal, Alyssa tucked him back in his pants and looked up at him.

"I don't like this movie. Can we watch something else?" She tilted her head adorably, her lips still shiny and slightly swollen. He'd never seen anyone more beautiful in all his life.

"We can watch whatever the hell you want."

* * * *

Gray fell asleep while they were watching the movie she picked, and she covered him with a blanket before going to bed.

Now he wasn't in her bed and she missed him.

As she was deciding whether or not she wanted to go wake him so he could come to bed, he stepped in her room and crawled into bed next to her, pulling her close.

"Snuggling isn't required after oral." She laughed, but shifted so she could get closer. She'd taken great pleasure in watching him enjoy what she was doing to him earlier. She loved that power, and had forgotten what it felt like. It had been so long. A lifetime ago.

"I like to talk to you while I fall asleep," he confessed.

"And you wondered why I bought you a kid's toothbrush. Do you want me to tell you a bedtime story?" she joked.

"Maybe. You got any good ones?"

"No." She shook her head, remembering her personal stories were off limits.

"Maybe you could tell me what happened to you?" he suggested.

"What do you mean?"

"I mean the way you won't let anyone in, and how you avoid anything remotely resembling a real connection with another person."

"Oh. That."

"Yeah. That."

"It's like you said, my bitchy blood."

He wasn't dissuaded.

"Come on. I know you don't like to trust people. But have I given you any reason not to trust me?"

"That's kind of the problem. I don't know who I can trust and who I can't, so by default, I trust no one."

"Please, tell me. Trust me with this one thing. Please." He made it sound simple. It was just a story. Part of her past she hadn't managed to get over. Maybe telling him would be a step in that direction. Or maybe he would look at her differently.

"You go first. What is the worst thing that happened to you?" She made a habit of turning his questions back on him as a distraction. It usually worked.

"All right. I'll go first, but you'd better not leave me hanging when I'm done. Will you share yours if I share mine?"

"I promise I'll tell you every gory detail." She shook his extended hand to finalize their agreement, then he began his story. She was expecting him to fall asleep at some point before she needed to tell him anything.

"I fell in love in twelfth grade. Her name was Mandy. She stayed back home and went to college there."

"Where is that? Home."

"Connecticut." They both paused for a moment. Probably trying to figure out why he'd never mentioned it before. Then he went on. "I wanted to go away to school. She promised me we would be able to stay together for the four years we would be apart. Then she screwed my best friend."

"Ouch."

"What made it worse was she started screwing him the minute I left and I didn't find out about it until I was a junior. He even told me he was doing this hot girl who had a boyfriend, throwing it in my face without using names."

"Rude."

"I know. It makes it difficult to trust people."

"Including yourself?"

"Yes. Definitely. I always wonder, am I good enough to keep a woman's interest or will she go off with some other guy?" They both nodded. "Same thing happen to you?"

"Not exactly." She frowned. Her distraction technique hadn't worked this time, and he seemed far from sleep.

"You promised. It will be okay, Liss."

She couldn't believe she was going to do this. Her mother was the only person in her life that knew her story, and they never spoke of it. Somehow she knew Grayson wouldn't judge her, or try to pity her.

While Kenley was officially her best friend, she'd never felt comfortable discussing it. For some reason, speaking to Gray felt more natural. She let out a breath and decided to go for it.

"You know where I grew up." He already knew so much about her, maybe this wouldn't be bad. Maybe it would even feel better to talk about it.

"Trailer park," he said.

"Right. I worked my ass off to get scholarships so I could go to college and make more of myself than a struggling single mother, like my own mom."

"And you did it," he said. "I'm proud of you, for whatever that's worth." He shrugged it off.

"I was on the pill before I ever even planned to have sex, just in case. And I was going to find a great guy who would want to marry me."

"I think most girls have that on their agendas at that age."

"Well, I found a great guy who wanted to marry me." She took a deep breath. "But now he's in prison."

Chapter 15

"What?" Gray pulled back to look at her face. Alyssa knew he hadn't been expecting that. Who would? "Seriously?"

"His name was Donnie. We started dating as freshman at Syracuse. He was perfect. Very polite and caring. He did romantic stuff like plan a picnic in his dorm room, and walked me to class even if it meant he'd be late for his own class. Things like that."

"I think I might vomit," Gray joked.

"We moved in together and I wasn't surprised when he asked me to marry him. We were engaged the summer before our senior year. We were busy getting good grades and making plans for our wedding. His family didn't have much. His father was on permanent disability. His mother was overworked and trying to take care of his four younger siblings. We talked all the time about having a better life. Getting jobs in New York and being yuppies." She laughed at the memory, but then turned serious.

"In January of our senior year, we walked out of class together, and the police rushed in and arrested him. They said he was being charged for sexual assault and rape."

Gray pulled her closer to him, though his warmth barely fought off the chill of that memory. It was the exact moment when everything went from perfect to perfectly awful.

"Of course, I didn't believe any of it. I knew Donnie wasn't capable of doing something like that. If anything, he was boring in bed, always wanting it missionary. On special occasions, we might do it with me on top, but never anything wild. Never any place but in a bed. He thought oral was disgusting. He didn't even make any noise during his release. There was no way he could have done it. I was sure.

"They set his bail fairly high because he had no real ties to the community. He didn't have the money to post bail and his parents weren't able, or willing, to help. I tried to raise the money, but I was only working part time at a coffee house. I had nothing to put up, not even a car. The money we had saved for our wedding wasn't enough, so he had to stay in jail.

"I supported him and visited every chance I got. He told me repeatedly that it was a mistake and how they would release him soon. Every day I woke up thinking it would be the day they would clear up the misunderstanding and he would come home, but that didn't happen.

"It actually got worse. A third girl came forward from his high school. I was so angry. I wanted to find these girls and scream at them for ruining our perfect life with their lies. That was until I walked into the courtroom and saw them sitting there.

"All three of them, with their long brown hair and big brown eyes, looked over at me. Their eyes were haunted and empty. They seemed hollow, and I knew someone had done something horrible to them. They had been victimized. It was clear on their nearly identical faces, but still I didn't believe it could have been Donnie. He never so much a raised his voice to me.

"Day after excruciating day, the evidence stacked up against him. His DNA matched the semen found in all of them, which made no sense. He'd always worn a condom with me, even though I was on the pill. We knew we couldn't afford a kid, so we took extra precautions. His attorney was arguing the accuracy of the tests to no avail. It was a positive match.

"When they were done with the scientific babble and pointing out his lack of alibi during the crimes, the women took the stand to tell their stories. It was atrocious. The person who had raped them was brutal. He'd beaten them and said violent things. Things Donnie could have never had said to anyone.

"Then the second to the last woman mentioned the rapist wearing a navy blue hoodie and gloves, and how his sleeve had pulled up showing a small section of skin. She had scratched his arm. The skin under her nails matched Donnie's DNA, but that still wasn't what finally convinced me." She shook her head, still baffled by her ignorance.

"It was that stupid blue hoodie. I used to borrow it sometimes, and then all of a sudden it was missing. Every time I asked where it was, he told me a different story. He didn't know. It had ripped so he'd thrown it out. He got bleach on it at work. I kept asking just because he kept making up something else each time. And I did remember that scratch on his arm.

"I had asked him what happened, and he told me he didn't remember. At the time I thought it looked pretty painful, and wondered how someone could forget being scratched that badly.

"In the courtroom, I looked over at him sitting like a stone, wearing his orange jumpsuit and I saw the thin white scar on his arm. My world stopped.

"I left and didn't go back. I knew then that he had done it. I didn't know why or how, but I knew I didn't know the real him at all. I never heard the last woman's story. I just needed to leave."

Grayson didn't say anything for a very long time. He pulled her over to him and held her very tight. Maybe he thought she was going to cry, but she wasn't. She had cried everything she had left to cry.

"The nightmares?"

"The man in my dreams does the things the women described. He's wearing a blue hoodie, but I never see his face." She took a quick breath.

"I can understand why you would be afraid to be close to someone after that," he said.

"Everyone has secrets," she said numbly. Of all the people she had met since finding out the truth about the man she had planned to marry, she felt the most comfortable with Grayson, but that didn't mean she could allow herself to be happy with him.

He paused before responding, then nodded and pulled back so he could look in her eyes.

"Yes, everyone probably has secrets to some degree. But most people don't have hideous secrets like that. Normal people have secrets like… they're still using their roommate's toothbrush or they *did* eat the last doughnut the other morning."

She laughed, which was probably what he was going for.

"You can't keep this bottled up inside of you, Liss. It will eat away at you until you're hollow inside. You need to have a good life and find a way past this." Except she didn't deserve to have a happy life after failing to stop a monster from hurting other people. If she'd just paid attention to what was happening in front of her, instead of planning a wedding, she might have spared at least one of Donnie's victims.

"It's hard to move on when you're not sure where things went wrong the first time. Obviously, he had this problem before he met me, but he seemed so nice. How could I have been so blind?"

"You weren't blind. He was just very good at hiding who he really was."

"And how would I know I wouldn't fall for it again with someone else?"

Gray let out a sigh. It was clear he didn't have an answer.

"I wrote to him after he was convicted, asking him why he did it. I thought if I knew maybe I could figure out how I'd missed it. Maybe I would know what to look for the next time, but he couldn't even give me that. He *still* denied everything. He swore they had the wrong person and he was going to be released soon so we could be married. If he could have just told me the truth…" She hung her head. "Maybe if I hadn't been so giddy every time he called me his almost-wife I would have seen some clue. I was so stupid."

"You weren't stupid. Who would ever suspect such a thing? Especially from someone who was so nice to you? No one would, Liss. No one."

She liked the way his fingers felt as they brushed though her hair, but she had no idea what he really did when he went to the gym or stayed late at work.

She didn't really know him.

No one really knew anyone.

* * * *

This was horrible. Worse than horrible. There wasn't a word for it.

Gray knew she had been hurt. It was obvious by the way she avoided relationships, but he had no idea it was this severe. He pulled her closer, wanting to take all of it away.

"I swear I don't have anything heinous like that in my past. The worst thing I'm guilty of is occasionally taking a long lunch break. I'm safe, Liss. I promise, you can count on me."

She nodded in a noncommittal way. She wasn't ready, but he'd gotten through. She'd told him her story. It was huge, and now that he was on the inside of her wall he was terrified.

He really wanted to help Alyssa because he cared, but he knew he wasn't qualified. He didn't have the ability to be what she needed in order to heal.

He held her as she fell asleep, his mind still racing to find a way to help. Then at about three in the morning, he had an idea. He wasn't qualified, but he knew someone who was.

The next morning, he snuck out into the hallway with his phone before Alyssa woke up.

"What, brat?" his older sister, Izabelle, answered.

"I need a favor."

"Like an *I need you to lie to mom and dad* favor, or an *I need bail money* kind of favor?"

"I need you to see if a psych eval was done on a prisoner and see if you can take a look at it and give me your thoughts."

"I so did not see that coming," she said flatly.

"I know. It's for a friend."

"Who is it and where are they being detained?"

"Donald Rice. Onondaga." He'd gotten the details out of Alyssa before she fell asleep the night before.

"Let me see what I can do. I'll get back to you after I take a look."

"Thanks, Iz. I really appreciate this."

It was two days before Izabelle got back to him with her results.

"How in the hell did you get mixed up with this sick son of a bitch?" his sister asked when he answered the phone. Since he was watching a movie with Alyssa, he excused himself and went to talk in his room.

"My friend was engaged to him, she had no idea he was a rapist."

"I can believe that. He doesn't seem to know he's a rapist either."

"What does that mean? Like multi-personality disorder?"

"He's delusional."

"I could have guessed that myself."

"Not like normal guy delusional, but like seriously messed-up delusional. His doctor put him under hypnosis to get to his repressed memories. Of course, it's not admissible in court, but it is helpful to know how to treat the patient."

"What did the file say?"

"His mother was apparently turning tricks for extra cash, and this Donnie walked in on his mom getting roughed up by one of her customers. He was thirteen and tried to stop the guy, but he wasn't big enough to help."

"Shit."

"He already had some other social issues before this happened, but this incident during puberty forced him to repress those feelings of helplessness and anger. You can only keep shit like that inside for so long before it comes out.

"The notes say the women he attacked looked like his mother, so I'm guessing he was probably acting out the scenario but with him being the one in control. Then when the act was over, he repressed it each time. It's very hard to treat a person like this because you don't have anything to grasp onto. He won't admit he did it, so there's no remorse or guilt. There's nothing.

"Apparently, they tried to go with a guilty by reason of insanity defense, but Donald relieved his public defender and refused his right for counsel, claiming it was a misunderstanding and he was innocent."

"She couldn't have known he was like this?"

"Like I said, *he* doesn't even know he's like this."

"My friend is having a rough time moving on. She doesn't trust anyone. What can I do?"

"Friend?" she said skeptically.

"Roommate? Whatever."

"Whatever?" she asked even more skeptically.

"It's not important. Just tell me how I can help her."

"It would depend on how close you are. I'm not just trying to find out the extent of the relationship for my own curiosity. I would need to know your position before I could offer a suggestion."

Gray swallowed uncomfortably. What was his position?

"I care about her, but she keeps me out, so we're just friends at the moment. Mainly because she isn't capable of anything else right now."

"And you're sure you're not drawn to her because she's a project? You used to have an issue with taking on damaged people so you could feel validated."

"Don't analyze me, Iz. You know I hate that. Just tell me how I can help her."

"She might need closure. Maybe if she could hear him admit to what he's done."

"She knows he did it," he said.

"Still, knowing the facts is different than actually hearing him take responsibility for hurting, not just those women, but her too."

"But if he's delusional, he's not going to admit it."

"Probably not."

"So you haven't helped me at all." He held his hand up even though no one could see.

"That's how we therapists work." She laughed at him. "Are you coming home for the family reunion? You could bring your friend."

"I'm not sure. We'll see."

"Okay. Let me know if there's anything else I can do."

"Thanks. See you soon."

Closure. Grayson had no idea how he would go about getting closure for Alyssa, but he wasn't about to give up on her just because it was difficult.

* * * *

"Everything okay?" Alyssa asked when Gray came back from his room. She knew he'd been on the phone. Not that she'd heard any of the conversation through the door since he'd been whispering.

"Yeah. Everything's great. I was just talking to my sister."

"How is she?" She knew how much he loved his older sister, regardless of how annoyed he pretended to be.

"Good. She's asking me about the family reunion. You want to go with me?"

"Not even a little bit." She laughed.

"All right then." He frowned and went to make a bowl of cereal for a snack.

"You're not even going to try to negotiate? Maybe offer me something in exchange for my going?" She crossed her arms over her chest.

"I don't want to go either. I'd like to avoid having my mother and sister tell embarrassing stories about me." He shrugged and took a big bite.

"I'm in."

"What? No!" He practically spit cereal all over the place.

"I'm going."

"You can't go without me." He pointed at her with is spoon.

"Why not?"

"Because it's a *family* reunion."

"Are you trying to make me feel insignificant because you have a family and I only have my mom? Thanks for rubbing it in, Gray. That hurts." She clasped a hand to her chest while batting her eyelashes.

"Okay. Okay. We'll go." He shook his head. "I don't know what just happened here," Grayson conceded as he crunched on his cereal.

"When is it?"

"Two weeks."

Alyssa never liked to plan things out too far because plans changed. People changed.

Police showed up and took people away.

Gray hadn't said much about Alyssa's revelation. He didn't pile on the pity either, for which she was grateful. He just seemed like his normal self. It was a relief and had been a step toward trusting him a little more.

She didn't know how long this would last, but she didn't want to waste any of it. She left her room and snuggled up next to Gray on the sofa.

He stroked her hair and kissed the back of her hand. It was a sweet gesture. One that made her bones and the wall around her heart soften just the tiniest bit.

Chapter 16

Doug tried not to smile in the middle of the meeting, but he'd just gotten a text from Chanda, and smiling was an involuntary reaction to seeing her name on his phone.

I'm off today. Can you come over when you get off work?

He was already looking forward to it. He had something planned, and was even going to get her flowers. Not that flowers were any guarantee that this would be a success.

He'd gotten a bit of good news on the money front and was happy to spend some of it on her.

I have a surprise for you. Her next text came in, complete with a smiley with heart-shaped eyes. In addition to the large smile on his face, he was also hard as a rock.

"You okay?" Gray leaned over to whisper.

"I think I'm going to take half a day off."

"Good for you. Chan's off too?"

"Yeah."

"I think I'm taking a long lunch."

Doug noticed his friend's gaze move across the table to the blonde he lived with.

"And you balked about going out on a Wednesday night." It seemed their mid-week adventure to ladies' night was paying off for Grayson.

They laughed and then nodded in unison to something Randy said.

The second the meeting was over, Doug was out of his chair and heading to his office. Using his tablet to hide his hard-on, he closed his office door and hurried through his emails.

I'm just wrapping up a few things and I'll be leaving early. See you in a half hour?

See you then. I can't wait, she answered.

Neither could he. But he had a stop to make, and things to tell her before he carried her off to bed.

"Don't fuck it up," he muttered to his crotch as well as to himself.

* * * *

Chanda opened the door before he even knocked. She'd been out on the balcony waiting for Doug to get there.

Her earlier excitement over her surprise had turned to throat-closing doubt. What if it was too much? What if she was reading too much into their relationship?

It was too late now. He was standing at her door. With flowers.

"Hi." He held them out. "I could barely wait long enough to finish my work. I think I may have sent an email to the wrong person, but I don't even care. I'll deal with it tomorrow. I'm here now, and I have something to say."

"Do you want to come in first?" He was still in the stairwell that led up to her loft.

"Yes. Okay."

She took the flowers from him and stepped back so he could come inside.

"These are beautiful. Thank you." She knew he didn't have a lot of extra money. Thanks to his ex-wife. Doug was happy to support his daughter and pay for the house where she lived as well as his apartment.

Though he stepped inside, he didn't move any closer. He looked nervous.

"What is it?" she asked, unable to move. Surely he wouldn't have brought flowers if he wanted to break up with her. But he wasn't smiling. In fact, she worried he might throw up.

"I'm in love with you, Chanda. And not just because I like the sex—which I like very much—but I love *you*." He winced and shook his head. "I wasn't going to blurt it out like that. Hold on. I have a list here." He patted his pockets and pulled out a folded piece of paper. "Shit. This is my agenda for the Fletcher project. I hope I didn't give the list to my assistant." He rubbed his forehead. "I was in such a hurry to get over here and tell you. I was worried I might chicken out."

"Doug. Take a breath." She smiled at his bumbling. "Go back to the beginning."

Doug took a breath. His wide shoulders moving up and down, stressing the dress shirt he wore. She wanted to take it off so he had more room to move.

"I love you. I know it's a lot to deal with. And don't worry if you don't feel the same way. I don't expect you to." Of course he didn't. His ex-wife hadn't just depleted his funds and kept his daughter away from him. She'd also demolished this man's confidence.

He didn't realize he was a catch. There were not a lot of men in the world as sweet and kind as Doug. The sweet guys she did find were rarely as quick-witted and clever, or as responsible while also being a fun-loving. Doug was the whole package.

And while he might not have ripped abs, she found his solid body to be the sexiest she'd ever had against her. Especially when he used it to make her feel so spectacular.

"Doug. Stop after the first sentence."

Again he let out a breath and fixed his gaze on hers.

"I love you, Chanda." He pressed his lips together, as if he really wanted to say something else, but was holding it in. "So much," he added quickly and covered his mouth with his palm.

She laughed and reached up to kiss him. He kissed back, making that low groan she loved. His arms were around her, pulling her against his hardness.

"You're not freaking out," he mentioned as his lips moved to her neck. "Can I take that to mean you're okay with my feelings?"

"Very okay. I wasn't expecting you to say it. Especially with your history."

"I know. You'd think I'd be gun-shy of the whole thing, but in truth, my history made me realize this was real so much sooner than I might have if I hadn't had a comparison."

"It's different than the last time you fell in love?"

"I didn't fall in love the last time. I wanted to have someone the last time. There's a difference. It's not about me. It's not about what I want or need, but about how I can give you what you want and need." He let out a laugh and shook his head. "That is not what I wrote down at all. That was ridiculous."

"I get it. And I feel the same way. In fact." She pulled away from him, remembering she had a huge gesture to share with him.

Taking his hand, she led him up to her loft. He was already unbuttoning his shirt in anticipation, but his brows pulled together when she passed her bedroom to take him to the door to her spare room.

With everything to lose she opened the door and pushed it open.

"I did this for you."

* * * *

Doug stepped into the room, expecting there to be a sculpture. Hoping fervently it wasn't a nude in his likeness.

Instead, he found himself standing in a purple room. The word *Lucy* was painted above the small white bed with the purple leopard-print blanket.

On the one side was a matching dresser and a door with a full-length mirror. He'd been in this room before and knew that closet used to hold a shelf of paint. This room had been for storage. Plastic crates had lined the wall opposite the big window.

The floor had been bare wood, but now it was covered in a purple sparkly rug.

He gasped at the animals painted on the wall. They were some of Lucy's favorites. A manatee, an otter, and a giraffe—its head cut off by the ceiling.

"I thought she might want to help me color in the animals. That's why I left them as outlines. Hopefully, she won't make every animal purple," Chanda said next to him.

"You made Lucy a bedroom." It was a stupid thing to say since he was standing in it, but he couldn't help himself.

"I'm tired of getting screwed out of bunny pancakes every Sunday morning. Now she will be able to stay. After an inspection by child services, of course."

His throat was so tight, he thought he might break down in happy tears. But the words *child services* shook him. He couldn't have this dream. No matter how much he might want it.

He frowned and turned toward her shaking his head.

"It won't help. I have to have a bedroom for her in my residence."

She tilted her head adorably and raised her brows.

"Then we'll have to make this your residence."

"Oh." He nodded in understanding. "Right. If I have my mail delivered here it would be considered my residence. Good thinking." He gave her a thumbs-up while she laughed.

"Or…" she ran her hands up his chest and around his neck to pull him down. He rested his forehead on hers feeling like a giant compared to her. "You could actually move in here and make it your residence."

Six seconds later, her words made sense.

"You're asking me to move in with you?"

Her answer was to hold up a key.

"I know it won't be as close, but you would be able to petition for equal custody. And Queens isn't *that* far."

She didn't know. Because he hadn't gotten the chance to tell her. "My wife is getting married and moving to Manhattan. I was going to be moving here anyway." Could this be happening? Could his life finally be taking a turn toward happiness?

He kissed the woman who was directly responsible.

"She is going to love this room," he said taking in the squirrel hiding in the corner.

"She is going to love having more time with her dad."

"Thank you. Thank you."

"My dad wasn't around a lot. He was always in the office. I'm glad Lucy has a dad who likes to be with her."

"Lucy's dad also likes to be with you."

"Well then, how convenient as I'll be living here too, and you're going to have to sleep in my bed."

"Hmm. Can I see that bed again? Just to make sure I fit and all."

She laughed and walked backward out of Lucy's bedroom toward hers. Scratch that—theirs.

* * * *

The next week, Gray walked in the apartment talking on his phone. He was laughing and shaking his head. It seemed he was having an enjoyable conversation.

"Okay. I'll see you later then. Bye." He disconnected the call and leaned over to kiss Alyssa on the neck. "I hope you don't mind but I invited Trent and Tiff over tonight for dinner."

"Why would I mind? It's your house. I can go hang out with Mia or something so I'm out of the way." Or hide in her room.

"No. I wanted you to be here for dinner too."

"Really?"

"Yeah. What do you say?"

"You don't think they'll read too much into it?"

"Trent has never been one for reading anything," he joked. "And all Tiffany can talk about right now is wedding shit, so she probably won't even notice you're there unless you're wearing a wedding gown."

"Okay. I'm in. What should we make for dinner?"

"We can just get pizza."

"Come on. We're having guests. We can do better than pizza. How about if we make lasagna and we could have a salad and garlic bread?"

"When you say 'we can make lasagna' do you mean *you*?"

"I mean me with your help."

"Then yes, I'm in."

"Awesome. I like to cook fancy meals and have people enjoy them."

"Why didn't you become a chef?" he questioned.

"Because I don't like people."

"Oh, right. I forgot." He chuckled at her.

"I'm going to run to the store. Did you need anything?" she asked as she picked up her keys and phone from the counter.

"No."

"Toothbrush?" she teased.

"No thanks. I seem to have taken over the one you vacated." He grinned at her as she stuck out her tongue. The truth was she was keeping her new toothbrush in her room so he couldn't use it.

Alyssa caught herself smiling as she put the box of pasta into her basket and moved toward the sauce.

What was she doing? Playing house? How pathetic it was for her to not only move in on Grayson's free-spirited bachelor pad, but to also move in on his friends and soon, his family.

She thought about backing out of the dinner, as well as the reunion, but she was too selfish to do it. She wanted to know the people in his life. His friends would have to be normal like him. They would tell stories of antics in college and they would be harmless antics not crazy things like multiple rapes and a conviction.

Alyssa wanted normal. She wanted easy. She wanted everything Grayson had. A caring family and no worries.

She remembered she had her own tiny family and pulled out her phone to call the sole member.

"Hey, sweetie."

"Hi, Mom. How are things going?"

"Good. Really good. How about you?"

"I'm really good too."

"Have you worked out the bed thing with Sasha?" Her mother chuckled.

"Actually, no. I moved in with someone else. Now I have my own bed. I even have my own room."

"That's great! What's her name?"

"Uh. Well."

"Alyssa?"

"His name is Grayson, but before you jump to any conclusions you need to know that we're just friends." Friends who have slept together many, many times.

"Friends?" Her mother must have been able to pick up the tone.

"Yes."

"Remember Liss, guys don't buy the cow if they get the milk for free."

"I never understood that metaphor. Guys don't buy cows and cows don't give their milk away. People *take* the cow's milk and sell it to many different guys. This metaphor is more about being a pimp than being promiscuous."

"You think you're so smart, don't you?" Her mother laughed.

"I do."

"I think you're smart enough to know what you're doing, and I'm glad you have a nice place to sleep every night."

"Thanks. He's a great guy."

"Good."

"How's work?" she asked to change the subject.

"Oh, you know. Nothing new. What about you?"

"I got a promotion. I have my own office. There's no window, but it's great."

"Congratulations! I'm so proud of you."

"Thanks."

"When are you coming to see me?" her mother asked.

"As soon as you have a weekend off." Her mother never had weekends off. Or many evenings. Her scheduled paired with her intense dislike of electronic communication were the reason her mother was just now finding out about the new job and her roommate situation.

"Hmm. I'll have to get back to you on that."

"Sure. I've got to get going. I'm making lasagna tonight."

"My recipe?" her mother asked expectantly.

"Kind of, but with real meat."

"Ooh, who you having over, the Queen of England?" her mother teased.

"Not exactly. Just some of his friends."

"Have a great time."

"Thanks. I'll talk to you later. Love you."

"Love you, sweetie."

She didn't know exactly why she hadn't told her mother more about Grayson. It wasn't that her mother would disapprove. She'd loved Donnie. Before she found out he was a rapist, of course.

Despite the lecture about milk, her mother had always told her to live life and make mistakes, then pick yourself up and live some more. It was a freestyle approach to child-rearing, but Alyssa appreciated it. Especially in those times when she was trying desperately to pick herself up and live some more.

With all the ingredients, she let herself back into the apartment, nearly dropping the bags.

Grayson ran over just as she was losing her grip.

"Why didn't you text me so I could have come down to help?"

"I've got it. No problem."

"So what do you want me to do? Tell me how I can help."

"A big pot full of water," she instructed.

"I knew you were a witch."

She smiled at him.

"Watch it, or I'll turn you into a toad."

They had the most fun as they cooked and arranged the noodles, meat, and cheese in the dish. She brushed the bread with butter and garlic and set it on top of the stove to go in the oven closer to their guest's arrival.

"Shower?" he asked when everything was prepared and cleaned up.

"Yes. Do you want to go first?"

He walked closer and gave her that predatory look.

"I was thinking we could conserve water if we showered together."

"It would save time too."

"Yes. I'm all about saving time." He leaned down to kiss her neck under her ear. With his arms around her waist he pulled her toward the bathroom.

"My mom told me I shouldn't give my milk away for free," she teased.

Grayson froze in the doorway.

"You told her you've been giving me your milk?"

"No, but she guessed."

"What are you saying? You want me to pay for it?"

She laughed. "No."

"You don't want to give me your milk?" He looked shocked.

"It's just funny that people still have sayings like that. As if not everyone is just handing out their milk to anyone who will take it."

Grayson laughed loudly in the small room and tugged off his own shirt and pants.

* * * *

He had to admit, he had been a little tense about Alyssa meeting his friends. That was before the shower.

The shower with Alyssa had relieved any stress he had as well as any he would have in the near future. It was that great. They had barely finished in time to answer the door when Trent and Tiff showed up.

So far so good. Alyssa and Tiffany seemed to be hitting it off, and Trent hadn't told any hideously embarrassing stories yet.

"So as my best man, I need to ask you a favor," Trent said with a slight wince. This meant it wasn't going to be good.

"What is it?"

"I need you to look after Suzanna at the wedding."

"No! No way. I did not sign up for that." Grayson waved his hands in the air in front of him.

"Come on, you know you're the only one I'd trust with my baby sister."

"I think you have it all wrong. You should be worried about who you force her on. That girl is a handful."

"What's wrong with her?" Alyssa asked curiously, leaning her elbow on the table and moving closer to hear the answer.

"First off she's a nympho," he told her.

"Is not," Trent defended.

"Yes, she is," Tiffany agreed quickly. "Sorry, but she is."

Trent let out a sigh.

"She gives her heart away too easily."

"She also gives away everything else too easily," Gray added behind the back of his hand, making Alyssa giggle.

"Come on, man. You need to be her date so you can keep the assholes away from her."

"Maybe he already has someone he wants to invite," Tiffany said nodding in Alyssa's direction.

"He told me they're just roommates. Right?"

"Right," Alyssa and Gray answered at the same time.

An awkward silence came over the table until Alyssa stood and began to clear the table.

"I'll help," Tiffany offered and Gray watched as they moved into the kitchen to talk about him.

"So what is with this girl?" Trent asked the second the girls were in the kitchen.

"She lives here and we sleep together sometimes. That's it."

Trent gave Gray a doubtful look.

"That's it? Since when do you do casual? That was my game and I ended up coming over to team relationship."

"Liss doesn't do relationships. So we're doing what she feels comfortable with," he told his friend.

"And you're okay with this?" Trent looked over his shoulder. "So what's the problem?"

"It's too much to go into right now." No way would he betray Alyssa by telling Trent her secrets.

"Is there any hope?"

"Maybe. I hope so." Gray was trying not to hope or think about Alyssa long term. Mainly because she had forbid it. But he had to admit, other than the trust issues due to the insane ex-boyfriend, she was perfect for him. "We'll see."

Chapter 17

"Sorry about that. You're welcome to come to the wedding as Gray's guest. Trent will have to find someone else trustworthy to watch his sister." Tiffany smiled.

Alyssa could tell by Trent's expression as they discussed his sister that it was serious, despite the joking around. The fact that Trent trusted Grayson with his little sister was a big deal. Trent knew Gray well enough to know if he was a good person or not. Donnie hadn't had friends. Just her.

"Unless the two of you really aren't together." Tiffany was still talking.

"No it isn't like that."

"Then what is it?" Tiffany pushed.

"I'm not sure what you'd call it," Alyssa said with an easy laugh as she tried to see the situation from the outside.

Living together, check.

Sex, check, and then some.

Making dinner together, check.

Walking to work together when it was convenient, check.

Eating lunch together, check.

Showering together, check.

Having friends over for dinner, check.

No wonder Tiffany was confused. Gray and she had all the elements of being in a relationship, but one: a future.

* * * *

"That was delicious," Grayson praised her with a big smile as they came back to the table.

"You helped."

"We make a great team," he said. It was true. They worked together like a well-oiled machine. In bed and out.

They all chatted for another hour, drinking wine and laughing over old stories. Trent enjoyed dishing dirt on his friend and Alyssa enjoyed hearing it.

To her surprise, Grayson didn't seem to mind. It was so comfortable.

When Tiffany and Trent finally left, an odd silence fell over them for a moment before they practically launched themselves at each other and ended up stumbling to her bedroom. The sex was quick and desperate, but satisfying all the same. Right on schedule, the guilt intruded in on the moment. She let out a breath and moved to get up.

Gray obviously wasn't onboard with this plan, instead pulling her back down next to him.

"I didn't get my allotted snuggle time."

"There is no snuggle allotment in our agreement."

"There is. The print is very, very small and written in invisible ink, but it's there and totally legal."

She laughed and gave in easily.

"What is happening with us?" she voiced her earlier confusion when talking with Tiffany.

"What do you want to happen with us?" he asked. She crossed her arms and gave him a look. She was the queen of answering a question with another question. It wouldn't work on her. "Okay. Fine. I don't know. All I know is that I don't care what you want to call it, Liss. I'm not willing to give up the best relationship I've ever had with a woman just because Trent and Tiff can't find a way to define it to their liking. We have a great time hanging out, so we are friends. We have amazing sex, so we are lovers. We share an apartment, so we are roommates. We work well together as co-workers. Take your pick. What does it matter to either of us to have a label? We're not label people. We're no bullshit people, remember?"

"Okay. You're right."

"Of course I am." He kissed her forehead as she snuggled up against him.

Whoever he really was deep down didn't matter to her. She was only in this for the roof over her head and the warmth in her bed. And maybe for a few laughs.

She was okay enjoying what they had. So long as he didn't expect anything else.

"So we're good?" she asked.

"Better than good."

Better than good sounded pretty damn great.

* * * *

After snuggling with Liss, Gray went to bed in his own room. He needed to put some distance between them. Things were getting...complicated.

Maybe that wasn't the word. Complicated sounded like a bad thing, and whatever he had with Alyssa was not bad. It was good.

He liked her. A lot. But for her sake, he would keep that to himself. She had made it pretty clear that emotional attachment was off limits. He didn't want her to leave. It would be impossible to build anything with her if she went back to Albany.

He wasn't into her just because of the sex, but everything else too. Living with her, cooking with her, watching crap television with her. Everything was better when she was there. Even sleeping.

He tossed and turned a few more times and eventually fell asleep. Not that he stayed that way for very long. He woke with a start when something warm and wet was stroking him. Down there. As he normally did when alone, he had gone to bed nude. Now someone was...He felt hot breath caressing him.

"Liss?"

He felt the warmth recede for a second as the covers pulled back slightly.

"Yeah?" she said as casually as if she was looking up from reading the newspaper instead of servicing him in the best way.

"Just checking."

She laughed and continued.

"God, you are so good at this."

"You think so?" she stopped to ask at an inopportune time.

"Yeah. The best part is how you don't stop to chat."

She laughed again and went back to her amazing task. But not for long.

"Why didn't you want to sleep in my bed?" she asked, her voice muffled by the blanket.

"Seriously? We're going to talk now?"

"You can talk while I finish here."

"I don't know." He closed his eyes unable to concentrate on her question. The pressure was building. He was close. So close.

He moaned and felt Alyssa smile around him. She liked having power over him, he could tell. He didn't care. He liked it too.

He shouted her name and a few praises to God as he gave in.

He hadn't even caught his breath when she crawled up beside him and took her spot.

"Can I stay?" she whispered.

"You can do whatever you want." He didn't care how long it took to convince her he was worthy of her trust. He wanted her in his life. They would find a way.

* * * *

Doug had gone to heaven. Or rather, he'd moved into a two-bedroom loft with the woman of his dreams.

Chanda had offered to move her studio out of the loft so there was more room for the living room, but Doug wouldn't have it. She'd already done so much; he wouldn't have her displaced so they could have a bigger television.

Besides, he'd rather watch her work than watch television. Every time he thought her project was perfect and couldn't need one more thing, she would do something to make it even better. Eventually, she would stop and smile in a way that beamed with her accomplishment.

"It's done?" he said quietly, in case she was still thinking it over.

"Yep. What do you think?"

"I think it's great." He paused, and smiled down at her. "What is it?" Not being an art guy meant her work often looked like a lump or a bunch of squiggles until she explained it. He felt like she was removing a film from his eyes when she enlightened him.

She laughed.

"This is called *Blended Family*. It's my interpretation of what a family looks like after divorce, when there's a child that will always bind them. This is the child." She pointed to the roundish orb in the center. "These spirals are her parents. And the tendrils coming off of those are the parents' partners. As well as the grandparents and aunts and uncles."

The spirals intertwined around one another. In some places they were smooth and flowing; in others they were kinked and bent. He felt them as much as saw them. He knew what those kinked parts were. The arguments and accusations.

"The most important thing is that the child is safe inside. What happens out here isn't as important."

"This is magnificent. You will sell this as soon as it's listed."

"I don't think I'm going to sell it. I think I want to donate it."

He didn't understand. She'd worked so hard on this project. She needed to make a living. Didn't she?

He looked around the apartment where they lived. He didn't know how much she paid for a two-bedroom loft in Manhattan with this much room, but surely it was more than she made at the bar.

He assumed she made a lot of money on her paintings and sculptures, but if she gave them away...

"Who are you going to give it to?"

"Remember that horrid office building where they have the family court?" She'd gone with him when he requested he be allowed to keep Lucy overnight and provided the documents that showed she had a room of her own. To say Lucy had been excited by her new bedroom was an understatement.

The office was dark and gloomy, and made even more so by the emotions generated by everyone involved.

He looked at the sculpture again, imagining it in the lobby. Maybe it would inspire some family to keep things civilized and positive for the sake of their child.

He leaned over and kissed her.

"I can't even...I don't have words to describe how blessed I feel to have you in my life. Your heart is...unbelievable."

"You might not think so if you knew I envisioned your ex-wife being there for the unveiling and due to faulty installation, it fell on her. It kind of goes against the spirit of the piece."

He laughed and pulled her closer.

"Your heart is unbelievably *real*," he amended.

* * * *

Grayson finally got off the phone with his frustrated client. The man had been yelling at him for more than fifteen minutes, as if it were Gray's fault that his business wasn't doing better.

They were dealing with numbers. There were no emotions with numbers, which was why Grayson loved them so much. Two plus two *always* equaled four, without question.

But now he was rattled. Unfortunately, it was after lunch and he couldn't expend the extra energy with Alyssa at their apartment.

He pulled out his phone to send her a text. He would have walked over to her office, but someone might have stopped him to chat, and he wasn't safe to be with humans yet.

What are you doing tonight? I'm having an awful day.

She answered him quickly:

Do you want me to make chicken encyclopedias?
With a smile he waited for the correction:
Enchiladas.
He replied, *Yes. Please,* and waited.
Do you think this looks trustworthy?
A picture then came in. It was a cowboy walking a horse into a parking garage. Clever.
Horses inspire trustworthiness. Good job, he responded.
Thanks. I worked on it with marketing.
He already felt better just thinking about dinner with Alyssa.

The more he thought of her, the more he found himself counting the minutes until he could get home and have her in his arms. They would be leaving the next morning for Connecticut for his family reunion, so this was their last night to be together before switching into friends for the weekend.

He met her at the elevator, his heart pounding in anticipation. Damn all their coworkers. He wanted to push her up against the wall of the elevator and sink into her.

"Grayson!" Chuck Borne called out. Someone held the door. "I need to see you before you go." Gray muttered a curse as he squeezed out of the elevator. He watched as the doors shut on his dreams.

For the next hour, he and his boss dissected the conversation with Grayson's client and tried to come up with a way to make the man happy while keeping to the laws of mathematics.

When Chuck stepped out to check on something, Gray took the moment to send Alyssa a text to tell her what was happening.

Focus on the future, she texted back.

I am. Sex and enchiladas. A three-day weekend with you and my family.

No, she answered. *Your client. Push what will happen in the future.*

Oh.

Chuck returned looking just as unhappy as when he left.

Grayson quickly looked over the reports for some uptick in the numbers.

"Girls!" Gray shouted in excitement.

"Excuse me?" Right. That didn't sound so good.

"The Girls' department had a profit. A small one, but it was still in the black. I'm going to drill down to see what it was. We can use this to focus on the upward trend of the next quarter."

"Good thinking. Dig into it and we'll call him back with the data."

"It wasn't my idea. Alyssa Sinclair came up with it."

"I didn't realize she was working on this account."

"She isn't. But we work well together." He remembered helping her with her presentation. They made such a great team.

Chuck nodded his approval.

Gray was able to leave forty minutes later after talking the client out of finding another firm. Alyssa's idea worked like a charm.

When he walked into his apartment, the smell of enchiladas filled his nose and happiness filled his heart.

Liss was wearing short cotton shorts with the waistband rolled over. Her skimpy tank top was one of those with the bra built in, but the built-in bra was no more than an extra layer of thin fabric. Her nipples were hard from being in the refrigerator where she was getting him a bottle of beer.

"Sorry about your day. Did you get it worked out?" she asked with a smile as she held out the bottle. "This should help."

The beer would definitely help, but at the moment, he was eyeing something that would improve his mood so much better than alcohol.

She'd turned back to chopping tomatoes on the cutting board.

"Do you want to talk about it?" she offered. Talk? No.

He glanced over at the oven timer, which displayed twenty-three minutes until dinner. More than enough time. Since he knew her so well, sex could be both satisfying and quick.

"I've wanted you all day," he whispered at her ear as he took her hand, sucking the tomato juice from her fingertips.

The smile she gave him was full of sin and good things as she worked the buttons of his shirt open and slid it off his shoulders.

He tossed his wallet on the counter before picking her up and setting her on the island to begin the frenzy of getting inside her.

He rolled up the tank top, exposing her perfect breasts. He took a moment to suck on each nipple before tugging off the shorts and her leopard print panties at the same time.

Her breath caught as she struggled with the button and zipper on his pants, pulling them down only far enough to gain access. Her fingers gripped him tightly and his head fell back for a moment, accepting the pleasure.

He still needed to be with her. Nothing else would get rid of the tension.

She dug through his wallet, finding the condom and rolled it on him with a skill that had him twitching.

Her skin made a small squeak as he slid her across the counter top to the edge. With one single movement he pushed the whole way inside her. The groan that escaped him expelled all the pent-up annoyance from the day. The air he pulled in was all Alyssa. The vanilla scent from her hair, the smell of her skin. The spicy scent of dinner in the oven.

"Grayson," she breathed against his bare chest as he shoved into her again and again. He had told her he liked to hear his name, but this wasn't just her following instructions. She said his name like she was his and knew it. "Liss," he gasped for another reason. He was close. Too close to stop. For a second, he was irritated that he hadn't satisfied her, but then he felt her muscles clenching and pulling him deeper into his release. "Alyssa," he groaned out once more.

The bad part about doing it on the kitchen counter was there was no place to go when his legs were unable to hold him up. He leaned against her heavily as she placed tender kisses on his neck and shoulders.

"Feel better?" she asked with shaky breath.

"God. You have no idea." He raised his head to smile at her. At the same time, they looked over to the oven. Three minutes to spare. "Dinner is underwear formal," he announced with a crooked grin. "Leopards are welcome."

In the past, they'd eaten pizza after sex in just their underwear, but they'd never eaten an actual meal at the table together just the two of them.

He smacked her ass lightly when she tugged up the boy shorts and returned to making the salad. Soon they were sitting down topless.

"To better days ahead," Alyssa said, holding up her glass of wine.

"It couldn't get much worse," he joked and touched his glass to hers. "How was your day?"

His attention was derailed for a moment, as Alyssa cut her enchilada, making her breasts jiggle in a very appealing way. What was it about boobs that made them so fantastic?

"…it's a small account, but it's mine." He heard the last part and his brows rose in surprise.

"You got the Pinehurst account?" he all but yelled, while hoping he wasn't asking a question she had already covered when he was hypnotized by her breasts.

"Yeah." She nodded and shrugged it off like it was insignificant, but he could see the happiness beaming out of her.

"Liss, that is great. Congratulations."

"Thank you for helping me with it."

"That is awesome," he said more emphatically, not taking any credit.

"It means I'll probably be as stressed as you are," she said, still trying to depreciate the event.

"This is a huge accomplishment. You're going to stun them and this will only be the start. I know it." He was so happy for her. "I'm sorry, we should be out celebrating. I came home with my bad day and completely ruined your good one," he realized as the guilt settled in.

"Trust me." She nodded over her shoulder toward the counter. "*That* did not ruin my day at all." She winked as she took a bite of her food.

Some emotion caught him up like a wave, his stomach fluttered at the strange sensation. He put his silverware down and slid his chair back.

"Come here," he said, holding out his arms, welcoming her onto his lap. She nestled against him, her breasts near his face. *Concentrate*, he told himself.

He kissed her softly, the spices on her tongue mixing with his. He would have been happy to kiss her for the rest of his life. Eventually, he pulled away and smiled at her slowly.

"When we're done with dinner, I'm at least going to take you down to the bar so I can buy you a drink."

"Not too many, we have a train to catch in the morning." She looked nervous.

"That's tomorrow. This is tonight. *Your* night." He brushed his fingertips through her hair, down to her shoulder and, of course, trailed along her chest until he was holding her breast in his hand. He stroked her nipple with his thumb and heard her suck in a breath. He stirred against her leg and a smile spread across her face.

He stood up from his chair, with her in his arms and took her straight back to his room to start the celebration properly.

Chapter 18

Gray was singing in the shower, which always made Alyssa laugh.

Not that he had a bad singing voice, but the songs he chose to sing were amusing. Not many guys felt comfortable singing Adele at the top of their lungs, but Grayson was quite secure with his masculinity. And rightfully so.

He had insisted on taking her out for a drink, but she wasn't really in the mood to worry with hair and makeup. She just wanted to be with Gray.

She had an idea, and quickly ran to the kitchen so she could get back to the bathroom before he finished the next verse of "Set Fire to the Rain."

He jumped when she opened the shower curtain with two glasses of wine, and the singing abruptly cut off.

"What's this?" He looked down at the drinks as her hair grew heavy with water.

"You wanted to celebrate by getting a drink, and I'd rather stay here, so it's a compromise."

With a big, beautiful grin he took his glass and held it up ceremoniously.

"To Alyssa Nicole Sinclair and her first account. May it be the first of many."

They clicked their glasses together and drank down the wine.

"Drinking in the shower?" He chuckled as she took his glass and set them out on the vanity. "People might say we have a problem."

She stepped closer letting her fingers trace the path of the water as it ran over his collarbone and continued down his chiseled abdomen.

"We might have a problem," she said as her hand reached even lower. He began to stiffen in her grasp and she grinned. "Nope. We're all good."

He laughed and pulled her closer, pressing her back against the wall and leaning down to take her mouth captive. After a second of intense kissing he pulled back and looked down at her, his hair plastered to his head.

"Thank you for moving in with me, Liss."

"Thanks for asking."

He let out a sniff and ran his hand through his hair tossing extra water around the shower.

"I didn't just ask. I begged you."

"Same thing," she said, giving him a naughty look. "Be careful or I'll make you beg for something else."

"I would gladly beg." He stepped closer, pressing his lips to hers in a way that made her moan. "But something tells me I won't have to."

He was right.

They ended up oversleeping the next morning and had to throw their stuff in their suitcases and run out to the cab.

They boarded the train in silence. She took the seat by the window so he could hang one of his long legs out in the aisle. The other leg encroached over into her space, but she didn't complain. He was definitely not a one-size-fits-all kind of guy, and for that she was glad.

She tapped her leg without realizing it until Gray laced his fingers through hers and pulled her hand to his lips, placing a light kiss on the back.

"You okay?" he asked.

"Sure. Why wouldn't I be? I mean, I'm going to another state to have a picnic with people who aren't going to understand who the hell I am, and we're not going to be able to explain it."

"This again?" he sighed.

"I'm okay with not having a name for whatever this is, but I'm guessing your family is going to want more specifics," she explained.

He let his head fall in her direction with a frown.

"You're right. Do you want to ditch?" He was giving her an out, which was one of the reasons she wanted to do this for him more than anything. Because he never expected anything from her.

"No." She shook her head and looked out the window. The truth was she wanted to meet his family. She wanted to meet the parents that had raised a guy who was so secure with who he was and what he wanted. She wondered if nurturing dripped off them.

Gray leaned down in his seat so he could kiss her cheek and speak softly into her ear.

"I would never ask you to lie, but I'm just saying it might be easier to let my mother assume whatever it is she wants rather than trying to explain it."

"You're probably right. Especially since, after adequate research, I'm still unable to find a suitable label."

"Me either. What's up with that?" He pulled away a little to look at her.

"I don't know. Apparently, we are the only two people on the planet who have ever been content to enjoy friendship and sex without forcing it to be more."

He nodded as he looked at the seat in front of him.

"I do worry I'm the weakest link. I've never done anything like this before. I've always ended up in a committed relationship. I had good role models in that department, which you'll see this weekend. My parents have always been happy together. I always assumed it was easy because they made it seem that way. I thought I'd get married and have a family—complete with the dog. I didn't even consider another way. Not until you. I'm happy with you, Liss. I'm trying my best not to mess up what we have because it's better than any of the actual relationships I've ever had. Even though we refuse to call it a relationship."

"I think awareness is the key." As it is for most things. "I'm nervous about meeting your family, even though I've been pretending it's not a big deal. I want them to like me." The truth just blurted out of her mouth.

"No pressure from me."

"I know, but I still want them to like me. And if I were being honest, part of it is because I don't want to make things difficult for you."

"I appreciate that. My concern is more about them liking you more than me. Then at some point, when I show up alone or with someone else, I'll be lectured for letting you get away."

"Should I not be lovable?" She grinned at him innocently.

"Do you think you could manage that?" He looked down at her and laughed.

"Probably not. I'm afraid it's not something I can control."

"Just be yourself and I'll deal with the fallout if it ever comes to that."

"*If*?" Her brows creased.

"We have a pretty good thing going here, Liss. Haven't you ever considered the possibility that we could just continue on indefinitely, growing old in this arrangement?"

"I guess I never thought about long term. That was kind of the whole point. That there was no pressure to make it work."

"What do you think now?" he asked, his tone turning extremely serious.

"I assumed at some point, one of us would want more, and would move on in search of someone who could give them that."

"Did you assume the person who would be moving on would be me?"

"Yeah."

"Because you're not able to heal?" he asked quietly. She nodded without looking at him. "I hope that's not true. I can't imagine how it was for you. I think about Jade, my last girlfriend, and I try to think of how it would feel to find out she'd committed some heinous crime. Even my girlfriend and best friend fooling around behind my back for years was not on that level of betrayal. I wish I could help."

"Believe it or not, you are. You haven't tried to push me into more than I was willing to give. It was the main reason I was reluctant to move in. But it's working. At least it is for me." She glanced up at him asking a silent question. Maybe this wasn't working for him.

"I'm not looking to make any changes. I know it's weird, but I feel safer with you than anyone else I've been in an official committed relationship with. Maybe it's like you said, there's no pressure in having to keep it together." He laughed as if surprised by this information. Alyssa felt herself relax. He wasn't holding out hope that she'd wake up and ask him to go steady.

"Then there's nothing to worry about," she said with a little snort. Ever since that icy afternoon when the cops shoved Donnie up against the cruiser and cuffed him, she had done nothing but worry. She hadn't realized it had gone on so long.

"Nothing at all."

They spent the rest of the trip sharing ear buds and listening to Alyssa's iPod. Occasionally, Gray would sing to her, making her giggle. She smacked him in the shoulder to make him quiet down before the other passengers complained.

He kept hold of her hand the whole time. She loved the way his thumb moved absently against her skin, and how he put the back of her hand to his lips every once in a while. He probably didn't even realize he was doing it.

At some point, she dozed off and woke with her head on Gray's shoulder as the train slowed and pulled into a station.

"We're the next stop. You might want to gather up your stuff," he suggested. "Make sure to pack your things safely. I'm not liable for anything broken or damaged when my mother grabs hold of you in a big hug and won't let go."

"How will I breathe?" she played along.

"I'll give you mouth-to-mouth." He threw her his sexy wink, which never ceased to make her heart skip a beat.

When they pulled into the next station, Alyssa immediately surveyed the crowd, hoping to pick them out so she could mentally prepare.

"Over here," Gray said, pointing to a graying woman with a happy face.

"Grayson!" she yelled, as they walked down the steps from the train platform toward the waving woman. "You must be Alyssa! Grayson has told us so much about you." Alyssa wasn't sure when this big information download had occurred, since she rarely heard Gray on the phone with his mother.

The woman latched on and squeezed. When Alyssa first saw Mrs. Hollinger, she was sure she'd be able to fend the woman off if need be. Gray's mother was in her fifties. Not frail by any means, but not huge either. From behind his mother's back, she gave Grayson a worried glance. Fortunately, Mrs. Hollinger released Alyssa before the lack of air could become a serious issue.

"It's so nice to meet you, Mrs. Hollinger, Mr. Hollinger." Alyssa nodded to each of them.

"Please. Call me Linda and everyone calls him Holly," she gestured toward the more reserved Mr. Grayson Hollinger II. "Let's get you home and unpacked. Then we'll have dinner," Mrs. Hollinger went on as they all walked to their SUV. "Izabelle isn't here yet. She was going to stay tonight, but she had an emergency with a patient so she's coming home tomorrow afternoon. Alyssa, do you have any food allergies, hon?"

"No, ma'am."

"That's good. Remember that guy Izzy brought to the picnic last year who couldn't be near peanuts?" Gray's mother twisted around in her seat to keep talking as Mr. Hollinger pulled out of the parking lot.

Alyssa reached across the seat and took Gray's hand. Whether it was meant to mislead the woman who was yammering on, or for comfort, Alyssa just knew she felt better when she was holding his hand.

"Mom, lots of people have peanut allergies. It's not that uncommon."

"But we had to tell great Aunt Rita she couldn't bring her peanut butter pie and then two months later, she was dead."

"Linda, I don't think it had anything to with the pie. It was probably the pack-a-day habit she'd had for the last forty-some years that did it. People can't die from an insult," Mr. Hollinger said giving Alyssa a wink in the rear view mirror.

"So, Grayson said you aren't dating," Mrs. Hollinger changed the subject while glancing at their fingers laced together on the seat between them. "Will you want separate rooms or how does this work? Back when I was dating your father, we called it dating so no one got confused. Now there are all these other levels that I just don't have time to decipher."

"We'll share my room," Gray said easily while Alyssa looked anywhere but at Mrs. Hollinger as her cheeks flushed.

"Maybe your sister will be able to make me one of her flow charts or something so I can tell how many steps away I am from having grandchildren," she said while shaking her head.

"Linda," Mr. Hollinger said, frowning at her.

"Sorry. No pressure. I'm not supposed to put pressure on anyone," she said with a bit of a huff. "No one cares about the pressure I'm under." The last sentence was muttered more to herself.

"It's okay, Mom. I don't feel pressured no matter how much you talk about grandchildren. Just so long as you know it's not going to happen." Gray leaned up and patted her shoulder.

"Jill Henderson is going to be a grandmother in two months. Jeremy is a year younger than you."

"Good for Jeremy. I'm happy for him and Mrs. Henderson."

"It wouldn't be so bad if your sister would cooperate. I just don't know where we went wrong. I don't know why you both seem to reject the idea of marriage and family so much. Were we bad parents?"

"No. You are the best parents anyone could ever have. You set the bar too high for Iz and me. We're never going to be as good as you, so why even bother?"

"Don't think for one minute I'm buying that." She shook her head making Gray snort a laugh and Mr. Hollinger smile.

Alyssa was enthralled with his family already.

* * * *

Gray relaxed as soon as Alyssa survived the hug. He knew everything would be fine.

"So what's really going on?" his dad asked when Alyssa and his mother were laughing in the kitchen.

"What do you mean?" Gray tried to evade the question, but he knew it was futile with his father. He was too observant.

"The girl. She doesn't look like a call girl you hired to make it look like you had a girlfriend."

Gray laughed with his father who had obviously been joking.

"She's not a call girl."

"Then what is she?"

"Does it matter?" Gray asked.

"It matters if the reason you're not telling me is because you don't know."

"I do know."

"Fine." He put up his hands. "That's all that matters."

Gray took a moment. His father was letting him off the hook. He wasn't sure he wanted to be off the hook yet.

"I'm not sure," he admitted quietly, glancing toward the door. "We agreed we weren't in a relationship. We are both busy with work."

"And have too many excuses," his father interrupted, his eyebrows mashed together.

"Maybe. We're happy with whatever we are. We talked about it a little bit on the way here."

"Just keep an open mind. I'd hate to see you miss out on a good thing because you were too stubborn to change your initial plan."

Gray wasn't worried as much about his open mind. He was more concerned about his open heart. For the first time in his life he wasn't worried about being hurt by someone cheating on him. His concerns now were that he would be hurt because the woman he cared about didn't return his feelings.

"We'll see what happens," he told his father as they went back to the kitchen to check on the women.

"Isn't she the cutest thing?" his mom crooned when they stepped through the doorway. "I love her to pieces, Grayson. You'd better not mess this up for me." He could tell his mother was only half joking.

After a quiet dinner at home, they played cards and went to his room.

"So how much do you want to run away right now?" he asked Alyssa as she slid into bed next to him.

"I don't. I had a lot of fun. Your dad was so cheating at cards."

"I know." They laughed together.

"I think your mother expects something."

"Let her." He shrugged it off.

"Thanks for inviting me."

"You're very welcome. I'm glad you're here."

Late the next morning, Izabelle arrived. For the next two hours, Alyssa was grilled with questions disguised as get-to-know-you conversation while they got ready for the picnic.

The guests started arriving at noon, which meant Alyssa was released from his mother and sister so they could interrogate the new arrivals.

"Let's go hide," Grayson suggested as he tugged her off to the far corners of the backyard.

"You have a huge family."

"Yeah. I know my aunts and uncles and first cousins. When we get to their kids, I'm not a hundred percent sure who belongs to whom."

"I don't even have a cousin." She shrugged.

"Wow." He wasn't sure if he felt bad or envied her. "I have plenty. Help yourself." He held his hands out wide, indicating she could have her pick.

"What about your sister? I always wanted a sister."

"You want Iz? I don't know. She kind of keeps my head on straight."

"Because she's a psychiatrist?"

"No, because she's my big sister."

"...and Grayson and his girlfriend are here." Gray could see his mother scanning the crowd. "Grayson!" she called when they were spotted.

"It was good while it lasted." He leaned down and pecked her lips. "I guess we need to mingle."

At some point during the picnic, Gray and Alyssa became separated. She seemed to be doing all right on her own as she laughed with his aunt, so Gray stayed clear of the women. Instead he went back inside to get another helping of potato salad and a brownie.

"She doesn't seem that bad," Izzy said, sneaking up behind him.

"She isn't."

"I expected her to be a train wreck." She stole the brownie off his plate.

"Sorry to disappoint." He frowned, taking the brownie back and shoving it in his mouth so she couldn't have it. It was a timeless strategy.

"I guess so." She pouted. "What are you going to do about the other issue?"

"What issue?" he mumbled with his mouth full of brownie.

"The guy in prison," she said flatly, implying he was dense.

"I don't see how there's anything I can do. I can't make the guy tell the truth, especially when the State of New York already failed."

"Maybe time has helped him remember the facts more clearly."

"Have you ever known anyone to remember something better over time?"

"It happens. I'm just saying she might not be able to move on with you if she never ends things with him. That would be a shame because I like her."

Gray looked down at his plate of potato salad and found it suddenly unappealing.

"I'm going to go save Alyssa from Dad and his friends."

He left his sister—and her prophecy of doom—to stand next to Uncle Jack. His dad was finishing the story of how he caught a marlin off the coast of Cabo—a story that became more riveting every time he told it, as fish stories often do.

"Wow. That is very cool, Mr. Hollinger," Alyssa said with wide eyes as she passed back his phone with the photo. "It's huge."

His father smiled at Alyssa. "Please call me Holly. At least until you start calling me Dad."

Gray's heart stopped for a second as he waited for Alyssa's response. He didn't know how she might react. Would she make a scene, denouncing him loudly so everyone knew they were only pretending to be in a relationship? Or would she walk away upset?

She didn't do any of those things.

Her eyes widened in surprise and then happiness beamed out of her like the light from the sun when it crests the horizon. She swallowed and gave him a little nod as if it was not a big deal, but Gray could see the way it had affected her.

She'd never had a father before, and the thought of one day being able to call someone Dad seemed to make her happy. Gray found himself liking the idea of sharing his father with Alyssa, on some level anyway.

They hung out with his family all day. When it was dark, and the crowd had dispersed, Alyssa helped them clean up.

"Do you want to get out of here for a while?" Gray asked as he tugged on the bottom of her shirt to get her attention. It was a little after ten.

"Sure."

They hopped in his mother's car and he pulled out heading down the road without a route planned. He just turned from street to street, occasionally mentioning a landmark here and there.

"And this is where my sack-of-shit, ex-best friend lives with my whore of an ex-girlfriend and their spawn," he said, pointing to a small house with a fence around the property. He may have sounded a little bitter.

"Wait, they're still together?" Alyssa asked.

"Yeah. Maybe I didn't tell you the whole story." He knew he hadn't. He hated the ending.

"Maybe you didn't."

"I told you I only found out about them when I was a junior in college."

"Right."

"The *way* I found out was rather upsetting." He took a breath and went for it. "When I came home at spring break in March she was about five months pregnant. I hadn't been home since August."

Alyssa's eyes went wide.

"Was she showing?"

"Yep." The memory of that betrayal caught in his throat for a second until he was able to choke it down.

"And then she told you whose it was?"

"Yes."

"And then what did you do?" she asked, as riveted by the story as if it had a marlin in it.

"Nothing."

"*Nothing?*"

"What was I supposed to do? Beat him up? He was going to be a *dad*. I couldn't beat up someone's *dad*," he said while shaking his head at the absurdity.

"And they're still married?" She looked over her shoulder at their house as he continued on slowly down the street. They moved out of the residential area and were passing a strip mall.

"Yeah. From what I've heard, they're both miserable. I'm not going to lie; it amuses me. It seems fitting, I guess."

"But you never got to be angry at them."

He shrugged. He'd been plenty angry. He just never yelled at them. He'd played it cool, like he didn't even care. But he'd cared.

"What's the point?" he said, shrugging it off.

"Pull into the parking lot here. I need to get something." Alyssa pointed at the grocery store in the strip mall.

Gray did as she asked and she jumped out of the car before he even put it in park.

"I'll be right back. Wait here."

Chapter 19

Grayson had planned to go in with her, but since she seemed to be in a hurry, he stayed in the car.

He hadn't thought about the betrayal in a while. He was over it. Or, he wanted to be over it.

The memory of Mandy telling him it was his fault because he went to school so far away made his blood boil all over again. And the way John avoided him and never so much as apologized or came up with an excuse made Gray squeeze his eyes shut. So maybe he wasn't quite as over it as he'd hoped.

The passenger door opened and Alyssa slid in with a smile on her face.

"Drive back to their house," she ordered while she settled the bag between her feet.

"Why?" He didn't understand.

"Just do it. Park two blocks from their house."

As he pulled out and headed back toward the house of doom, Alyssa opened a bag of beef jerky and held a piece out to him.

"Beef jerky?" he said with a laugh.

"It's the snack of criminals."

His brows creased, but he continued driving and chewing until he was parked a block and a half from their dark house. No doubt they were asleep as normal people would be at this hour.

"Come on," she said as she pulled a carton of eggs from the bag at her feet.

"What the hell are you doing with those?"

"We're going to throw them at their house. It's summer. They will stink and be a bugger to wash off, but as long as you don't wing them at anything breakable, they won't cause any real damage. Just enough to make us feel better."

"We're not fourteen, Liss."

"Let's be fourteen for a little while."

"This is crazy." He shook his head and looked out the window at the tiny house.

"Are you chicken?" she challenged—and that was all it took. He snatched the carton from her fingers and walked up the sidewalk.

Alyssa giggled as she glanced around quickly, apparently taking on the role of lookout.

Gray pulled the first egg out of the carton and weighed it in his palm before snapping it across the yard. It broke against the porch post, spraying slime all over the front door.

He smiled widely as he pulled out the second egg.

Alyssa only got the chance to throw three eggs and one of them didn't make it to the house, instead it landed on the grass and bounced onto the sidewalk where it broke and oozed its innards out into a puddle.

Gray was almost disappointed when he realized the carton was empty.

"Let's go," Alyssa hissed as she tugged him back to safety. They ran down the sidewalk full speed and jumped in the car. They were laughing hysterically as he sped away.

"I can't believe we just did that." He was still laughing when he pulled into the parking lot of the gas station. He let his head rest back against the seat so he could look at her.

Alyssa's green eyes blazed in the glow of the street light.

"Thank you for that, Liss. I know it was only eggs, but I feel somewhat vindicated."

"Good. Nothing says *screw you* like eggs that will most likely be stinking by morning."

"Remind me to never piss you off."

"You deserved better than what they did to you."

"Thanks." He leaned closer, enthralled by the way she spoke while still out of breath from running. He wanted to kiss her more than air.

His lips touched hers like they had many times over the last few months. It shouldn't have felt any different, but something flared between them.

Alyssa must have felt it too, because her eyes popped open for a second before she pulled him back to her lips. Giving into the flames completely, he found himself gasping for air again. They needed to go somewhere they could be alone.

"Come on. I know a place," he whispered.

* * * *

Without questioning him, Alyssa nodded and put her hand on his.

It was only six minutes to the lake, but Gray found it difficult to drive with his pants constricting him as they now were.

At the lake, he circled around to see if anyone else was there before he found a spot by the dock. As Alyssa got out and looked around, Gray got two blankets out of the trunk of his mother's car along with a bag of towels. She was always ready for an impromptu picnic.

Alyssa kicked off her sandals while Gray arranged the blankets on the worn wooden boards that were still holding the sun's warmth from the hot day. He looked up at Alyssa and was speechless.

The moonlight was shining through her golden hair, which hung down her bare back. She was beautiful.

Of course he shouldn't have been surprised. He'd known this since the second he met her, but sometimes he was still caught off guard by just how perfect she was when she wasn't even trying.

"Swim?" she asked with her head tilted to the side.

He nodded and smiled at her as she kicked off her shorts and jumped in the water nude.

"Come in. The water's warm," she said as she raised herself out of the water enough for him to see her amazing breasts, her nipples peaked from coolness of the air.

"You look like a mermaid, luring me into the depths," he mused as he unbuttoned his shorts and let them slide down.

"I'm sure I can lure you into some depths if that's what you're after," she joked. He jumped in recklessly, letting his entry throw water all over her.

After her squeal of protest she laughed. The sound echoed over the surface of the water, making them seem so much more alone. The water wasn't deep. Standing flatfooted on the sandy bottom, the water came to his shoulders.

"So who's the guy with the hockey mask and the chainsaw?" she said in mock horror as she pointed over his shoulder.

"Very funny." He swam after her, grabbing her and pulling her against him. Her wet arms slid around behind his neck and her legs eagerly wrapped around his waist.

"You're right where I want you now," she said with an evil laugh.

"Well, maybe you're right where I want you too."

"Hmm. Convenient," she allowed with a little giggle before she pressed her lips to his. Like before in the car, something flared again. Only this time, it engulfed him. He didn't fear it, he embraced it, wanted it. He wanted her, more than he'd ever wanted anyone.

Not just for the sexual release, but to be as close to her as humanly possible. To be connected to her on the deepest level.

She pulled back slightly to look into his eyes. Did she feel it too? Her eyes glowed silver in the moonlight, but he could still see something there. Surprise, maybe?

"Gray," she whispered.

He didn't answer. He didn't need to. He knew what she wanted. He moved them back to the dock and assisted her up onto the blanket before flinging himself over the edge of the dock to join her there.

They kissed again and again, and each time she lured him closer and closer. Just like a mermaid.

He reached for his shorts and slid them over so he could get to his wallet in the back pocket. As he opened the wallet, it occurred to him that he had just done this same thing a few days ago. The evening he came home and took Alyssa in the kitchen.

The absence of the foil pack reminded him he'd never replaced it.

"Liss? Do you have a condom in your bag?"

"I don't have my bag."

"Shit!"

"We don't have a condom?"

"No. I used it and never put another one in here." He rolled back over to her and stroked her face. "I'm sorry. I'm such an idiot."

She kissed him again and he continued to stir, as if his dick wasn't aware of the situation they were facing.

He pulled away, contemplating leaving her there to run to the gas station. How far was it? Six minutes there, six back. Twelve minutes away from her while she lay there alone on the dock, waiting.

"We are both safe, and I'm on the pill," she told him with a loud swallow.

"Would you be okay with that?" he asked, trying to hide the desperate edge to his voice.

"I think so. What about you?"

He glanced down at his engorged state. "I sure don't want to stay like this until tomorrow night when we get home."

"I'm sure it would be fine. I mean, I've never missed a dose, and I take them every day at the same time like clockwork. I haven't had any antibiotics in over a year. It's 98.9 percent effective."

"That basically means out of a million women, eleven thousand got knocked up."

"There are certain situations in which math isn't helpful," she said with a frown.

"Right. Sorry about that."

"Always honest," she reminded him while looking up at the stars.

"Do you trust me, Liss? I'm not asking for a big emotional declaration, but do you trust that if you ended up being one of those eleven thousand women I would do the right thing?"

She nodded and looked away.

"Yes. I do trust you. I want this." She turned to face him, connecting with him on some level deeper than sex. He hadn't asked for an emotional declaration, but he felt one all the same. Something was shifting between them.

"I want this too."

He'd never wanted anything more.

* * * *

Alyssa couldn't remember ever wanting anything more.

It wasn't just sex with Grayson, which she could have pretty much any time she wanted. It was having sex with Grayson at that moment, at that place.

She had seen the freedom when he threw those eggs. It seemed like the first step in his healing process. She could feel how much lighter he was now. She enjoyed being a part of it. If she couldn't find a way to heal herself, at least she could be part of Grayson's recovery.

His eyes were locked on hers as he pushed inside her; she couldn't look away. She didn't want to.

"Alyssa," he said her name quieter than he normally did. She had to admit she liked hearing him say her name while they were joined. It was as if he was claiming her for that time.

"Gray," she breathed, staring back at him.

He was everywhere. His body covered hers, his face filled her vision, his breath filled her lungs, his warmth filled her completely. As he moved, he seemed to fill every dark corner of her being with his light.

He normally told her how sexy she was when they were together. He didn't do that this time. His words were different, more intense. He told her she was beautiful instead of sexy and said he never wanted the night to end.

Normally, his confession would have had her reminding him of the rules, but not this time. She didn't want the night to end either. For this moment, she allowed herself to trust Gray. With her mind focused on that task, she was too distracted to notice the usual guilt that came from being happy with a man.

"I'm so glad you're here with me instead of living in that house with eggs all over it," she admitted.

"Me too."

He held her tightly when he released into her, filling her with fire and something else. Something emotional that she tried to keep away.

Despite their wishes that the night wouldn't end, it did.

The hard boards of the dock were not very comfortable and the chilly night air on their wet skin caused goose bumps. Not to mention the fear of falling asleep and being caught there by some early riser.

"Let's get back," he said, kissing her neck but not moving.

Eventually they moved. Slowly they dressed and folded up the blankets. He held her hand as they walked to the car, stealing glances at each other like it was their first time.

She wasn't sure why they were suddenly being so awkward, but there was something there.

Gray pulled her against him when they crawled into his bed. They lay there in silence for a long time. He trailed his fingers up and down her back, and kissed her hair while she played with his fingers and nuzzled closer.

Despite the signs of affection, neither of them spoke.

She awoke alone.

* * * *

Gray's things were gone. She didn't even worry that he'd run off. She knew he would have packed right away.

She smiled as she thought of all the little things she knew about him. From his preferences in bed, to what he ate, to how to get him to relax.

She showered and packed her own things before heading downstairs. She stopped on each step, studying the photos and portraits as she made her descent.

Toward the bottom, she could hear Grayson in the kitchen, his voice low but full of stress. Her feet moved quicker, wanting to help.

He was in the kitchen with his sister, apparently, they were fighting, but they stopped the second Gray spotted Alyssa at the doorway. She hadn't caught much of their words, just Izabelle telling him that he was setting himself up for disaster.

"Morning," Gray said with a big, genuine smile. He came closer and kissed her, and then took her bag and set it next to his by the door. "Hungry?"

"Yes. Starved."

He winked at her.

"Did you want...*eggs*?" he asked with a grin. Yes, her vandal therapy had done wonders for Grayson.

"Eggs would be great," she told him as his mother and father came downstairs.

"You're all packed to go?" his mother said with a pout.

"We have a ten o'clock train. Sorry," Gray said as she gave him a little hug.

"I hope you had a nice stay," Mrs. Hollinger said to Alyssa while patting her shoulder.

"It was great. Thank you for having me."

"You are welcome anytime, sweetheart. You are my favorite."

"Mom," Gray gave her a warning tone.

She just waved, dismissing him.

"Don't worry. I'm not going to go into the others with all their problems and baggage. I know you wanted to help them, but you're an accountant, not a psychiatrist like Izabelle. I'm just glad you've found someone normal who isn't a project." She smiled at Alyssa again.

Alyssa swallowed as her gaze met Grayson's. She couldn't read his expression. It was probably the first time since she'd met him that she didn't know what he was thinking.

Maybe she didn't want to know.

Izabelle walked them out, giving Alyssa a hug and a smile.

"It was really nice to get to know you. Thanks for looking out for my brother."

"Did he tell you about the—"

"Eggs? Yeah. Good job. I wouldn't have thought of it." She smiled and walked away as Alyssa got in the SUV.

Mrs. Hollinger talked most of the ride to the train station. She told Alyssa all the things she wanted to do the next time they visited. Most of her plans consisted of shopping, which made Alyssa cringe. Gray gave her hand a reassuring squeeze.

The chances of her ever coming back to Connecticut with Grayson were probably slim. She realized this thought caused sadness. Maybe not about the shopping, but about missing out on being with a genuine family.

She never once doubted her own mother's love, but it would have been nice if her mother hadn't spent all her time working. She'd taken on extra jobs so Alyssa wouldn't have to go without things. It turned out that Alyssa had to go without her mother.

They were quiet on the train for the first ten minutes. It wasn't that she didn't want to talk. She did. She just wasn't sure what to say or how to say it.

Fortunately, Gray took the initiative.

"I can't help but notice we're not talking," he said, leaning over so his breath touched her neck. "We're going to mess this up if we aren't honest with each other."

She nodded in agreement and said the first thing that came to her mind.

"Did it feel different for you last night?" she asked.

"Yes. It was different." He looked very intense.

"Maybe because there wasn't a condom?" she reasoned.

He shook his head looking straight ahead. "No. It was something else. Though the no condom thing was freakin' amazing."

"Do you think maybe it was the situation? Adrenaline?" She was desperate to come up with any excuse so it couldn't be the thing she feared.

"Maybe. Do we have to know? Can't we just go with it?"

"You're suggesting we ignore our feelings and maybe they'll go away," she said. "When has that ever worked?"

"We'll see what happens when we get home. Maybe it will wear off." He kissed the back of her hand and smiled.

"Maybe." She rested her forehead against his shoulder, trying to decide if she wanted that to happen.

When they walked through the door, she waited for her emotions to snap back, but they didn't.

"Home," Gray said with a contented sigh.

That one word and the way he said it nearly speared her to the ground. She had made a home with him. He was not just a roommate or a friend.

Before she had a chance to panic, his lips were on hers urgently.

He took the bag from her shoulder and let it drop to the floor without breaking the kiss. Then he pulled her close and started moving them down the hall.

"I'm not sure if this is going to help things go back to normal," she pointed out.

"Normal is overrated." His grin was so big it made her laugh, but only for a moment.

When they touched, it was just as intense as the night before. She trembled at the feelings moving through her.

"Liss? What is it?" He rubbed her arms, no doubt thinking she was cold.

"I'm scared," she whispered the truth, surprised by how easy it was to tell him her fears. When he moved to step back, she held on to him tighter, unable to let him go.

His chest moved under her cheek with a deep breath and his arms curled around her, holding her tightly.

"Tell me what you need and I'll do it. I made you a promise that I wouldn't ever ask for more than you were willing to give. Last night..." He pulled away enough to look down at her face. "I thought you wanted it too. I thought you wanted more. If I was wrong—"

"You weren't wrong." She pulled away and hung her head. This man was willing to give her space if she needed it or hold her all night if she wanted it. He was watching her, waiting for her to give him some clue of what she needed, and that look on his face...The look that told her he would do anything for her was the thing that scared her the most.

How had she gotten this close and not noticed how much she cared for him? And more importantly, what would she do now?

Chapter 20

Chanda was a wreck as she walked into the gallery alone. Doug promised he would be there for her exhibit. It was small, but she was excited to have her work displayed. And she wanted him to be there to share in the moment. Not to mention calm her nerves.

Where was he?

Blended Family was in place under the spotlight. The caterers had set up the food and were pouring the wine as the first guests arrived. Still no sign of Doug.

Becca, the owner, took her around to greet people. She was introduced to some big art collectors. Time flew and her nerves calmed. She loved talking about art with people who knew the difference between Claude Monet and Edouard Manet.

"You sold a piece," Becca whispered, barely containing herself. "And I think *Blink* is about to be sold as well. I'm so happy for you."

"Thank you." Chanda smiled and looked around the room, wanting to tell Doug about her sale. She pulled out her phone and texted:

Where are you?

Ten minutes later, she still hadn't heard back. Her big night was over in twenty minutes and he was missing it.

Worry took the place of annoyance. Nothing would have stopped him from being here. Something had to be wrong. Was he hurt? Was it Lucy? He had planned to pick his daughter up and bring her to the show. Lucy had been so excited to have a place to wear her sparkly new dress.

Chanda's breath caught when he walked through the door. She hurried through the crowd to get to him.

"Look at this turnout. I'm so proud of you, Chan. Have you sold anything?"

"Three pieces. Where have you been? Where's Lucy?"

"There was an incident when I went to get her. She's fine. I don't want to talk about it now. This is your night." He frowned at his phone. "For a little while longer anyway. I'm so sorry I'm late. And I ordered you flowers, but I didn't have time to pick them up."

Something about him seemed stiff. Whatever it was that kept him, it was important, but he shook it off and put a smile on his face.

* * * *

Doug was still riled up. He could feel his blood pounding in irritation. The nerve of that guy to step in. Letting out a breath, he gave Chanda another smile just as she was pulled away to go talk to someone.

He nodded that it was fine and spotted someone carrying a tray of hors d'oeuvres.

Food would calm him. He picked off a sample of each and moved around to each of her pieces, scoring a glass of wine along the way.

He was standing behind one of the bigger pieces when he heard someone whispering. Since he was hidden and didn't want to give up his spot, he stayed, focused intently on the mini-quiche.

"I wonder what her father is paying to put this on. She probably thinks she was asked here because of her talent." The two people laughed at the comment and Doug swallowed down the lump of quiche.

"I heard her father paid for that sculpture and donated it to the Pressroom. There's no way anyone else would have paid forty thousand dollars for that mess."

Doug understood how jealousy caused people to be cruel and rude. But after the night he had, he had to do something. He couldn't stand there hiding while these two idiots tore apart the woman he loved.

The only problem was that he didn't know if their accusations were true. Chanda hadn't spoken about her father other than to say he was a workaholic who had no time for her.

That didn't mean he wasn't rich.

Being a father himself, he knew how many boxes of cookies he personally bought so Lucy could get a pin on her sash. He would have bought every box because it was important to her.

Still, he was itching for a fight, and this guy would do.

"Excuse me?" Doug said, walking around the statue to address them face-to-face. "She works damn hard on these and they're beautiful. Forty thousand is a steal for her work."

The man sniffed at Doug. Sniffed.

Doug felt his fist connect with warm flesh. He heard a scream. He felt two hands push his chest. His world went sideways for a second, but he reached out to brace himself and came back swinging. Though the thing he'd braced himself on gave way.

After a few seconds had passed, there was a man at his feet bleeding from the mouth and one of Chanda's statues was on the ground in pieces.

The small orb rolled over to his foot and he realized it was the center of *Blended Family*. He'd destroyed it.

He looked across the chaos to see Chanda and knew he'd just destroyed them as well.

* * * *

Things felt different between Grayson and Alyssa. The feelings she experienced during their visit to Connecticut hadn't faded; they just changed into something else. Something comfortable. And Alyssa didn't do comfort with men.

Comfort meant trust. It meant letting down her guard. It meant not paying attention to the details. All things she now realized she had with Gray.

Originally, their relationship had mostly revolved around sex and fun. Now there was something else in the way Grayson stroked her hair while she fell asleep, or the way he smiled when they passed each other in the office. Like he was doing now.

"You want to grab some lunch?" he asked, looking over his shoulder to make sure no one was listening. She was the only person who knew he wasn't actually asking her to lunch.

"I can't. I have a meeting with Mr. Hasher."

"Really?"

"Yeah. He wouldn't fire me, right? I mean he'd have someone else do it, like a henchman?"

"He wouldn't fire you or have henchman do it. You've been working your ass off. Maybe you're getting a raise."

"That would be great." She could use the extra money.

Years ago, when she believed in things like trust, she'd taken cash advances from her credit cards to buy Donnie a real lawyer. He'd convinced her that the public defender was lazy. It turned out that the public defender was faced with a client who refused to plead insanity even though he was obviously insane.

Unfortunately, it had taken a few more weeks and eighteen thousand dollars for Alyssa to figure it out.

She was down to the last sixteen hundred she owed. Soon it would all be over and she'd be able to put it behind her forever.

Alyssa's meeting was moved from eleven to two and then from two to three because Mr. Hasher had other things come up. Did bigwigs just move stuff around to make themselves feel important, or did they do it to toy with people's nerves?

"I'm not getting fired. Just breathe. The last time it was a good thing. This is a good thing." She muttered to herself as she walked to his corner of the floor.

She waited the normal twenty minutes, and then went into his office when his assistant gave the nod. She was moving, though she couldn't really feel her legs.

He gave her a warm smile and gestured to the chair in front of him.

"Hi Alyssa. Have a seat."

"Thanks."

"I've been talking with the team and everyone was impressed with the presentation you gave for the Pinecrest parking complex."

"Thank you."

"We're always looking to expand, but just because we have the clients, expansion isn't possible if you don't have the team in place to give the clients what they expect from Hasher Borne."

"Yes."

"You've done so well with the Pinecrest account that we would like to give you their other accounts as well. They run a number of companies and they requested you specifically. Of course, your salary will be increased to compensate you for the extra workload. For now, I'd like you to run everything through Melanie and Grayson."

"Grayson?" she blurted without thinking.

"Yes, he's the financial lead on this account. And Melanie was the previous account manager."

"I see. Okay."

"If you have any issues, please let us know. It's a sizable account."

"Thank you for this opportunity."

"Everyone sees big things for you."

She nodded and left his office, anger and excitement battling for top emotion.

She smiled at everyone on her way to Grayson's office, and then went in and shut the door behind her.

He looked up, a smile breaking over his face as he leaned back in his chair. "Hey. How did it go?"

"You never told me you were the financial manager on the Pinecrest account." It came out as an accusation as she moved closer.

The smile fell from his face and he sat up in his chair.

"I am?" He looked confused as he hands moved over the keyboard in front of him.

"Yes. You are. Is this why I was given the account? Are you helping me? I don't want your help."

"I have thirty-seven accounts, Liss. I don't remember seeing Pinecrest." He sat back in his chair and nodded at the screen.

"I have them under Leedom Enterprises. There are four businesses under them. Pinecrest is one. I didn't realize it."

"We talked about them being part of Leedom when I was working on my presentation. It didn't ring any bells?"

"You're accusing me of getting you a promotion? Even if I could do that, wouldn't it be a good thing?" he asked.

"I've just been given all the accounts for Leedom. I wanted to get ahead on my own merits not because some guy is trying to get me into his bed."

"You are already in my bed, so that motivation hardly makes sense." He swallowed and stopped talking when she leveled him with her look of fury.

"I don't need your help. Why do you insist on trying to fix my life? I'm not one of your projects."

"I don't see you as a project. I see you as a friend. Ask Doug or Trent. I will do anything I can to help my friends. But I didn't get you this promotion. I swear. You're going to have to trust me."

She glared and he nodded.

"Right. You don't do that." He sighed and stood to come closer.

The adrenaline from her rage had abandoned her.

"While you might not believe me, I really didn't know. I'm happy for you."

He was trying to cheer her up. She shouldn't have been so angry in the first place. Maybe he wasn't lying. Maybe he really hadn't remembered the Pinecrest name on the account. It seemed reasonable.

He let out a breath and let his hands fall down to his side.

"I honestly didn't realize it was my account. But had I known, I would have suggested you because you're qualified."

"I want to get it—"

"On your own merits. I know. But I know your merits too. And if I had suggested you—which I didn't—it would have been because of said merits at work and not because of any other merits I might be privy to."

"Fine. I'm sorry I overreacted." Why couldn't she just be normal?

"Now that we both agree you're crazy, do you want to go out tonight to celebrate?"

"No, thanks. I have a lot of work to do." With that she left his office. Her earlier frustrations were now turned inward. Why did she have to assume all men had some other agenda? That they had a hidden life.

She shook it off and went to her own office to get started.

A few hours later, she received a call from Doug.

"Hello?"

"Hi, Alyssa. I was just given the Leedom account. I understand you're managing that account. Would you be able to send me a copy of the file so I can review it?"

"You're taking over the account?"

"Grayson offered a trade and I couldn't turn it down. I hope that's not a problem." She wondered if Gray had taken on the notorious Knott account in exchange for Doug taking the Leedom account.

"No problem."

"Good."

Doug didn't sound like his normal fun-loving self. She might have thought this was his business persona, but she'd seen him in too many meetings.

"Okay. I'll send it right over."

"Thanks." He hung up without another word.

Alyssa didn't put the phone down; instead, she keyed in Gray's extension.

"If you're going to yell at me, I'm going to hang up," he threatened.

"Why did you do that? I didn't ask you to give up the account." She made sure not to yell.

"It was the right thing to do. I don't ever want it to become an issue or for your promotion to be questioned. Especially by you."

"Thank you."

"I get that you don't trust me, so until you do, I'm going to do my best to convince you I'm safe."

"Did you trade Doug for a crappy account?" she worried.

"I can't talk about my client's profile. And since you're not on the account, I'm going to have to officially say, 'none of your beeswax.'"

She laughed at his *official* announcement, and then let out a sigh. From his reaction, she was positive he'd gotten the bad end of the deal with Doug, just so she would be more comfortable.

"Thank you, Gray."

"No problem. Now get to work."

Her client seemed to like what she'd done so far, but she still needed to tweak the project into perfection. She packed up her laptop to work from home. She didn't mind putting in the extra time to find a way to save her client money.

Gray made her put her laptop away by eight so they could have dinner together and snuggle on the sofa.

Since her outburst, she'd been thinking about her relationship with Gray—because it was obvious it was now a relationship. They were too close. It was apparent he cared about her. She knew she cared about him. Way more than she ever wanted to.

In fact, she was pretty sure she was in love with him.

This wasn't supposed to happen. She'd had rules to save herself from this.

Sure it felt great to see his face light up when he saw her, but how long would that last? How long before the pain? At any moment, she might learn some horrible truth that would break her heart and send her life into a tailspin.

She needed to get things back to where they were safe.

By Friday, she'd convinced herself it was possible to go back to the way things had been when they were just roommates. They only needed a little distance.

No sex, no snuggling, no emotions. She could do this.

"Don't get attached," she told her reflection as she changed to go out. She didn't allow herself to dwell on how she'd much rather slip on a pair of shorts and spend the evening on the sofa with Gray. She needed to do this.

Distance was the first step in getting control of her life, and her heart.

As if intent on demolishing her resolve, Gray came home.

"Honey, I'm home!" he called through the apartment with a happy tone. "It's Friday!"

Alyssa stepped out of the bathroom in her heels.

"Holy shit!" he stammered as he looked her over. A smile took over his face as his gaze moved up and down her body.

"Guess what?" she said with a huge smile.

"What?"

"Leedom liked my budget proposal. They signed off on it today."

"That's awesome! I knew they'd like it. Let me change and I'll be ready to go out—"

"Actually, I'm going out with Mia to celebrate."

"Oh." The disappointment on his face almost made her backtrack. She couldn't. "Well, have fun."

"I will. I need to get going."

"Sure. Maybe we could go out tomorrow night?" he asked, his blue eyes searching her face.

"Yes. Tomorrow should work." He only seemed slightly relieved.

"See you when I get home."

Twice on the way down in the elevator, Alyssa almost went back up. She shook her head and continued on to meet Mia.

She needed distance. This was healthy.

* * * *

Gray watched Alyssa walk out of the apartment as his chest tightened uncomfortably.

What could he do? He couldn't chase her down and beg her to stay with him. Actually, he could have done that, but then he was certain she would have kept on going and not looked back.

Damn it! He wanted them to be close. It didn't have to be such a horrible thing.

He understood why she was scared. The asshole to whom she'd been engaged had devastated her, but it didn't mean Grayson would too. He didn't know how to get out of Donnie's shadow. Unless...

What if the whole *just friends* thing was her way of keeping him from pushing her into something she really didn't want with him? Doubts flooded his mind, calling up those old insecurities as he went to change. Mandy hadn't been satisfied with him.

He tossed his work clothes in the direction of the hamper and pulled out a T-shirt and sweatpants. He was planning to order in some Chinese and spend the night on the sofa in front of the television until Alyssa came home.

But then what? No matter what he did, he didn't see a way to get out of this labyrinth of doubt and suspicion. He couldn't prove he wouldn't hurt her until she trusted him enough to get close and see he wouldn't hurt her. It just went round and round with no way to get any further.

"Fuck this," he said as he dug around in his closet for a dress shirt and the skinny jeans Alyssa had dared him to buy. She said they were hot, and it was time to put them to the test.

His conviction only lasted until he got down to the sidewalk. He realized he wasn't up for the club scene. Instead, he walked down the street to MacGregor's. It was still fairly early, so he sat at the bar and ordered his usual fish and chips.

Shirley, the early bartender was still there. She was a large woman who called everyone Sugar. He and Alyssa had picked up the habit one evening when she was working. They had called each other Sugar for a few days after. Gray liked it more than he should have. He realized he liked everything about Alyssa more than he should have.

He needed to get over her before she broke his heart.

A few hours later, he was still sitting in the same spot, trying to figure out how to manage moving on and putting Alyssa back in the friend box.

"You look like someone stole your best friend," Mac said as he put a second beer down in front of Gray.

"Kind of."

"You're here without your sexy little sidekick?"

"Yeah. Looks like it." He couldn't argue. Alyssa was sexy, and she had been with him every time he came into the bar lately.

"I thought the two of ya were joined at da hip. You have a fight?"

"No." He shook his head.

"I see." Mac nodded and went about making a drink for another customer. "Why don't you check out the blonde at the end of the bar? She looks to be your type."

"No thanks."

"Come on, man. Don't be like that. At least take a look."

Reluctantly, Gray looked up. The bar had filled while he'd sat there feeling sorry for himself. He leaned over so he could see down the length of the bar, and his eyes shot wide open.

"Right?" Mac said with a grin. "I told ya."

"I want to buy her a drink," Gray said with a slow nod.

"Aye, I thought you might come around." He mixed the drink and carried it over while Gray watched.

She shook her head, refusing the drink at first. Then Mac pointed down at Gray. He gave a little wave when her gaze met his. He watched as her eyes widened in surprise. She smiled at him. His chest tightened at her reaction as he got off the stool to go meet her.

His night was looking up.

Chapter 21

"You come here often?" Grayson was rewarded for his humor with a melodic laugh that warmed him to his toes.

"As a matter of fact, I come here quite a lot."

"Hmm. I wonder why I've never seen you." He continued to play the part as his gaze studied every curve.

She laughed again and turned to her friend.

"Mia, this is Grayson, my roommate. Gray this is Mia."

"Nice to meet you," Gray said, holding his hand out.

"I work at Hasher Borne too. Liss has told me many things about you." She smacked Alyssa in the arm. "You said he was okay looking."

"*Okay*? I'm only *okay*?" Gray complained with a frown.

"No, baby. You're way more than *okay*." Alyssa was a bit drunk, which made Grayson smile wider.

"Uh-huh," Mia said with an eye roll. "I think I'm going to go take that blond guy up on his earlier offer. I can see we're done here."

"Thanks for tonight, Mia," Alyssa said, resting her head lightly on the woman's shoulder.

"Yeah, yeah. I know when I'm being replaced by a penis." Mia waved them away with a smile as she got up and went to a table with a few guys sitting there. She shoved one of the guys in so she could sit down.

"She'll be okay?" Gray checked.

"She's fine. We know them."

"How was your night?" he asked.

She shrugged and took a sip of the drink Gray had bought her. Maybe that hadn't been a good idea. She was safe with him. He'd make sure she got home.

"Kind of boring actually."

"You didn't have any takers in that outfit?" Gray asked doubtfully.

"I had some offers." She bit her bottom lip, not saying anything else.

"And…?" He sipped his beer going for nonchalant. Why weren't they together? He could tell by her earlier reaction she wanted to be with him. Would she ever admit it to him? To herself?

"I've been out of the loop for a while." She shrugged again, and he knew that was all she was going to say.

When she finished her drink, he held out his arm.

"Are you ready to go home?" he asked.

"Yeah." She gave Mia a thumbs-up and Mia returned it while a guy was kissing her neck.

Alyssa was sober enough to walk in the heels, but Gray still put his hand at her back. Mainly because it felt so nice to touch her.

His earlier plan to give up on her abandoned, he kissed her in the elevator in their building. She had her hands on his ass, pulling him against her.

"I love these jeans," she mumbled.

"I love—" He stopped. Now wasn't the right time. "Love that you love these jeans."

He helped her get undressed since she was a little wobbly. He even hung her dress up on the hanger.

"You're a good guy," she said as he handed over one of his T-shirts.

"But not good enough, right?"

"Too good."

"Why would you say that?"

She didn't answer, and went to brush her teeth. He took his turn when she was done. When he came out, she was crawling into his bed. A small piece of him wanted to tell her to go to her own room, so he could maintain the small detachment he'd managed to gain. The rest of him was happy for the reprieve. One more night.

He slid in on his side and she moved into her spot. They felt so right.

"We said we would be honest with each other, but what if I want to tell you something that will upset you?" he asked.

"I'd want you to tell me anyway. That's what honesty is all about."

"You've met my parents, you've seen how happy they are together—even when they're picking on each other."

"Right."

"I always assumed I'd have that by now. Someone who laughed at my fish stories and told me to watch my cholesterol because she wanted me around for as long as possible."

"You didn't tell me you have a cholesterol problem."

"I don't. It's an example."

"Are you accusing me of wanting you to die early from an unchecked medical problem? Have you had your cholesterol checked? It might be hereditary."

"I missed you tonight," he blurted it out before he lost the courage. "I'm sure that breaks the rules, but I can't help it. I can't expect you to trust me one moment when I'm keeping my real feelings inside."

She let out a breath and sat up.

"It totally breaks the rules, but I'm glad you told me the truth. Then I don't feel so bad to tell you I missed you too. I was trying to convince myself I wasn't getting attached, but the truth is that I only want to be with you," she admitted. "I don't know what to do next."

"It doesn't matter. We're together now. We'll figure the rest out later." He pulled her closer, not having an answer but relieved she hadn't shut him down. Her admission should have made him happy, but she seemed so heartbroken, he couldn't feel any real happiness.

"Don't let me go." Her voice faltered.

"Never," he promised. This was how it should always be.

She was the one he should always be with.

If only he could convince her.

* * * *

Chanda threw her ribbon tool across the empty space and let out an obscenity. Her voice echoed back to her. She couldn't work like this. She couldn't create anything.

She'd been so angry at Doug after he wrecked her show she hadn't even let him explain. She'd kicked him out and told him she never wanted to see him again.

Now she was rethinking that. In truth, she'd regretted her words as soon as she'd calmed down. Which had been only a few minutes after he left.

She picked up her phone and frowned at the blank screen. She hadn't gotten so much as a text from him since that night. Of course, when someone tells you that they don't want to see you ever again, it's not a huge jump to assume he won't reach out.

The buzzer rang for the front door and she rushed to get it.

"Hello?" Her heart pounded in anticipation of hearing his voice.

"Hi Chanda, it's Becca. I have your check from the exhibit."

She never thought she could feel such disappointment from having someone show up with a large check.

"Come on up." She buzzed the woman in and opened the door at the top of the steps.

"How's it going?" Becca glanced around at the supplies she'd thrown around.

"My muse is on vacation."

Becca frowned and held out the check.

"I'm sorry about the sale for *Thunderbirds* falling through."

"Well, when your boyfriend starts a fist fight in the gallery, it kind of hurts sales."

"I heard a rumor." Becca frowned. "I think I know why he might have hit Mr. Brenner."

"Why?" Chanda desperately wanted an answer as to why her world went to hell.

"Mr. Brenner made a comment to Ms. Faum that your father buys your work and donates it. He inferred that no one would buy your work otherwise."

"That's not true."

"I know that. But apparently, it's widespread gossip throughout the art community."

"Doug hit him to defend me?"

"That's what it sounds like."

Regret choked her once again.

She'd dated a lot of asshole guys in the past. After the exhibit, she thought Doug was the same, just better at hiding it. She should have known he wouldn't have done anything to intentionally hurt her.

He'd been standing up for her and she kicked him out of her home and her life.

* * * *

Alyssa looked up as Mia slipped into her office Monday morning and shut the door.

"I'm in love," Mia announced.

Alyssa made a show of looking at her calendar.

"We went out on Friday night. You said you needed to get laid."

"Yes. Turns out I also needed to fall in love. And I did both."

"All I did this weekend was my laundry." Alyssa frowned.

"It was the guy I met at MacGregor's. The blond guy."

"You weren't even going to go for it. You said you'd put more effort into Saturday night."

"I know, but then you bailed and I wasn't ready to go home."

"And it was good?"

Mia wasn't the type to fall in love. Sure she was always searching for Prince Charming, but she still had trust issues from all the times Prince Charming turned out to be a troll. But Mia's trust issues were the normal kind, not the Department of Corrections type.

"His name is Andy and he is so sweet." Mia's eyes fluttered as she held her hands in front of her.

The skeptic in Alyssa doubted Andy was so sweet. He'd been found in a bar.

"He's only in town visiting. His friend lives here and was showing him where he hangs out. How crazy is it that I might not have met him if my friend hadn't wanted to celebrate that day?"

"So he's leaving?"

"Yes. Back to Philly." She winced and tilted her head to the side. Alyssa could almost hear it before she said it. "I'm thinking about moving there with him."

"*What*? Are you crazy?" Alyssa stood up, ready to jump on her friend to stop her from running off to Philadelphia.

"Crazy. In love. Same thing." Mia smiled all dreamy-like as Alyssa made a choking sound.

"No. No way. I'm not going to let you run off to another state with some strange guy you just met."

"Liss, this is it. I'm telling you. It's going to be okay."

Okay? First Kenley—the virgin non-dater—leaves town, marries her boss, and is having a baby. Now Mia's following the same path? What the hell was happening?

"I'm going to have to take the train to Philly to identify your body!" The bum-bum from the opening of *Law and Order* played through her mind.

"Relax. That's not going to happen. He knows some people, and he can get me a job down there."

"I swear if you say he's a talent agent, I'm going to shake you."

"Look, I know this isn't for you. I understand. I felt the same way. I didn't think I could ever let go and trust anyone. But when you find the right person, it's a lot easier than you would expect."

While she was truly concerned for her friend and her life choices, Alyssa had to admit, part of her reaction was because she found herself wondering if maybe she could have it too.

No. No she couldn't. Even if she wanted more with Gray, she didn't deserve to be happy when she'd caused someone else so much pain.

"I'll be here for you," Alyssa said with her jaw clenched. It wouldn't help to continue her rant. It was obvious that Mia was going to do this with or without her permission.

Mia let out a sigh.

"You mean you'll be here for me when this all goes to hell and I need a place to crash while I suffer a breakdown."

"Probably not the crashing part, since it's not my place, but yeah."

Mia stepped closer and rested her hand on Alyssa's arm, smiling like she knew something Liss didn't.

"I'm not going to have a breakdown or need an escape plan. I've found the one."

Alyssa bit her tongue to keep from saying, "The one who will lock you in his basement while he wears your shoes."

"What does Freddie say?"

"He's ecstatic. He says he only has one more of his princesses to marry off." Mia pointed at Alyssa and raised her brows. "You don't even know what's coming. You're next, sweet cheeks."

"Am not."

"Are too."

"Am not."

"Am not, what?" Grayson asked by the door. "Sorry, I knocked and thought someone said come in."

"I said 'coming.' As in she's not ready for what's coming. And look. You showed up." Mia thumbed over to Grayson. "Did you see that?"

"Shut up."

"You okay?" Grayson pointed at her pout.

"This one is running off with some strange guy to Philadelphia. All my friends are growing up and I don't wanna." She stuck her tongue out at Mia who returned the gesture adding devil horns.

"Stop it, both of you. If you're good, I'll take you for ice cream later."

"I'll be good," Mia offered.

"Sorry, my offer was meant to cheer up Liss, not consort with the deserter who I have no shot of getting into bed. I'm sure they have ice cream in Philly." Grayson's joke made them all laugh.

"It probably sucks." Alyssa added, and Mia gave her the finger.

"Enough, girls. Liss, I came in here to tell you we have a meeting. The grown-up kind. So get your crayons and come on."

"Shit!" Alyssa grabbed up her tablet and folder as she headed for the door. "We're not done with this conversation."

"Yes, we are." Mia waved and started off toward the elevator.

"Last I saw her, she was sitting on some guy's lap," Gray mentioned.

"Not *some* guy, apparently. *The* guy."

Liss sat next to Gray in the meeting room, mainly because it was the only seat available, but also because she felt unsettled and being close to Grayson made her feel more secure. He was like a security blanket with a penis.

As the meeting started, Alyssa found herself thinking about where this was going. Being close to a man was a bad thing, something she wanted to avoid. Somewhere in the next hour, she was so focused on how she was feeling about Grayson, she wasn't paying attention.

"...and we want to congratulate Alyssa for taking on the Leedom Enterprises account. I'm sure it's the first of many we'll be able to throw her way."

She jumped when Randy said her name. Everyone smiled and clapped. She nodded in thanks, hoping nothing was said before that. No one asked for a speech, and the meeting continued, so she could go back to her analysis.

"You okay?" Grayson whispered while reports were handed out.

"Yeah. I'm good." She wasn't good. She was freaking out. If Mia could flip from the detached single person to love-swept automaton in the span of a weekend with a perfect stranger, what hope did Alyssa have of fending off Mr. Perfect sitting next to her?

It was the damn feelings from that night on the dock that had messed up everything. Ever since then, she was having difficulty getting things back to normal. Well, she was going to do something about that. Their first encounter was nothing more than attraction and sex. It had worked for her many times before. She would go back to what she knew worked. Plain old sex without any connection.

Right now.

Or as soon as the meeting was over.

* * * *

Something was up with Alyssa. Grayson was sitting two feet away from her and could feel the tension snapping in the air.

He had an idea it had something to do with Mia and her new development. While he had doubts about a relationship developing into love in only two days, he did feel optimistic that it was possible to turn a committed single person into a romantic. Maybe he had a shot with Alyssa. They hadn't talked much about their confessions from last Friday night. They'd chatted, and talked about work, but she'd slept in her own room on Saturday and Sunday night. He hadn't pushed.

When the meeting was dismissed, he was surprised when she followed him back to his office. And even more shocked when she closed the door and slid his guest chair over in front of it.

"You okay?" he asked.

"No. I need sex." Giving the door a look and a nod she stepped up in front of him and reached for his pants.

"*Now*?"

"Yes. Now. Just sex. No funny comments that only we would understand. No telling me I'm pretty or sexy or any of that. Just sex without emotions or speaking."

"I don't have a lock on my door." He studied the chair and frowned.

"That's why I braced it shut with the chair."

"There's no way to explain why we're in here alone with the door braced—which I doubt would even hold if someone pushed on it."

"Then you'd better be quick about it. Because we're doing this."

"We can't—" She'd opened his pants and grasped him firmly. "God. Okay." And just like that, he was onboard with this stupid, stupid plan. "How do we do this with the least amount of difficulty?"

"I think pants down, me bent over your desk."

"Christ." He had to pull away before he went off from just the thought of it. However stupid, it was still very hot. "Do you want to face the door or the window?"

"I don't care, just hurry before someone comes in to talk with you."

"Just let me check my emails to make sure no one has scheduled a meeting."

"All you do is go to meetings."

"It's not *all* I do. Apparently, I also have sex with my coworkers at ten-thirty in the morning." No messages. Good.

"Gray, you're being cute. Stop being cute. This is supposed to be just lust."

"You think I'm *cute*?" He winced. "I have my pants around my knees. Cute? I'd prefer sexy or maybe wicked hot. Cute? I don't—whoa. Okay, this is really happening."

Her pants were now down at her knees and she was leaning over his desk facing the door. That was probably the best choice. If someone came in he might be able to convince them she was choking and he was administering the Heimlich.

He didn't have time to think about a better excuse or anything for that matter. She had an agenda.

"You're going to have to get closer. You're not that big."

"And now you're insulting me? I kind of need a minute. I wasn't really prepared for this. I thought you were coming in to tell me you noticed Derek scratching himself when he was pointing out the levels of integrity."

"Grayson Hollinger III, get over here and do this before I pull my pants up and leave."

"I have to say the bossing with the name thing is really good." They hadn't been together for a while so his body was definitely on board with the plan, but he wasn't the type to use someone without some kind of affection. No matter how much the other person might demand he do so.

He rested his hands on her hips and leaned back before pushing into her. She cried out.

"You're going to have to be quiet," he whispered by her ear. They worked together perfectly. She was able to keep a handle on the normal cries of passion, but her breathing was so heavy, he worried Doug might hear from his office next door. It didn't matter.

She was clenching the profit and loss statement he'd spent an hour on this morning. No worries, he would just print a new one. Did he have tissues in his desk? He probably had some extra napkins from the coffee shop. Would it be rude to offer her a napkin with a smiling coffee cup on it? She probably wouldn't care.

A small moan was the only warning she reached point B. The spasms caught him off guard, and he didn't resist as he rode them out with her. He hoped his groan of release was quieter than it sounded in his head.

He didn't pull out of her right away and to his surprise, she didn't try to wiggle away. He opened his second drawer and found he also had plain white napkins as well as the smiley coffee cup ones. He handed the whole pile over, except for the one he kept for himself, and moved away.

"I don't know about you, but that was the hottest fifty-seven seconds of my life." He wasn't even exaggerating, his computer was on, counting away the seconds right in front of him. She stood and buttoned her pants.

"How's my hair?"

"I didn't touch it." No matter how much he wanted to.

"I'll see you later."

"You feel better?" he asked as she moved the chair out of the way. He'd done what she asked, but maybe he misread the situation. Maybe this hadn't been about needing sex at all.

"No," she answered and walked out without looking back.

Chapter 22

Well, that hadn't worked, Alyssa thought as she made her way to her office. She'd been trying to get things back to the way they were. But she should have known better. Things had always been fun with Grayson from that very first time. They'd laughed and didn't take things too seriously.

But things felt way too serious now.

She hadn't planned on a quickie in his office being romantic, but somehow it was. Even down to the way he'd handed her those napkins. It was as if that smiling face on the coffee cup was saying, "Now this is a kind man. He cares about you." She laughed at the thought.

"Alyssa?" Mr. Hasher had called her name. She stopped and changed direction hoping she didn't look like she'd just had sex. "You have a minute?"

"Uh, yeah. Sure." Did he know? Was she going to be fired? Was Grayson? This was her fault. He hadn't wanted to do it. Well, obviously he did to some degree. Maybe she'd point out how it hadn't even taken a minute and that Gray had checked his emails first. Damn.

Thoughts of Kenley came to mind. What if Alyssa ended up like her? Without a job, she'd have to move home.

The owner of the company didn't say anything as they moved toward his office. No waiting the normal twenty minutes this time. She would have welcomed the extra time to get her knees under control. Of course it didn't work that way.

He frowned as he took his seat and steepled his fingers.

"I think we have a problem," he said. Oh God. Now she'd done it.

* * * *

Grayson didn't know how to respond. She'd been speaking so fast, he barely made out the words, but eventually, after a few repeats, he was able to get the whole story.

"So what happens now?" he asked. They were almost to their building. It was raining so he held the umbrella for them, noticing the rain amplified the vanilla scent of her hair.

"I'm not sure. I guess they'll give me another account. It's not *my* fault the owner of Leedom Enterprises decided to sell the business abruptly and run off with his son's fiancée. Who does that? It's so rude, not to mention incredibly icky."

"Maybe the person who buys it from him will want us to continue to work the account."

"Maybe. I had big plans for that company. Stupid old guy with his Viagra."

"I think he's only like sixty." Grayson had to laugh at her.

He especially enjoyed the part of the tale where she thought she was going to throw up all over Mr. Hasher's desk.

"You thought he knew what happened in my office?"

"He was so serious and my face was so hot."

"Well, he might not know, but Doug does." He came clean.

"Seriously?"

"You were too loud."

"I was not! You were." She frowned and let out a sigh once they were inside.

"Are you okay?"

"I'm going to go take a shower and spend the rest of the evening not working on the Leedom account."

He brought her a glass of wine while she was in the shower, and by the time she came out, he'd made tacos.

They ate in front of the television and then he nudged her to sit on the floor in front of him so he could rub her shoulders and neck. She was so tense.

"Feel good?" he guessed when she moaned in appreciation. She nodded and he bent to kiss her neck.

This was the only place he wanted to be. And she was the only person he ever wanted to be with.

They hadn't mentioned Mia's earlier announcement or her reaction to it. He was biding his time for now. Instead he focused on making her feel good. And he could tell from the way she let her head roll from side to side that so far, he was successful.

He leaned up when she didn't say anything. Then he heard a sniff and saw the worst thing ever.

Tears streamed down both cheeks as she looked up at the ceiling, her jaw clenched tight.

"Shit! What is it? Did I hurt you, Liss?" He removed his hands from her shoulders. She didn't seem hurt. At least not physically.

A sob caught in her throat and she shook her head.

"You didn't hurt me. I'm fine."

"You're obviously not fine. What is it? Please tell me."

Again she shook her head.

"Alyssa, let me help you."

He placed his fingers on her chin and guided her face toward him so she had no choice but to look at him. "Tell me."

"I'm scared."

"Of what?"

"Of...you." Her voice shook as she tried to hide her face from him again. He released his grip immediately, though he hadn't been holding her hard enough to cause pain.

"*Me*?" he choked. "I would never hurt you." Again he looked her over, thinking she was suffering from some physical pain he had caused.

"I know that. It's just this." She moved her hand back and forth between them.

"This?" He didn't understand.

"I didn't want to go out with Mia last week. I wanted to be with you. I always want to be with you." Her words finally clicked.

"I only ever want to be with you too," he confessed.

"We said we weren't going to let this happen," she said as she pulled away from him. "We're getting too comfortable with each other. And what happened with Mia and the Philly guy has me worried that I could end up wanting the same sort of thing with you."

"That's not necessarily a bad thing, Liss. We're happy together. Why can't we just go with it?"

"And what happens when it doesn't work out? I'll be right back where I was, with deeper scars and heavier baggage."

"You don't know that. Maybe this could be good."

"I can't. This isn't what I signed up for. Don't you get it? I'm too messed up. Anytime you work late or go to the gym, I wonder if that's really where you are. It's none of my business so I never ask, but I keep waiting for the cops to knock on the door to take you off to prison. I don't let myself plan too far ahead because you might not be here."

"I *will* be here. I'm not a rapist or anything else. I'm just a regular guy who wants to try to have something real with you."

"I don't do *real*, Grayson. I told you that from the beginning."

"Then what do you want? Tell me how you want to handle this?" He couldn't hide his panic. She looked like a caged animal about to run away and never come back. He couldn't let that happen. He couldn't lose her. Not until he had a chance to fix things.

"I think we should go back to just being roommates. Nothing else."

Gray knew that would never work. Their attraction was undeniable. They wouldn't be able to keep their hands off each other. But he was afraid if he refused, she would bolt.

"Okay," he agreed hastily, holding up both hands. "We'll do it how you want, until you feel safe enough to trust me. I'm not going anywhere, Alyssa. I'm willing to wait however long it takes for you to trust me." He realized now it was too late to save himself. Everything he wanted was in the hands of this woman.

"I'm not going to change my mind. I can't change my mind even if I wanted to. It doesn't work that way. I'll never be able to trust anyone. I'm broken," she said, wiping tears from her cheeks. "I'm not meant to be happy. It wouldn't be fair."

This was not the first time she'd alluded to not deserving happiness.

"Of course you're supposed to be happy. You didn't do anything. You didn't hurt those girls. Donnie did."

"I didn't stop him!"

"What do you mean?"

"I could have figured out what he was doing and stopped him."

He stared at her for a moment wondering how she could think that. He wanted to tell her she was wrong, but he knew from the look on her face, he'd never convince her. She believed this for too many years.

He wanted to be the one to pick up the pieces and help her mend, but he didn't know how. He remembered something Iz had mentioned about closure, and decided it would be worth a shot. He'd do anything to help her. Even visit her ex-fiancé in prison.

Over the next week, they kept their distance from each other. They didn't even watch television together. Most evenings, Alyssa took her dinner to her room and stayed in there.

That was fine, it gave Grayson the time he needed to make travel plans and talk to his sister.

By Tuesday night, everything was in place.

* * * *

Something was up with Gray.

"I have a work thing I have to go to this evening. It might be late when I get back," Gray said on Wednesday morning as they got ready for work.

"Okay."

As if a reflex, he leaned down to kiss her, and then quickly pulled back. When he stood and didn't meet her eyes, she knew he was lying.

She knew it as sure as if he had been wearing a T-shirt that said, "I don't have a work thing tonight. I'm doing something I don't want you to know about."

"Have a nice day," she said, trying to get him to look at her.

He just nodded and left.

For a few minutes, Alyssa tried to fight off tears. Stupid, irrational tears she had no business having. She and Gray weren't together. She'd even told him he should go out with someone. But now that it seemed that was happening, she hated the idea.

When had she become fickle? She disliked fickleness.

Mia stopped in her office.

"Let me guess, you broke up with the guy?" Alyssa said as she pulled her laptop from her bag.

"No. I gave my notice. I was able to get a job in Philadelphia. And no, it's not porn. It's a legit job, thank you very much."

"I'm sorry. I'm happy for you."

"I don't think you're happy at all. What is going on?"

"Nothing."

"Liar," Mia called her out with an expectant frown. "Spill."

"I told Grayson I didn't want a relationship, like I've been telling him since we met. I think he's going out with someone tonight."

"Like you told him to do," Mia said with her brows raised.

"Yeah."

"You are so stupid." Mia rolled her eyes. "What the hell is wrong with you?"

She couldn't go into all the scary details about what was wrong with her. They had jobs to do.

"Too many things are wrong with me."

"You're in love with him, Liss."

"No way."

"You wouldn't give a shit if he went out with someone tonight if you didn't really care about him."

"I *don't* give a shit. He can do whomever he wants." If she could say it without cringing, it might seem believable. Mia wasn't falling for it.

"From the way he was looking at you, I'm pretty sure he's got it all kinds of bad for you. There's no way he's seeing someone else. This is ridiculous. Why are you fighting this so hard?" Mia huffed and started to walk away. Then she returned. "And you are being stupid. I know. I used to think it was safer to not get close, but you know what? Not every guy is going to lie to you. Andy isn't that kind of man and neither is Grayson."

"I wish I could be sure that was true." She couldn't imagine Grayson hurting anyone or lying. But then she hadn't imagined Donnie was capable of such a thing either.

"It doesn't really matter if we want to or not. Sometimes our hearts take over. Do you love him?" It was a question now.

"Maybe."

"And you told the man you love to go be with someone else?"

"When you say it like that, it sounds pretty stupid."

"I don't know what happened to you before. I know you're hauling around a whole bunch of pain and heartache. You need to find a place to dump it so you can move on."

"I can't."

"You have to find a way. This guy makes you happy. I can see it. You deserve to be happy."

"No, I don't," she whispered under her breath as Mia's phone rang. She held it out so Alyssa could see the caller before she answered.

"Hi, Kenley. Why are you calling so early in the morning?" Mia's face broke into a smile and she nodded. Alyssa pulled out her phone to see that it was still on vibrate, and that she'd missed call and a text message:

The baby is here.

When the picture of the prune-faced angel wearing a tiny blue beanie came through, her heart twisted with loneliness. She had no idea she still wanted this.

She thought she'd pushed all those hopes and dreams far enough away that they would never see the light of day again. But she wanted things. Normal things.

Too bad she didn't deserve to have them.

* * * *

Grayson stood outside the prison with his hand tapping his leg nervously. Even the building looked menacing. Maybe that was on purpose. Maybe it was supposed to make people want to walk the straight and narrow so they wouldn't end up having to live in a place that looked so unappealing.

To make things worse, the sky was a dark gray with unsettling clouds moving in. He could smell rain in the air. A storm. How appropriate.

He walked inside, making sure to read every bold-lettered sign thoroughly so he didn't accidentally do something that would keep him from leaving when his visit was over.

I can't believe I'm doing this, he said to himself as he waited in line behind a bunch of scary-looking younger women and older women with defeat in their eyes.

He filled out the proper paperwork, and signed the consent form before he sat on the orange vinyl loveseat in the waiting area. One by one, people came and went until finally his name was called.

Chapter 23

Gray's feet pulled him quickly toward the exit of the prison. He couldn't wait to be out of there. He was nearly hyperventilating by the time he got outside. He sucked in the damp air. The puddles in the parking lot rippled slightly as he walked to the rental car. He tilted his head to the last of the rain, letting the drops cleanse him.

The anxiety remained as he drove to the train station. What had he been thinking?

When the guard had called his name, he stood to follow him to the visiting room, but he couldn't go through with it. It wasn't fear that kept him from walking up to Donnie and begging him to help Alyssa. It was the knowledge that if Gray had any chance of a future with her, they were going to have to find the path together, and Donnie had no part in that.

Gray might not know how to help her yet, but he'd known the answer wasn't inside a prison.

Due to an earlier storm, there was a maintenance problem with the track, so the train stopped two stations out of Syracuse for what they said would be a few hours. He might have driven the four hours back in a rental car if he wasn't already so exhausted. He might have switched to a bus, but he found he wasn't in a hurry to get back.

He didn't want to go home until he'd come up with a plan.

From the beginning, they'd agreed to be honest. No bullshit. No games. But he was keeping the truth from her now. He loved her, but he couldn't tell her. He couldn't set himself up to be turned down again. And Alyssa wouldn't just turn him down. She'd be out of his life as quickly as she could pack her things.

As he sat at the bar near the train station, he glanced up to see a dark-haired woman smiling at him. He smiled back. Not in a way that would make him look interested, but unfortunately she interpreted interest anyway.

She came to sit next to him with a smile on her face.

"You look lonely over here all by yourself," she said.

He was lonely, but nothing this woman had to offer would fix that.

"Can I ask you a question?" Gray said.

"Okay." The woman looked uncertain, but the smile didn't leave her face.

"What is worse? Facing the very slim chance you could have your heart broken, or being alone for the rest of your life?"

The woman's brow creased at the question, but she seemed to be thinking of an answer.

"I'm going to guess you mean someone other than me."

"Yes."

"I'd have to say being alone. It sucks. Loneliness makes us do stupid things." She frowned at the drink in her hands.

"Right. That's what I was thinking too."

"Your girl doesn't agree?"

"My girl doesn't want to be my girl because she got blindsided by someone else."

"And you're so sure you won't ever mess up and hurt her the same way? Can you guarantee you won't?" the woman challenged.

"I guess not. I know she's the only woman I've ever wanted like this. No one knows what happens next. Shouldn't it be about *now*?"

"*We're* both here now." Was she still trying?

"I'm in love with her. I'm not going to do anything to mess it up."

"Then maybe she's missing out."

The woman moved on and Gray pulled out his phone to call Alyssa. He wasn't just late any more. He probably wouldn't be there until after eleven at this rate. He paused. What would he say? That he'd come to Syracuse to visit Donnie of all people? No. She would not appreciate that.

He sent a vague text and ordered another beer, silently hoping the train would never be able to leave.

* * * *

Alyssa lost track of time waiting for Grayson, and had fallen asleep while reading a book. She woke up around midnight with the book on her chest and her light on. She went across the hall to find his bed empty.

She checked her phone, there was a text:

Something came up. I'll see you tomorrow.

She had no right to be upset or jealous. They were not together. Not in a relationship. That was how she had wanted it for this very reason.

Trust was not something she could handle.

She continued to tell herself to let it go over and over as she tried to go back to sleep. It didn't matter if he was with someone else. That's what she'd wanted, for him to move on and be happy. What they had wasn't supposed to be serious.

It was only an hour later when she heard the key in the door. A few seconds later, her bedroom door opened and she felt his presence as she pretended to be asleep.

After a soft sigh, her door closed and she heard the shower turn on.

In the morning, she was up and dressed before she heard anything from his room. Just as she was heading out, he shuffled into the kitchen and poured a cup of coffee. His hair stuck up and he was only wearing boxers.

She wanted nothing more than to wrap her arms around his waist and press her cheek to his back. He would turn in her arms and smile down at her. It was a scene she remembered from a few weeks ago. Before things got so messed up. When it had just been fun.

"You're going to be late for work," she said when she met up with him in the kitchen.

"Yeah. Sorry I didn't make it back sooner."

"Why would I care if you don't come home? You're a grown man and we're not in a relationship. You can do whatever you want."

"Don't. Just don't, okay? It's too early in the morning to deal with how much you don't want anything with anyone ever. I get it." He was snappy this morning. Rather than press, she simply nodded and left their apartment.

He understood her, even though it was clear he didn't like it. She decided to let it go, but she found herself thinking about him all day. Had he been out with someone he really liked? Would he want this new woman to move in? Would Alyssa have to find a new place to live while he got married to someone who didn't know him as well as she did?

Stop it, she said to herself. She needed to get it together. She could not be jealous. Only people who *cared* got jealous.

That night, Gray worked late and said little when he finally got home.

"Did you eat?" she asked.

"Yeah. Sorry, I should have let you know." There was something in his voice she didn't like. Pity?

"It's fine. Why would I care if you ate?" she asked, causing him to look at her strangely.

"Is everything okay with you?"

"I'll be fine. I'm just distracted with work. I'm going to go to bed early."

Grayson went to his own room. Alyssa heard the murmur of a quiet conversation as she passed his door. He didn't come over to say good night. Not that she expected him to.

She tossed and turned for a few hours before she finally fell into a restless sleep where men in dark hoodies chased her. It went on like that the rest of the week.

Gray was gone when she woke on Friday.

"What the hell?" she said to no one as she made coffee.

As she dressed, she decided what she needed was to find someone else to get her mind off Grayson. She could go out after work and stay out just like Grayson had. There was nothing to stop her. She didn't need to feel guilty in any way.

He'd looked at her with pity? She would show him how much she didn't need his pity.

She stopped by Mia's desk before going up to her floor.

"Hey, why are you slumming it down here on twenty-three?" Mia laughed.

"We're going out tonight. It's going to be fun."

"Oh-kay." Before Mia could ask questions or bow out of their plans, Alyssa turned and went up to work.

They would go to a club. It would be fun. Just like it used to be.

* * * *

Gray called Alyssa in her office on Friday afternoon. He still didn't feel comfortable facing her. He feared she would see what he'd done written on his face.

"Alyssa Sinclair." Her name, spoken in her professional tone, sent a shiver of pleasure through him.

"I feel like I should be charged by the minute to hear you say your name like that," he joked. She didn't joke back.

"Did you need something?" Yes. He did. He needed things to go back to how they'd been. Except he didn't want that either.

"I just wondered if you wanted to get a drink tonight after work. I haven't gotten a chance to talk to you much lately." Mostly because he'd been avoiding her as much as possible.

"I can't. I have plans." She didn't elaborate on those plans, and he didn't ask for details.

She'd said they were just supposed to be roommates. He was trying to go along with her request. But roommates could hang out on Friday nights. It wasn't unheard of.

"Okay. Well, maybe I'll see you around later."

"Maybe. I have to go now. I have a meeting."

He wasn't sure if she really had a meeting, but he said good-bye and hung up.

They were drifting apart and he didn't know which way to move. No matter what he did, he was doomed.

He'd been quiet since coming home from the prison. He still hadn't figured out how to get her to open up and give him a chance.

He'd been desperate for some way to help her. If he could help her heal, maybe they would have a chance to be happy together. But now there was this *thing* between them.

By three in the morning, he knew she wasn't coming home.

He fell asleep on the sofa, so she woke him when she came in at ten the next morning.

He looked her over, seeing the dressy outfit and the messy hair.

"You stayed the night with someone?" Even as he said it, he knew he had no right to ask or be upset. Not having the right didn't make him any less upset though.

"Yes."

"Come on, Liss. This is stupid. We had a good thing going. I can satisfy you as well as anyone else. Why would you go out with a stranger?" This was a valid point. Not the reason he was upset, but still valid.

She rolled her eyes trying to play it off, but he thought his head might explode. Another guy had touched her?

Without a word, she walked down the hall to her room. He followed.

"I don't understand. You could have just told *me* you wanted sex. I was right here. I'm safe."

"Where do you get off judging me when you were doing the same thing on Wednesday?"

"I wasn't doing the same thing at all. I was—" He couldn't finish the sentence. Not yet. "I wasn't *with* anyone."

"Whatever. That's the whole point of you and me. No expectations, right?" She patted his shoulder as she passed him to go into the bathroom. He heard the shower turn on as he paced in the hall.

He needed to calm down before he said something that made things worse. The more he paced, the more he realized he didn't care if he pissed her off. She's said no games and he was going to hold her to it.

He tapped on the door before he just barged in.

"What?" she asked.

"Are you trying to sabotage what we have? Is that what this is?"

"We don't *have* anything, Grayson. We're roommates who used to hook up sometimes. That's it."

"What if..." Was he really going to say this? Out loud? "What if I wanted something? Not a relationship, but some form of exclusivity."

"No."

"*No*? You can't just say no. We have to discuss it."

"No, we don't. People in relationships discuss things. Roommates can just tell each other no."

"This is ridiculous. Why would you want to go out with someone else when I'm right here?"

"Do you hear yourself? You're getting all crazy."

He left, slamming the door behind him like a crazy person. Then he walked back in.

"You could have at least texted me so I knew you were safe. I worried about you all night."

"I didn't ask you to worry about me."

"That's too bad." He was making a mess of things, but he couldn't seem to stop. "I'm worried you're going to try to go back to the way you were. You weren't happy like that."

"It's none of your business."

"I care about you, Liss."

"I'm just someone who rents the room across the hall, remember?"

"If you still think that, you're lying to yourself."

He left again, knowing he was throwing a fit like a little kid.

She had him all tangled up in knots. He didn't know how to make her care.

"Fuck!" he yelled into the empty kitchen.

He caught a glimpse of a naked Alyssa as she walked to her room. She looked up at him with wide eyes and then ducked inside her room without a word.

He decided to leave. It wouldn't do him any good to stay there and keep fighting with her when he was angry.

The more he walked, the angrier he became. The day had come and gone; it was dark when he finally looked around to see where he was. The whole city looked different.

He decided that maybe he needed a new perspective on everything. When he'd taken Alyssa up on her offer of a one-night stand it was because he'd wanted to prove to himself that he was capable of just having a good time. While he knew what he felt for Alyssa was different than those other relationships, he'd still fallen into the same trap. He didn't know how to stop wanting the commitment his parents had.

He walked into the club, hell bent on finding someone to get him through this.

* * * *

Chanda was miserable. She missed Doug. Ever since finding out the reason for his outburst, the guilt had compounded daily. She wanted to see him, but didn't even know where he was living now.

She flung the clay back on the board and went to clean up. She couldn't work like this. Despite the sun shining through the loft, her work was full of darkness. Guilt had her all tied up in knots. On her way to her room, she stopped and opened the door to Lucy's room. She missed the little girl so much. She hadn't just lost Doug, but Lucy too.

She picked up the polar bear Lucy always liked to sleep with. Was she having trouble sleeping without it?

Feeling like she had a purpose for the first time in days, Chanda tucked the polar bear into her bag and set off to pay a visit to Doug's daughter.

After the second ring of the doorbell and a series of knocks, the door finally opened, revealing an irritated Julie.

"Yes?"

"Hi. Can I speak to Lucy? She left her bear. I wanted to drop it off."

"Chanda!" Lucy came running before her mother had the chance to decide what to do.

"I brought Snowflake. I found him in your room."

"Can I come with you?" she asked, ripping Chanda's heart out.

"No." Julie snapped. "I told you, you have to stay with us."

"I want to see my daddy!" Lucy complained, pulling the bear against her chest. Tears gathered in her eyes, so much like her father's.

"Shh," Chanda said with a smile. "You'll get to see him in a few days. Remember how we talked about taking turns?"

Lucy shook her head.

"I'm not allowed to see him anymore because Daddy yelled at Mommy's boyfriend." The tears fell as Chanda stared in confusion.

What was going on here? Doug wasn't allowed to see his daughter?

She remembered back to the night when he was late. He'd said there was an incident and Lucy had to stay with her mother.

"What happened?"

"Doug came to pick up Lucy. And I told him she couldn't go to the gallery because she'd used crayons on her walls—something she apparently got from you." Julie tossed her hair in a very annoying way. "Doug got angry and started yelling. Mitchell threatened to call the cops. It was a big scene and our new neighbors witnessed the whole thing. I suggested he leave and not come back until after we meet with the caseworker next week."

Chanda stepped back as if the woman had struck her. Because she had allowed Lucy to paint on the walls at the loft, Doug had lost the two days of custody he was able to get?

"Don't worry, Lucy. I'm sure everything will be fine."

The door was closed in her face and Chanda turned to go. She needed to find Doug and help fix this.

* * * *

Gray had to do something. He couldn't go on like this; it would kill him. And he couldn't get over Alyssa by having sex with some random women. He'd had his chance at the club and blown it.

He'd spent the night on Trent and Tiff's sofa and when he'd gotten home, Alyssa had smiled and went out for a run as if she didn't care at all what he had done all night.

Her disinterest was too much. He couldn't take it. He needed to get away from Alyssa before she broke his heart. Far away.

On Monday morning, he went straight into Randy's office and sat down.

"What's up?"

"Any openings in the San Diego office?"

"For who?"

"Me."

"No." Randy shook his head quickly.

"I need to get out of here. I can either move to the San Diego office of Hasher Borne or I can move somewhere else with another firm. What's your pick?"

"I don't like either of those choices."

"Too bad. Pick one."

"Fine. I'll see what's available." Randy frowned.

"Make it quick. I really need to leave soon."

"Why? Did you murder someone?"

"No." Gray got up to move for the door.

"Is Alyssa going with you?" Gray stopped and hung his head. He hadn't realized Randy knew about them. In hindsight, it was probably pretty obvious. The way he'd suggested her for the job initially, and the way they walked into the office together every morning. Not to mention the visits to each other's offices.

"No."

"Oh. I see," Randy said sadly. "I'll let you know by Thursday."

"Thanks."

Alyssa wasn't at the apartment when he got home. She arrived an hour later with a bunch of groceries and out of breath.

"Why don't you ever let me know you're coming home with bags so I can meet you and help you carry them?" he snapped at her.

Guilt was a sick son of a bitch. For some reason, it made you think you had a right to be angry at the person you'd wronged. It made no sense.

"I can carry three bags of groceries, Gray. I carried them the whole way from the market."

"If you would communicate, maybe I could go to the market with you and help you carry them back to the apartment." He couldn't shut up, even though he knew he was being a huge ass.

"Okay. Next time, I'll let you know when I'm going. I did ask yesterday if you needed anything. I guess I didn't make myself clear." She kept her eyes on the floor.

He needed to fix this.

He grabbed her by the arms and pressed her back against the refrigerator. His lips crashed down on hers roughly. All the pent-up tension and anger came out in that kiss. She kissed him back, but her body was tense. He tried to relax a little so he wouldn't scare her, or worse hurt her. The kiss slowed and then he released her to rest his forehead against hers.

"Why can't we make this work? Please. Just say we can try."

Alyssa looked away for a second and then met his gaze.

"There's nothing to work out." He watched her face to see if she was trying to hide her true feelings. All he saw was a mark on her lip where he'd kissed her hard enough to bring the blood to the surface of her skin.

"I'm sorry." He ran his hand over his face. "I don't know what to do."

"You don't have to do anything. I'm not your problem. Feel free to go out and spend the night with whomever. It doesn't bother me."

"I haven't slept with anyone." He got two ice cubes out and put them in a baggie for her lip. "We said we would be honest with each other. I don't feel comfortable telling you where I was, but I wasn't sleeping with anyone." Holding out the bag, he frowned. "I'm sorry about your lip."

He wanted to crawl in a hole.

"I haven't slept with anyone either. Not that I owe you an explanation." That last part was said with an air of defiance.

"What? But you—"

"You assumed, and I let you. You were giving me pitying looks when you got back that morning you supposedly had a work thing, and I knew you were lying to me. I wanted to sleep with someone so I could move on, but I couldn't do it. I went to Mia's instead."

"You didn't sleep with anyone?" This information bounced around inside his head.

"No one but you since I met you."

"I haven't been with anyone but you. I stayed at Trent's and the work thing wasn't a work thing, but it wasn't a date thing either."

"Oh." She frowned.

"We promised each other no bullshit and it's all we've been doing. Is it wrong for me to want to be with you? Why can't we try? If it doesn't work out—"

"It won't work out and I'll end up hurting you. I don't want that. You shouldn't feel bad about what you want. You haven't done anything wrong." She sighed. "It's normal for people to want things to progress, but I can't do it. I thought being up front would keep us from being sucked down that path, but things have gotten too complicated."

He could tell she truly didn't want this. Not like he wanted her. She wasn't capable of anything more than convenient sex and a place to live with a few laughs and dinners thrown in.

How could that be?

He remembered the way she'd looked at him on the dock by the lake. There was something there. He'd felt it.

Hadn't he?

The familiar doubts crowded in. He had been pretty sure Mandy had feelings for him too. He obviously wasn't the best judge. He couldn't trust himself.

"So I was going to make Hamburger Helper. You want some?" she asked lightly.

"No. I–I'm not hungry. Thanks anyway." He went to his room and hid there for the rest of the night.

At eleven, Alyssa tapped on his door.

"Gray?" She tested the doorknob, which was locked. "Can I come in for a second?"

"No." That tiny word nearly ripped him in two as it came out. He couldn't do this anymore. It was time to let go.

"Okay. Good night."

She'd been upfront from the beginning, and his heart hadn't been paying attention. His heart was paying attention now.

Chapter 24

Unable to get Doug on his phone, Chanda's next stop was the Hasher Borne building. She'd never been there, so she asked the receptionist for his extension and then went outside to call from her cell.

"Doug Phillips. How may I help you?"

"It's me. I need to talk to you. I'm in the lobby. Can you come down here please?"

"Sure. I'll be right down."

Seeing him get off the elevator comforted her. She didn't realize how much she missed him until he was within arm's reach. But while Doug was standing next to her, he was also missing.

His eyes were dim and his usual easy smile was nowhere to be seen.

"I'm sorry to just show up like this, but you didn't answer my calls."

"My phone was broken in the...scuffle. I can't afford a new one right now." His voice was flat and lifeless. He didn't seem angry—not that she would have blamed him—he was just empty.

"I heard some details about what happened at the gallery. You were trying to defend me? Why didn't you say anything?"

"Because I shouldn't have hit that guy. Even to defend you. I was itching for a fight, and I ruined your event because I was angry about something else."

"About the fight with Julie?"

He looked surprised that she knew.

"I dropped off Snowflake and Lucy told me she wanted to come see you. Julie said she had to wait until the consult next week. What is going on?"

* * * *

Doug wasn't sure he had the energy to go into what happened. He guided Chanda over to one of the benches on the wide sidewalk.

"Julie only got angrier. I should have remembered that telling Julie to calm down only makes her get louder. Lucy started crying and then the boyfriend came to the door threatening to call the cops unless I left. I decided it would be better to go than to get into an altercation with my ex-wife's boyfriend in front of my kid so I left. But before I got to your show, Julie had sent a text telling me how upset Lucy was and that they would need to hold off on visitation until after we talk to the case specialist."

"And then you tried to smile and act like nothing was wrong at my show."

"I didn't want to ruin your night with my drama. But then..."

"You should have told me what happened. If you weren't up for it, you shouldn't have even come."

"I wanted to be there for you because I love you. I wanted to see your shining moment. Instead I wrecked it. I'm so sorry, Chanda." He rubbed his forehead unsure how things had gotten so bad. He should have known he couldn't be happy for long. He'd been tempting fate.

"I'm sorry too."

He didn't know why she would be sorry. She hadn't done anything wrong. But before he could say that, she had her arms wrapped around him, her face in his chest.

"This is all my fault."

Was she crazy? He moved back and stared down at her. While he didn't want to break contact with her, he couldn't let things get out of control. It would just hurt worse later.

"It's not your fault. It's mine. I took my anger out on that guy. Christ, he was so scrawny. I could have really hurt him."

"You fought for me, Doug. Now I'm going to fight for our family."

* * * *

By Wednesday, Gray didn't think he'd make it until the next day to hear if there was anything open in San Diego. He contemplated flying there and waiting until they had a position for him, no matter how long that might take.

Avoiding Alyssa was becoming more and more difficult.

It wasn't like he needed to avoid her because she was giving him a hard time or being nasty. It was the exact opposite. She was still indifferent and pleasant, just like always. It was killing him.

"You okay?" Doug asked.

"No. I'm not. You look better."

"I'm back with Chanda," his friend smiled.

"She took you back after you demolished her art show?"

"Yeah. Can you believe it?"

Actually, he could believe it. That was what people did when they loved someone. They didn't give up.

"Good for you."

"She's got some secret plan to get my visitation with Lucy back. She told me to relax and let her take care of it."

"You're not relaxing."

"No. I'm scared. You don't know what it's like being called before child services. All your words get twisted around and you end up looking like the villain."

"Why don't you hire a lawyer?"

"I can't even afford a new phone, Gray. How am I supposed to get a lawyer?"

"Maybe I could—"

"No. It's my thing. I'll take care of it."

"If you need me." If anyone ever needed him, he would be there. Nobody did.

"I heard a rumor," Doug said, looking over his shoulder.

"About?"

"Seems you're looking to go somewhere warmer?" Shit.

"Yeah. I think it's time to move on."

"Your family is closer here."

"And I will fly out to see them as much as I do now."

"What about Liss?" Doug challenged. It was clear he knew Alyssa was the reason he was leaving.

"She'll be fine."

Doug snorted at this and shook his head.

"And I thought *I* was bad at this."

* * * *

Doug left work early to go to the meeting with the family counselor. Chanda had been working on what she called her *secret weapon*. When he'd asked, she said she wasn't positive she could pull it off and didn't want him to get his hopes up.

Now as he walked up to the office—his only hope being able to see his daughter again—he saw Chanda waiting for him with a big smile on her face.

He rushed to greet her, and only noticed the man standing next to her when he was a few feet from her.

"Doug, this is my father, Thomas Donavan. Dad, this is Doug, the man I told you about."

Shit. This was not exactly the time and place to meet her father. Doug wasn't prepared. Not that he would ever be prepared to meet a woman's father.

He was certain he'd pummel any guy who showed up on his doorstep for Lucy. Though from this side, he hoped Chanda's father wasn't as protective as he was.

"It's nice to meet you." Doug offered his hand making sure he seemed respectful. Had he been staring at Chanda's breasts when he saw her? Her blouse was cut low and—yes, no doubt he had been looking. This guy was going to kill him, and Doug couldn't blame him one bit.

"Chanda's told me about you." Okay, so that wasn't the best greeting, but it was better than getting a fist in mouth right before he went into an important meeting.

The man's bushy gray eyebrows pulled together when Chanda squeezed her father's arm. Chanda told him her father was an American who met her mother in Cambodia when he was there on business. He'd pictured the man being small like his daughter.

He wasn't. Instead, he was tall and looked quite capable of handling Doug whom Chanda was now hugging. While he didn't want to push her away, he worried about poking a stick at the bear.

"My father is an attorney. He's going to be your attorney."

It took a second for the words to make sense.

"He's coming inside for the meeting?"

"I will be handling the meeting. You will sit there and be quiet while I take care of this mess." Chanda's father straightened his jacket and began walking.

Doug had never been able to afford an attorney. He'd just gone into the hearings hoping for the best. The best being that the judge would see he was a good father, despite the spin Julie put on things.

The man headed for the door to the building and Chanda moved to follow him.

"Is he any good?" Doug worried. Chanda just laughed and nodded.

"He's the best there is."

* * * *

Chanda tugged nervously on the dress she'd put on. No ripped jeans or T-shirt with a snarky logo today. This was important. She'd even taken out her lip ring.

Doug noticed when he kissed her.

"You look so normal," he commented with a frown. "I don't like it."

The sweater covered her tattoos and her make-up was less... scary. She hoped it helped their case.

Since these weren't formal proceedings, everyone gathered in a small room filled with a large conference table.

Chanda smiled at the look on Julie's face when they walked in. Her father looked quite formidable in his suit. And despite not feeling comfortable, Chanda knew she played the part of sophisticated girlfriend quite well.

The caseworker looked bored as she straightened a stack of papers and turned to the group.

"According to Ms. Phillips' attorney, we are here to determine if Mr. Phillips should be granted visitation. I'm told there was an incident at the home of the child." She turned expectantly to Doug.

Chanda's father interceded.

"I spoke with a witness to the said incident and I wish to provide this affidavit from the neighbors. They both stated the incident was clearly escalating due to the actions of the mother. They also stated the father said he would leave even though the child cried for him to come back. At that time, the father bent down to talk to the girl, telling her he would see her as soon as he could, but that right now he had made her mother mad and didn't want her to be upset."

Chanda pressed her lips together as her heart broke for the man next to her. She took his hand and gave it a little squeeze.

"I ask the court to dismiss this allegation entirely. As no law enforcement was called to take a formal complaint, the only recourse we have is to take the word of the witnesses."

The woman in charge took a moment to read over the document and then handed it to the other attorney who frowned before leaning over to whisper to Julie.

Since they were only sitting across the table, Chanda heard the other woman say, "I think it would be best to let it go."

Julie didn't look happy but gave a quick nod of agreement.

Chanda's father then pulled out another document.

"While we are officially convened, I also want to provide my request to have the custody arrangement reconsidered."

"What?" Julie shouted. Her lawyer hushed her and reached for the copy she was provided.

"Joint 50/50," the attorney read while Julie exploded.

"Never! That will not happen. She's *my* daughter."

"Ms. Phillips, I'll ask that you please sit down. Lucy is also Mr. Phillips's daughter." The caseworker scowled at Julie and perched her glasses so she could read the document.

Doug was holding Chanda's hand so tightly she could no longer feel her fingertips.

When the woman finally opened her mouth to speak—an eternity later—Chanda thought she might pass out from holding her breath.

"I see that Mr. Phillips has been the sole supporter of Lucy's financial needs."

"Ms. Phillips doesn't work. She instead provides a home for Lucy," Julie's attorney said.

"It appears Mr. Phillips was paying for that home. And now she and Lucy live with someone else?"

"Yes."

"Mr. Phillips, you have proven you can provide a safe home with a room for Lucy. You've provided financial support. I ask you—not your attorney—if there is a reason Lucy should not spend equal time with both parents."

Doug swallowed and shook his head.

"No reason, ma'am. I'll make sure she's taken care of no matter where she's living."

"Then I grant temporary 50/50 custody. We'll reconvene next month to examine the results. As dictated by the court, no parent is liable to pay support when the custody is equal between them. Meaning each parent is to supply the child's needs during the time period said child resides with that parent. And, it being equal time, no parent owes the other parent for additional expenditures."

"I'm going to lose my child support payments?" Julie's eyes went wide and then narrowed on the woman in charge. "Hold on just a second. I need those payments."

The women took off her glasses and looked at Julie in a way that made even Chanda nervous.

"I believe what you meant to say was that *Lucy* needs those payments."

"Yes. Of course, that's what I meant. I can't take care of her without that money."

"Your attorney has been given the projected income a person with your degree is expected to make. Support is based on actual payroll records, or if none are supplied, we use these projected figures. You have the potential to make the wage calculated on that document. My suggestion to you would be to supply your actual payroll records if you feel this number is too high."

"I don't have any payroll records."

"Then this figure stands. If you cannot provide for your daughter, the court can give full custody to Mr. Phillips until a time when you can."

Julie's lawyer whispered again, too quickly for Chanda to hear. Julie nodded. "We're fine with the judgment for today."

Not waiting to be dismissed, Julie jumped up from her chair and glared at Chanda and Doug.

Chanda knew Doug well enough to know he would have given anything he had to make things easier for Lucy. Even agreeing to custody and alimony that weren't to his benefit.

"This isn't over." Doug frowned. "She's going to fight this." If there was one thing Julie was good at, it was fighting.

"I expect your ex-wife will be very unhappy when I'm through. But my daughter is important to me, and I am fighting for your daughter as if she was my own."

Chanda was touched by her father's words. He'd always been so busy, she hadn't realized he cared that much. Her parents were still happily married so there'd never been a need to fight over her. Still, it made her smile that she meant that much to him.

"Thank-you, Daddy." She leaned her head on her father's shoulder, hoping he could make things better as easily as he had when she was younger. Except her problems were more complex now.

Chapter 25

Grayson heard back from his boss first thing Friday morning.

They had room for him at the San Diego office. He thought this news would make him feel better, but it didn't.

There was no way he would have been able to walk any slower on his way home that evening. He looked up at their building and cursed. He didn't want to walk in there and see her smiling face of indifference.

He forced himself to go inside, letting his bag slide down his arm to rest by the door.

Alyssa was sitting on the sofa with her legs tucked under her.

"Hey, how was your day? You worked really late." She stood. "I made chicken stir-fry. You want some?"

"No thanks. I'm going to go take a shower and go to bed."

"Do you feel okay?"

"No."

* * * *

Alyssa asked if Grayson needed anything as he rushed to his room, but he didn't answer.

She'd always been under the impression that when guys had an argument they said what they needed to say, cleared the air, and then made up and went back to being buddies.

Gray wasn't making up or going back to being buddies. She knew she'd hurt him, but she couldn't allow herself to love him. Somewhere, out in the world, was a woman who had been hurt because Alyssa had once been blinded by love.

Love meant not seeing what was right in front of you.

As she tried to come up with a plan, his phone rang from his bag by the door. She tried to tune it out, knowing his voice mail would pick up after the fourth ring, but instead it rang again right away.

Then again.

And again.

She looked annoyingly toward the hall, still hearing the water running in the bathroom as the phone started yet again.

"For the love of God!" she huffed, and got up to go answer it. She saw two letters that made her smile. I-Z

"Hey, Izzy. What's up?" she asked as she knocked a wrinkled piece of paper out of his bag.

"Hi, Alyssa. Where is he?" she asked, sounding angry.

"Um, he's in the shower. Do you need me to take the phone in?"

"No."

"What's wrong?" There was a long silence. She guessed Izabelle was deciding whether to side with Alyssa or her brother.

"Please tell him I'll call him back later to discuss the email he sent me," she said.

"Okay. Sure. I'll let him know." It was obvious the email exchange had not been good. They said their good-byes and she put his phone back in the pocket of his bag and moved to replace the wrinkled paper, until she noticed a familiar name written at the top.

"Oh, no," she gasped as she started reading. It was a consent form for visitation with Donnie and it was filled out for Grayson Hollinger. He'd gone to talk to Donnie?

Her hands were shaking so badly that she could barely hold the paper still.

Just as she was finished reading the date of the visit, Gray walked into the living room in a pair shorts, his hair still wet from the shower.

He stared at her with wide eyes.

"No." He rushed over and took the paper from her, but it was too late.

"Why do you have that?" was her first question.

"It's not how it looks."

"Why did you go to see him?"

"I didn't see him."

She shook the form at him as proof.

"I went there to speak with him, hoping he could offer some closure. I was desperate to help you heal, but before I went through with it, I realized he wasn't going to be able to help you."

"So I'm just some broken toy you're trying to fix, but the parts are no longer available so just toss me out?" She remembered what his mother had said about the projects he'd taken on in the past.

"No. It's not like that."

"What is so wrong with me that you feel I need to be fixed?"

"You…" He obviously thought better of answering that question. Instead he shook his head and let it fall. "I can't do anything right with us. Is it wrong that I want to help you? Is it wrong that I care about you?"

"I never asked you to care about me." She tossed the form at his chest and went to her room.

She wasn't his fixer-upper project.

As she lay there sobbing herself to sleep, she realized the effort he'd made to help her. To go to a prison. As misguided as the idea was, she knew his heart was in the right place. One day, she would thank him. But it wouldn't be any day in the immediate future.

Somehow she managed to fall asleep, only to be awoken by her phone ringing by her head.

"Yeah?" she asked, not recognizing the number.

"Hey Alyssa, it's Chanda. Can you come down here? Gray's blitzed and I'm going to have to put him out. I'd have Doug help, but he has Lucy." For a moment, Alyssa contemplated letting him stay down there all night, but she couldn't. He'd gone to Syracuse to try to help her. She could at least make sure he made it home safe.

"Sure. I'll be right there."

In the ten minutes it took her to find shoes and get to the bar, Gray had already been put out on the street.

Chanda peeked out with a frown.

"Sorry. I didn't have a choice. It's a legal thing. Mac said we had to kick him out. Do you want me to call a cab?"

"No. I'll take care of it. Thanks for calling me."

"He's going through something. He didn't ever get to the point, but I'm pretty sure it has to do with his feelings for you."

"I don't know what to do. I told him this was never going to work."

"Maybe you're both trying too hard. It's a common mistake."

"Maybe."

"Let me know if you need any help." Chanda waved and closed the door.

Liss turned to Gray and sighed.

He was slumped over on the bench. His right pants leg was wet and smelled suspiciously like urine. She wondered briefly if it was from a dog or a human. Then decided urine is never good, no matter the source.

"What's going on?" she asked him and got an incoherent mumble for an answer. "Come on, big guy. Let's get you home. You reek."

"I don't want to go home if she's there."

"Who's she? *Me?*"

He blinked and then let out a sigh. She guessed that was all the reply she needed.

"Look, I know you're upset, but I can't leave you outside all night where people or things will piss on you. So get up and come home. Don't be a baby."

"I am a baby. No, I'm worse than a baby, I'm a teenage girl. I'm all about feelings and shit," he slurred while attempting to stand.

"Feelings really suck, don't they?"

No answer.

He was able to walk, though he was leaning heavily on Alyssa's offered shoulder.

After the first half block, she realized walking was going to take too long and she hailed a cab. The first driver took one look at Grayson and kept going. The second one didn't seem as selective, but frowned as she maneuvered him into the backseat.

"He'd better not get sick in my cab," the man threatened.

"I think he's okay. It's not far. Just two blocks."

Two blocks later, she shoved at Gray until he woke up again. She tugged him out of the cab. She'd never seen him so bad off and wondered what he had been drinking.

"Were you doing shots?" she guessed.

"Yeah," he told her. "A whole bunch of them."

"I see."

He groaned when the elevator moved, and for a moment Alyssa thought it was all over. He took a deep breath and reached for the wall to steady himself. When the door opened on their floor, they stepped out.

Alyssa opened the door and Gray headed straight for the sofa.

"Oh no, you don't. We need to get you out of those clothes and cleaned up first. Someone pissed on you."

"Did I piss on me?" he muttered, looking down.

Alyssa hadn't considered that possibility, but studied him again.

"I don't think so. Not that it would matter. You still need to get cleaned up first."

She guided him to the bathroom and helped him with his clothes while she turned on the water.

"It's very 'roary' in here," he said, making her laugh at his made-up word.

"Come on." She helped him get the offending pants off and tossed them toward the trashcan. Then she pulled down his boxers and assisted with his socks while he managed to get his shirt partway over his head. "Here. Let me," she said, pulling it back down and undoing the buttons before pushing it off his shoulders.

She glanced down at her denim shorts and T-shirt and decided to go in with him to help, worried he'd drown otherwise. She washed his hair and lathered up the soap, paying special attention to the offending leg. As she stood up, she saw he had taken notice to her bending down in front of him and his body had responded to her closeness.

He made a strangled sound as she stood and turned him to rinse. He slumped back against the wall and hung his head.

"Why can't you love me, Liss?" She didn't know what to say so she said nothing. "Please just love me the way I love you. Everything would be so much easier if you could love me. Why...?" He faded off as he leaned his head back against the wall. Water dripped from his nose, lips and chin as he squeezed his eyes closed. "I wouldn't ever hurt you. Please, Liss?"

In that moment, she didn't see him as the guy she was trying desperately not to fall in love with to save her heart, but as the man who already had her heart, and wanted to give her his own in return. Grayson was safe. It was that simple. The fear washed away and the answer was easy.

"Okay," she whispered and leaned up to kiss his wet lips. Water poured all around them as she let her feelings for him well up around her like the steam in the small room, comforting and warm.

Gray stumbled back and she steadied him while she turned the water off. When the water stopped, his hands were on both of her cheeks, pulling her to his mouth again.

"Alyssa?" he whispered against her wet neck.

"Yes. I love you, Grayson. I'm sorry I've been fighting it. I was so scared."

"Please don't be afraid of me, Liss."

His lips claimed her as he leaned against her heavily. She quickly understood the shower was not the safest place for someone who was intoxicated.

"Come on," she said and helped him out of the shower. She helped him dry off then looked down at her dripping clothes. Rather than make puddles, she slipped her clothes off and led him to his room. When she got him settled—in the nude because she wasn't going to struggle to get him redressed—she stole one of his T-shirts and pulled it on.

He was already snoring softly with his arm out as if in invitation. She slid in next to him and closed her eyes.

"I love you, Grayson." She waited for the panic to settle in, but it didn't come. She relaxed and let the rightness of the moment cover her like a warm blanket.

It was easy to fall asleep in his arms, listening to his steady breathing and his heart reassuring her with each beat that he would be there for her always. Safe.

She awoke before him. No doubt, he would sleep until noon. She went out to get breakfast. She wasn't just making breakfast, though; she was also smiling.

And thinking.

Where would this go from here? Love changed things. They already lived together, but would he want to get married someday? What about kids? She found herself wanting all of those things. Because she loved him.

She was ripped from her joyful moment by Grayson as he shouted from his room.

"Fuck!" he yelled. "Fuck, fuck, *fuck*!"

Alyssa dropped the frozen waffle and went running to help the man she loved.

Chapter 26

How could he have done this? He could not believe how stupid he was. He couldn't even remember who he'd brought home. Had Alyssa heard them?

"What's wrong?" Alyssa asked as she popped her head in his room. He was still lying in bed naked, so he pulled the sheet up quickly to cover himself.

"Uh, nothing."

"Are you sure?" She took a step into his room and he felt his shame multiply.

"Did you…?" He sighed. "Did you happen to see a woman leaving here this morning?" He hung his head, unable to look at her. He was never going to be able to convince her he was a good person after all of this.

He took a breath and held his head up. It was only a week, two at the most. He would be leaving, and she wouldn't have to deal with him anymore. He wouldn't have to deal with living with a woman he loved who didn't love him back. It would all be over. He would send her an email on her birthday to show he remembered, and that would be the extent of their relationship.

Two weeks.

"A woman?" Alyssa looked confused as she turned to look down the hall.

"I apparently brought someone home last night, but I don't remember. Is anything missing?"

Alyssa looked down at her T-shirt and bare legs. Except…it wasn't her T-shirt. It was his, and he knew it had been in his room before he left the day before.

Bare legs?

He swallowed loudly, trying to gather the courage to ask the unaskable question.

"I was with *you*?" he said in barely a whisper.

For a moment, he thought he might be sick. She'd made it clear she didn't want to be with him. She stared at him with big eyes and then shrugged.

"I slept in here, but nothing happened. You don't remember… *anything*?" Her voice sounded tiny and far away.

He shook his head quickly, unable to look her in the eye. He was focused on his shirt she was wearing and saw her shift her weight from one foot to the other.

"I'm so sorry, Liss. I know you wanted things to go back to—" He stopped short in that thought. "Wait. Were you drunk too? Did I take advantage of you, Liss? Christ!"

"No! No. I wasn't drunk. I came to get you. I helped you get home, and showered. Then I stayed with you, but we didn't have sex."

He must have been in pretty bad shape if she slept next to him despite her plan to keep a twenty-foot buffer between them at all times.

"I'm sorry." He couldn't say it enough.

"Do you want waffles?" she offered. He knew her well. Better than anyone beside himself. She was trying to play it off as if she were fine, and he cowardly wanted to let her. Even if they hadn't had sex, he still crossed a line. He shouldn't have put her in a position to have to come rescue him from his own stupidity.

"Uh, yeah, sure. That sounds good."

She vanished out of his room like a racehorse out of the starting gate.

He took his time getting dressed, noticing he was clean. She said she helped him in the shower. That must have been uncomfortable for her. He stopped himself from chasing her down to apologize yet again.

The thought sparked a fleeting memory of them kissing under the stream of water. It was an excellent memory, but he pushed it away painfully. He didn't deserve to have a memory of that.

She was quiet when he came out to the kitchen fully clothed.

"I think we need to talk," he said, but she shook her head quickly.

"No. We don't need to. Nothing happened. Just snuggling."

"But we agreed we weren't doing that anymore."

"It was nothing. No big deal. Just forget it." She put his plate in front of him. "Oh that's right, you already did." She was trying to be funny, but neither one of them laughed.

"If you don't want to talk about last night, fine. But we need to talk about something else."

"So talk," she said holding up her fork in annoyance.

The way she refused to take any of it seriously was beginning to piss him off. He was a human being with feelings. Didn't anything get through her walls?

"I'm moving to San Diego in two weeks. You'll need to find a new roommate if you want to keep the apartment. I can spot you for a few months."

He regretted spitting it out like that because obviously, he had finally made those impenetrable walls shake. She had that same sick look he had a moment ago when he realized what had happened between them. Only this time it was much, much worse.

"I'm sorry. I should have given you more notice, but we haven't had a chance to talk much lately, and I…" *Don't want to leave you*, he finished in his head.

"I need to go meet Mia," she said as she pushed her uneaten breakfast aside. "I'm late." Only then did Grayson notice she had changed into real clothes instead of just his T-shirt.

"I tell you I'm moving across the country and you've got to go?" He couldn't believe she would be this cold.

"What do you want me to do? Mia and I have plans to go to Connecticut to see the new baby. And I've got two weeks to find a roommate or a place I can afford on my own. What else do we need to talk about?"

"I told you I would help for a few—"

"I don't need your help. The last thing I need is anything from you." Her voice shook with real emotion as she snatched up her phone from the counter and headed for the door.

"What the fuck is wrong with you?" he asked himself out loud when she was gone.

* * * *

"Leaving?" Alyssa said to no one as she waited for the elevator. "He's just leaving? He tells me he loves me, begs me to love him back, and once I do he says he's *leaving*?" She couldn't believe her life at the moment.

When she'd gotten out of his bed that morning, everything seemed perfect. How could it end up in such a mess so quickly? This could only happen to her.

Her visit with Kenley and the new baby was torture. It was nearly impossible to keep a smile on her face all afternoon. Kenley didn't buy it either. She'd asked once already, but Alyssa just shook her head and smiled wider. She wouldn't let her heartbreak interfere with Kenley's happiness.

Being with the happy family forced Alyssa to face the future that waited for her in New York. She was alone and had no one to blame but herself. Kenley had a family. Mia was leaving for Philadelphia soon. And Gray...

"What's going on with you?" Kenley asked when they were alone. "Don't say you're fine or I'll start talking about how I cry with joy every time I'm breastfeeding."

Alyssa sniffed and shook her head.

"I've been overly emotional myself, and I can't even blame it on hormones."

"The guy? Grayson?" she guessed. Liss nodded and pressed her lips together, feeling the tightening in her throat.

"I told him I loved him. Can you believe that?" She let out a snort of disbelief. "I wasn't even drunk. I meant it."

"He doesn't feel the same way?" Kenley asked.

"It doesn't matter. He's moving away."

"Last time I checked, there wasn't anything keeping you here. Take it from me, sometimes starting over somewhere you didn't expect to be is a great thing."

"I'm not cut out for this kind of life. I should have known better. I don't deserve it."

Kenley sucked in a breath, her eyes wide.

Alyssa hadn't meant to say that. She didn't want to have to explain.

"What does that mean? Of course you deserve to be happy."

"Just forget what I said. I'm just being silly over a guy. I'll be fine."

Alyssa managed to convince Kenley she would be fine; however, Liss had her doubts it was true.

* * * *

Doug came home from work to find both his girls wearing aprons and covered in clay. It was a welcome sight, one he looked forward to seeing frequently now that Lucy would be staying with them more often.

"What are you making?" he asked as he picked up Lucy and bent to kiss Chanda on the head.

"I'm making a sculpture of a lion."

"I see." It didn't look like a lion one bit, but he didn't care. Not when his daughter was smiling like that.

"Chanda is going to come to my school tomorrow and teach us how to make an animal."

"She is? That is very nice of her."

"Chanda is very nice."

"Yes. I couldn't agree more." He kissed Chanda again and let Lucy slide down to the floor.

"I'm going to go put on my new princess dress," Lucy announced.

"Wash your hands first," Chanda called with a smile.

It was that moment. Simple and ordinary when he knew.

After the divorce, he vowed to never marry again. He was sure most men had the same thoughts after having their balls handed to them.

Doug's reason for not wanting to try again had been more than just the pain of a failed marriage. He realized in the months leading up to the separation that he'd made a mess out of all their lives.

He'd taken the easy way out and married Julie so he wouldn't have to date, or entice someone into caring about him. He'd been lazy and married the first woman who said she loved him back.

It was easy to see, years later, that he never loved Julie. And because he basically coasted through the rest of the marriage, he could now understand why she hadn't been happy. The guilt made him shiver, even though he knew that Julie was responsible for the role she played as well.

She'd gotten pregnant on purpose, knowing they were having problems in their marriage. It had been her plan to take him for child support, but she needed the child first. Lucy was the best thing to ever happen to him, but her presence didn't heal their damaged marriage. Instead, it gave them something new to disagree on.

He thought he'd never marry again because he didn't want to fail someone else, including himself. But as he stared into Chanda's eyes, he knew he wouldn't fail at this. It was so simple that there wasn't any reason not to try.

"I love you," he told Chanda, feeling it down to his toes. He knew he cared about her enough to follow through. Every day he would put in the effort so she knew how important she was to him.

"I love you too. Are you okay? You look a little pale."

"I'm better than okay."

"Don't be mad about the princess dress. It was on sale and she looked up at me with those eyes. I can't help but give in."

"I've been told she has my eyes."

"She does."

"So does that mean you would give in if I looked at you all pleading and begging?" He bent to kiss her neck and she giggled, squirming closer to him.

"What can I say? I'm a pushover," she confessed.

He'd seen how fierce she could be. She definitely wasn't a pushover. But if he had an advantage, he would very well use it.

"I'm going to use this skill to get what I want," Doug said.

"I don't think they make princess dresses in your size." They laughed as Lucy thumped down the steps in a glittering atrocity.

"You look lovely, your highness." Doug bowed elegantly. "And you, my queen, will be mine after bedtime," he whispered only to Chanda.

* * * *

Alyssa and Grayson were back to being strangers. Over the last two weeks, she'd thrown herself into her work to keep from dealing with her life.

Grayson was busy packing and taking care of last minute arrangements, while Alyssa stayed in her room in denial of the fact he was leaving.

There was no farewell party or even a toast at the bar. He'd refused.

The moving company came in that Saturday and took all of his boxes and furniture. Their home echoed as he walked back inside, picking up his bag and handing her his key.

"Well, I guess this is it. I have a plane to catch."

"Okay. Good luck." She took the key without looking at him. She was sure if she did, she'd end up on her knees, begging him to stay with her.

He leaned down and gave her a hug. She just stood there woodenly, unable to respond. With a sigh, he turned and walked out the door.

She heard his footsteps as he entered the hall and shut the door. She knew that was it. She wouldn't ever see him again, but she couldn't move to make him stop.

She didn't deserve to be happy.

Tears filled her eyes and flowed the rest of the weekend.

On Monday, she went into the office with red swollen eyes, causing everyone to stare and gossip. Not that she cared at all. Her manager had planned to give her another account, but after taking one look at her, she retreated back to her office and gave it to someone else.

Again, she didn't care.

She texted Grayson a few times. Asking how his flight was. Was he getting settled okay? They were just random questions in an attempt to connect with him again in some way. She missed him so much, it felt like he'd accidentally packed up her soul in one of his boxes and taken it to San Diego with him.

He never texted back.

Even her email went unanswered. She didn't give up. She told him about the weather and how he'd gotten some mail. She told him how she hadn't found anyone to rent his room to yet.

Two weeks later, she was no better. If anything, she was getting worse. He still hadn't answered.

She was watching television in her pajamas on Saturday afternoon when the doorbell rang.

She pulled open the door after checking to see who was there.

"Hey, Iz," Alyssa greeted Grayson's older sister.

"Hey." She frowned at Alyssa's appearance. "Gray asked me to stop by and pick up some mail."

Alyssa couldn't hold it back. She burst into tears, sobbing uncontrollably as Izzy wrapped her arms around her and led her over to the sofa.

"What's wrong?"

"I miss him so much."

"You do?" Iz seemed surprised.

"Yes. I didn't want him to leave."

"Huh. He told me you didn't care about him. He said you probably wouldn't even notice he was gone."

"He did?" Alyssa cried harder.

"Yes. But I probably shouldn't have told you that."

"He was wrong." Obviously. She was a mess.

"I didn't want him to go either, but he wouldn't listen to me when I asked him to stay. What did he say when you asked?" Izabelle said while rubbing Alyssa's back.

Alyssa sat up, wiping her eyes with the back of her hand.

"I–I didn't ask him to stay."

"I'm confused."

"So am I," Alyssa conceded. "I think I need to see someone. I'm so messed up. I didn't think I deserved to be happy with Grayson so I messed it up. I saw myself doing it, and I still couldn't stop."

"Why would you say you don't deserve to be happy?" Izabelle had slipped into psychiatrist mode. Alyssa felt excited for a second.

"You're a shrink! You can help fix me!"

Izzy held up her hands in front of her and shook her head.

"As much as we love being called that, no. I don't take on patients who I know personally. You would need to see someone else. I can refer you to someone if you'd like, and I'll be here if you need to talk, but I can't offer any advice. I'm compromised."

"Sure. Yes. I want to talk to someone. I'm ready."

"Good. It might have been better if you'd been ready a month or so ago, but at least you're doing it." Izzy smiled.

"I know. My timing is off."

"Go get dressed. We need a drink." It was a strange therapy for a psychiatrist to employ, but Alyssa didn't question it.

The next Tuesday after work, Alyssa sat in the lobby of Dr. Drenner's office.

The tiny woman was in her fifties and had photos of St. Bernards and family members all over her office.

Alyssa spoke until she was hoarse at the first meeting and the second and the third. Dr. Drenner wasn't bringing much to the table. She was just listening and asking more questions to get Alyssa to talk.

Eventually, she folded her hands together and nodded.

"Why did you leave the courtroom before the last woman took the stand to testify?" the doctor asked.

"I realized he was lying. I didn't need to hear her story to be convinced."

"You told me three times that you left without hearing her story. Why did you mention it so many times?"

"I don't know. Aren't you supposed to have all the answers?"

"No. I'm supposed to point out the answers to you."

Alyssa tried to think about why she might have said it three times. She didn't know. She hadn't even realized she mentioned it more than once.

"I don't know," she finally said.

"The sweatshirt convinced you of his guilt."

"Yes. And the scar on his arm," Alyssa explained.

"The scar put there by the second victim."

"Right."

"And you knew he was lying about both things after he'd attacked the second woman?"

"Yes." Alyssa was getting frustrated.

"And you questioned him about the cut and the sweatshirt."

"Yes. I already told you all of this. Why does it matter?"

"It matters because you keep getting stuck on it. Tell me again," the doctor insisted.

"God! This is ridiculous."

"Maybe. Tell me again. Tell me about the sweatshirt and the cut."

At first, Alyssa crossed her arms, silently refusing to go through it all again. What did it matter? It was over. She just wanted to forget.

"It was the end of November." She gave in, hoping there was some trick to getting through this. "It was cold out and he came home without the jacket. He had a winter coat, but he rarely wore it to work because it made his coat smell like fried food. He hated the smell of old grease."

Alyssa took a breath, remembering him rubbing his arms when he walked into their apartment.

"I asked him where his coat was and he said he left it at work. It didn't make sense. Even if he'd forgotten it, he would have remembered as soon he walked outside and felt the chill.

"He went straight for the shower. When he came out, he had a bandage on his arm. I asked him what happened and he said he didn't know. It was a long cut. I couldn't imagine he wouldn't have known.

"Over the next week or so, he never came home from work with the jacket. He told me a different story each time. I knew he was lying. I should have pushed him on it, made him tell me the truth, but I didn't." Alyssa's hands were shaking.

"Why didn't you?"

"I didn't want him to think I didn't believe him. I didn't want him to get angry and leave me. We were going to get married. I couldn't risk it."

"So you didn't push him for the truth even though you knew he was lying. What did you think happened?"

"I didn't think anything happened. I didn't know. I just knew he was lying."

"Did you think he was having an affair?"

"No. I don't know."

"You must have thought something had happened to the jacket. You must have known it wasn't normal for someone to lie to someone they loved over something so insignificant."

"I figured it wasn't important."

"You didn't want to know," Dr. Drenner said sternly. "You didn't want to know the truth."

"No, I didn't." To Alyssa's surprise, she found herself crying. Big guilt-ridden tears rolled off her cheeks onto her dress pants.

"And what would have happened if you'd made him tell you?"

"I don't know!" she yelled at the doctor.

"Yes you do. What would have happened if you had made him tell you the truth? If he'd told you he hurt someone?"

"He wouldn't have."

"If you'd asked him, really asked, he might have told you. Then what would have happened?"

"I'd have turned him in."

"Would you have?"

"*Yes*! And then Bridgette wouldn't have ever been hurt! She wouldn't have had to live through that. It was my fault! I didn't stop him from hurting her. I could have and I didn't!" Alyssa broke down, repeating the words that had been dammed up in her for years.

The doctor gave her the time she needed to cry it out, offering tissues.

Alyssa took a deep breath when she'd regained control and Dr. Drenner gave her a small smile.

"He never would have told you. Never. And there was no reason for you to suspect it was something so gruesome. You never could have known what he did. He didn't even know it himself. You were protecting yourself from being abandoned. You weren't turning a blind eye to a horrendous crime. It's easy for you to look back now and see how you should have known, but you didn't. You couldn't have. No matter how much you would have asked or pressured him about that sweatshirt, you wouldn't have been able to spare Bridgette. You can't keep punishing yourself."

For the first time, Alyssa realized the truth. It was a sweatshirt and a cut. Not a bloody knife or a smoking gun. The police had used the sweatshirt and the cut to prove the crime after the fact, and somehow Alyssa had twisted it to believe she should have seen it first. But the shirt and cut, on their own, wouldn't have meant anything without a reason to suspect him.

Alyssa left the office feeling slightly better. No one else would have jumped to the conclusion that her loved one was a rapist from a missing hoodie and a cut.

She'd believed Donald because she loved him. And part of her still loved the man she'd thought he was. But that man was gone. Or never was. She needed to find a way to let him go so she could move on.

Chapter 27

"How's San Diego?" Trent asked.

"Great," Grayson said with an enthusiasm he desperately wished were real.

"You sound so convincing."

Gray should have known better than to try to lie to Trent.

"Tiff and I stopped by to see her."

"How is she?" Gray asked right away. Izabelle had refused to share information with him, calling it juvenile and unhealthy.

"She's good, I guess. She and Tiff talked about wedding shit. Liss is coming to the wedding. Are you okay with that?"

"Of course," he snorted. It was only August, by the following June, he would be okay with it. He hoped so anyway. The pain was still as strong as it had been when he left. "Is she seeing anyone?"

"I don't know. Tiff didn't say." Gray wanted to reach through the phone and strangle his best friend for not asking the right questions.

"Did she find a roommate?"

"I don't think so. Tiff said she was packing."

"Packing? Where is she going?"

"I don't know. Why don't you call her and ask?"

"Because I don't care." He was certain if he said it enough times eventually it would be true.

"Right. Maybe you need to move on."

"That's great advice coming from someone who's getting married."

"If you felt for Alyssa the way I feel about Tiff, no way would you have just split," Trent said.

"What if Tiff didn't want you? What would you have done then?"

"I would have convinced her that she did want me."

"Whatever. I have to go."

Grayson hadn't so much as gone to a bar in San Diego. He didn't want to hook up with some random woman in an effort to get rid of the pain in his heart. He knew it wouldn't work. He only wanted Alyssa. He would only ever want her.

He had made a few friends at the new office, but they were all happily married with kids. Something he couldn't handle quite yet. He still wanted that life.

Doug had called next. With his expenses reduced, he could now afford a new phone. Apparently, he was also able to afford a diamond ring.

"I want to be ready, you know? I want to give us plenty of time to get to know each other better. I don't want to rush into it, but I got the ring so I'd be ready when the time was right."

"Good for you."

"And you'll come back for our wedding? If she says yes?"

"She'll say yes, and of course, I'll be there."

"Good." He stalled for a moment, and Gray thought he probably knew why.

"What is it?"

"Liss."

"I don't want to talk about her, Doug. I can't handle it right now." Or ever. It hurt too much.

"Fine. Take care of yourself out there."

"Good luck on the proposal."

All of his friends were getting their happily-ever-afters.

Pissed off at the world, he got dressed and went out.

After a few drinks, Gray flipped through his phone, looking at the photos of Alyssa smiling and laughing as they lay in his bed. They'd been so happy in the photo. They had no clue how bad things were going to turn out.

He pulled up her name and let his thumb hover over the "call" button. What would he say if she answered?

He put the phone away and ordered another beer.

* * * *

Alyssa stood outside the prison taking in the sturdiness of the building. She'd been standing in the parking lot for nearly twenty minutes and hadn't come any closer to going inside.

Gray had come here to do the same thing once. At least he made it inside and filled out the paperwork.

Alyssa could only stand there waiting for something to feel right about this.

When she told Dr. Drenner about how Grayson thought she needed closure, the doctor agreed to a point. She said Alyssa needed to find a way of letting go and ending the relationship. Apparently, she'd been so busy piling on guilt and reeling from the pain Donnie had caused those other women that she hadn't dealt with her portion of that grief.

The end of a relationship that was based in lies seemed insignificant to being attacked. Her heartbreak was a small thing. Unfortunately, that small thing had festered.

"I need to say good-bye. I need to end this officially."

She took two steps toward the prison and stopped once again. Only this time, she realized why. The Donnie she loved and lost was not the man in this building. She knew at the trial that her Donnie was gone forever.

She got back in the car and drove to Thorndon Park. She pulled in near the rose garden and got out without hesitation. There were still some varieties of roses blooming, and she walked straight for the bench where her life had been changed the first time.

With a breath, she sat down and looked out at the view with splashes of colors.

This was where Donnie had proposed. Where he promised he'd love her for the rest of their lives. She remembered the feeling of safety those words brought her. From that moment on, she would no longer be facing the world alone. She'd always have someone next to her.

At the trial, as her world crumbled, she'd been tossed back into that loneliness again.

"If you had died, I would have mourned for you. I would have hurt for you, and I would have moved on. It would have been better if you had died," she whispered. "You're not worth mourning for, or hurting over. You're just nothing. It's like you were never real."

She let out a sigh and looked up at the perfect blue sky.

"I'm done. I'm moving on."

With a deep cleansing breath, she got up and walked to the rental car.

She was exorcising all her demons today, and there was another stop she needed to make.

Chapter 28

Alyssa parked in the same spot she'd parked many times in her life.

Her mother's small yard was neat with a short plastic fence bordering a tiny garden that marked the end of her lot. The window air-conditioner was humming like crazy, and a puddle had formed on the narrow sidewalk under the unit.

She hadn't even made it up to the deck when the door opened and her mother squealed in excitement.

"Alyssa! What are you doing here? Why didn't you tell me you were coming? Is that your car? Is everything okay? How long are you staying? What can I get you to drink?"

"I didn't know I was coming. No, it's a rental. I'm fine," Alyssa answered as many of the questions she could remember.

"Come in, come in," her mother demanded as if Alyssa would have driven all this way and not come in. "I have to leave for my shift in a half hour, but we can chat until then."

Alyssa took in the cluttered but clean living room-kitchen area and shook her head.

"Mom, I need to ask you a huge favor, and I want you to say okay."

"Of course. What do you need? I have some money. I was saving it for new brakes, but I can put that off for a few more months."

"I don't need money. I need you to call off work and sit and talk with me."

Her mother looked so shocked someone would have thought Alyssa had asked her to be a surrogate to her alien triplets.

"Call off work?"

"Yes. I don't think you've ever called off. They will understand, and I—" This was difficult to say because she'd never said it before. "I need you, Mom. Please."

"Okay. Give me a second."

Without another word, her mother flipped open her cell phone and sent an honest-to-goodness text. It took forever as she pressed the keys three times until she got the correct letter.

How did people function like this? Alyssa wondered. She would get her mother a smartphone for Christmas. And maybe classes on how to use it.

"So what are we going to talk about?" her mother asked after she received a text back that her boss had approved her sick time.

"We're going to talk about all the things we don't talk about. Like Donnie, and what happened between you and grandma. I want you to tell me about my dad, and I'm going to tell you about Grayson, the man I'm in love with, except I totally blew it."

"Wow." Her mother still looked shocked. "I think this calls for drinks."

Her mother served them *cosmos* made from vodka and Hawaiian Punch in Tupperware, and then they got down to it. For the rest of the night and into the early morning, they talked and laughed and cried.

"So what are you going to do about Gray?" her mother asked, her lids drooping with exhaustion.

"I'm not sure. He moved to California to get away from me. I can't very well show up there and make him talk to me."

"Why not? You did it to me, and I have to say, this is probably the best night of my entire life." It was pretty high up on the list for Alyssa too. "Why have you stayed away?"

"We never talked about what happened with Donnie, and I thought you saw me as silly to have trusted a man like that. Or any man. You never did. You were always so strong."

"Hold on just a minute. It's easy not to try. You don't need strength for that. It takes more strength to trust someone. It means you know you'd be able to pick yourself up if you had to. It means you trust *yourself* enough to know who you can believe in and who you can't. I've taken the easy way out. I had you and it was easy to focus on taking care of you and not worrying about anything else. Don't mistake that for strength, Alyssa."

Liss swallowed and nodded, understanding the truth in her mother's words.

"Let's get to sleep. I have plans."

Her mother smiled, and clapped her hands.

"Good for you."

Alyssa's plan included Grayson, and she smiled as she pulled out her phone to schedule the flight the next morning at breakfast. Her mother had already left for work, but it was okay. They'd promised to keep in touch more. She'd even shown her mother how to Skype.

Two days later, Alyssa was standing outside the San Diego office of Hasher Borne. She was waiting to build up enough courage to go in. Twenty minutes had gone by and still she wasn't quite ready.

It didn't matter, because he walked out of the building.

Alyssa's heart thumped in her chest with joy and then...pain.

He was with a woman.

She was younger than Alyssa, talking animatedly while he laughed.

Alyssa hadn't considered he'd have a girlfriend. She should have known. He wanted the happily-ever-after like his parents had. It made sense to see him hugging this woman. He waved as the brunette walked away, she turned to smile and wave at him and he smiled back with affection.

Before her brain had a chance to weigh in on the decision, her body turned and her feet were taking her away from the scene as quickly as possible.

"Alyssa?" The sound of his voice stopped her in her tracks. Her heart forced her to stay.

* * * *

It was her.

Grayson watched as her shoulders hunched slightly. Slowly, she turned toward him, giving him a chance to get his expression in order.

She winced as he walked closer.

"What are you doing here?" he asked. It came off sounding harsh, but he was so surprised he didn't know what else to say.

"Is that your new roommate?" she asked instead of answering.

"What?" Oh. The woman he just hugged. Why did she care? "No. That was Suzanna, Trent's little sister. She stopped by to see if I wanted to go to lunch. I'd already eaten."

Alyssa nodded and bit her lip.

"What are you doing here?" he tried again.

"You didn't answer my emails." She made this sound like it was a reasonable explanation.

He squinted up at the sun and took a breath.

"I know. I figured we would inevitably lose touch. I didn't want it to drag out. I didn't want it to become a thing." He gave her a smile. "Most people get the hint and let the other person fade off into the sunset. They don't hunt them down on the other side of the country to yell at them." He couldn't believe she was standing there in front of him. He had to fight the urge to grab her and pull her close. He loved her just as much as he had in New York. Maybe more. It wasn't getting better. Iz had been right.

It didn't matter how far he ran, Alyssa was a part of him.

"Yeah, well, most people aren't missing you like crazy," she said.

His eyes searched her face, waiting for the joke.

"You miss me?" He couldn't believe his ears. Could he hope...? No, surely she meant as friends and roommates.

"Yes."

"Trent said you were moving out of our place, I'm sure you'll have fun with whoever you're moving in with now."

"Actually," she bit her lip. "I'm not living with anyone. I stored my stuff at my mother's place until I figured out where I wanted to be. I've been doing some soul searching. My therapist suggested it."

"You're seeing a therapist?" Hope reared again. He worked hard to subdue it.

"Yeah. It turns out I was letting guilt keep me from being happy."

"Guilt is a mother." He reached for her hand, but stopped before he touched her.

"Yes, but I've been able to get rid of some of mine. I realize I deserve to be happy with someone. I'm working on allowing myself to be happy."

"That's great, Alyssa. Really great." He did want her to be happy. He just wished it could have been with him.

"I need to be honest," she said.

"Honest is good. It worked for us, right?" Up until a point, then everything went to hell.

"That's just it. I wasn't completely honest with you. I need to tell you something, no expectations. I just want to say it so I can move on."

"Okay." His heart hummed with hope. "Go ahead, I'm listening." She shuffled her feet nervously and looked everywhere but his eyes. "What is it?" he encouraged. "You can still tell me anything." His words seemed to give her courage. She made eye contact and dropped a bomb.

"I'm in love with you," she said, letting out a deep breath at the same time.

"Are you messing with me?" he asked immediately, his head swimming.

"No. It's the truth. I know I said I didn't want that, but I do."

"You're telling me you love me?" He couldn't believe he was hearing this.

"Yeah."

"And I'm supposed to, what? Tell you I don't feel the same way?"

"Right. You could maybe let me down easy. That would be a nice touch."
She forced a laugh.

"What about how I feel?"

"How you feel is pretty evident by the way you moved across the country to get away from me, and won't call me back no matter how entertaining my messages are."

"Let me ask you this. When did you realize you loved me?"

"I think I first felt it on the dock that night in Connecticut."

"You didn't tell me."

"I was trying not to love you. I was hoping it would go away."

"I didn't want it to go away."

"Really?"

"Come on. You know I love you. I eventually remembered mumbling something to you about it in the shower. Begging actually."

"You were drunk. That was just drunk rambling. Everyone says they love people when they're drunk."

"I meant it."

"You left."

"I couldn't just be your friend anymore. It was killing me. You didn't sleep with anyone, but I knew eventually you would. It was more than I could take."

"I couldn't ever be with anyone else," she admitted, and his heart leapt in joy.

"We messed this all up," he said with a sigh. She nodded in agreement. "Maybe we can do better in San Diego."

She jerked her head up to look at him.

"What?" she choked.

"You love me. I love you. I'm sure as hell not going to break up with you or let you down easy or give you closure." He leaned his head in to kiss her and then rested his forehead against hers. "Move to San Diego." He nodded to the building. "Put in for a transfer. Be my coworker, my roommate, my friend and my wife. Marry me, so we can be happy and have a real life together. Let's make a new point B."

She laughed.

"You still don't seem to understand the concept of a one-night stand."

"Maybe we'll do better with a one-*life* stand."

"With lots of expectations?"

"The more the better."

About the Author

Photo by: Vanessa Jean Photography

Allison B. Hanson lives near Hershey, Pennsylvania. Her novels include women's fiction, paranormal, sci-fi, fantasy and mystery suspense. She enjoys candy immensely, as well as long motorcycle rides and reading. Visit her at allisonbhanson.com.

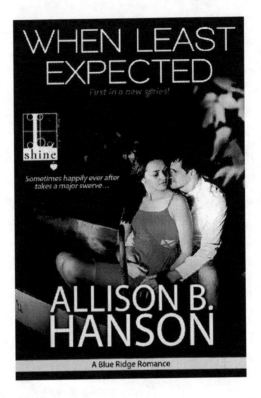

WHEN LEAST EXPECTED

First in a new series!

shine

Sometimes happily ever after takes a major swerve...

ALLISON B. HANSON

A Blue Ridge Romance

Whispering breezes, clear mountain lakes—and her ex.

Alexis Montgomery thought her marriage was fine. Sure, they were going through hard times, struggling to get pregnant—but she and Ian had chemistry, friendship, and love. Or so she thought, until she found the separation agreement waiting for her on the countertop.

Ian Montgomery feels like life is spinning out of his control. He's got a new girlfriend, even if he can't remember why he's supposed to want one. His family clearly likes his ex-wife more than they like him. And then he inherits the romantic family cabin in the rolling Blue Ridge Mountains, where he and Alexis honeymooned. Or rather, they both inherit it. Together.

A weekend alone with fresh air and fresh wounds seems like the worst thing that could happen to an ex-couple trying to keep it civil. But life is full of surprises—and Ian and Alexis are in for a big one...

A romantic cabin in the mountains. And a man who knows how to get lost...

With a brand-new M.D. behind her name and a wonderful man by her side, Nichole Atherton thought she had her happily-ever-after all sorted out. Then her fiancé told her he was gay. Nic can fake a smile better than anyone, but she's hanging by a thread. She just has to make it through her best friend's wedding...and an encounter with his nightmare little brother, Tucker Matthews.

Weddings make Tucker antsy—he's got a bad track record with "forever." The family screw-up became a screw-up famous rock star, and bottomed out fast. Now he's putting his life back together, and the last person he wants to see is perfect Nichole. No matter how hot the fantasies he had about her growing up, Nichole is out of his league and he knows it. It's just too bad they have so much chemistry.

NEVER LET GO

ALLISON B. HANSON

A Blue Ridge Romance

Just one gorgeous weekend away from reality. Then they can go on like it never happened...

Riley Fisher doesn't have time to chase after men. As a single mother working two jobs, she barely has time to eat or sleep. But a girl has needs. So when handsome veteran Sam Brooks asks her out, she decides she deserves some R&R. She doesn't expect anything else from him—after all, he's hardly the type to get serious.

Sam came back from Afghanistan lucky to be alive, despite PTSD that hits whenever he lets down his guard. His therapist told him to forget about relationships. When he meets Riley, he's not planning on breaking the rules. She's cute, petite, and a total smartass—not even his type. But she's hard to forget. Especially once he runs into Riley and her toddler on a rustic mountain getaway and sees what he's missing. Her kid makes him laugh all day. And Riley makes him burn all night.

Too bad a relationship is impossible. But they can enjoy the attraction. It's not like they're going to fall in love...

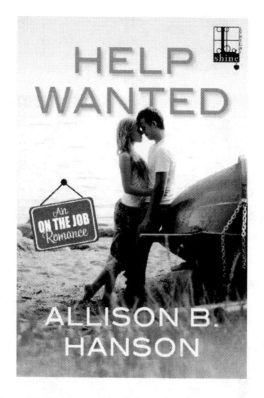

Who said mixing work and pleasure was a bad idea?

For Kenley Carmichael, getting fired for sleeping with the boss's husband is almost funny—at 28, she's still a virgin. Not that her now ex-boss would believe it—Kenley's got the face and figure to attract plenty of men, even if she's never found the right one. A job at New Haven Custom Boats is a chance to start fresh and learn a whole new skill set. Trouble is, she can't stop wishing her incredibly hot new boss would introduce her to some decidedly un-businesslike pleasure . . .

Zane Jackson needs a new assistant, but when his pregnant sister hires her replacement, she chooses a girl who reminds him of the kind who broke his heart in high school. Zane might not be that shy boy anymore, but sweet, sexy Kenley makes him feel every bit as awkward as he did then— and even hungrier to kiss her. She's the perfect woman for the job—but he wants her to be so much more.

Interoffice dating can only lead to trouble—unless it leads to true love . . .

Printed in the United States
by Baker & Taylor Publisher Services